W9-BMA-487

The Casualties

rookie in middle
Sonics open their season tonight
Mohamed Sene as starting post.
STORY, C2

WEDNESDAY
NOVEMBER 1, 2006
THE SPOKESMAN-REVIEW

things to come

rowing in a home win over Oregon for
od measure. As a result, WSU is already
wl eligible and is playing not to create a
ember destination but to improve it.
lead coach Bill Doba said he would
gladly taken the team's current re-
on Oct. 1.

onestly, that'd probably be (good)
d. "Of course, you'd like to win them

portant thing to come out of the month f
WSU, confidence has to rank a solid
cond.

After getting contributions from b
key players (Alex Brink has compl
nearly 80 percent of his passes in the
two game's) and other players (Jed C
stepped in) the second, right en
had made a big catch the Coug

The Casualties

NICK HOLDSTOCK

THOMAS DUNNE BOOKS
St. Martin's Press ❧ New York

THOMAS DUNNE BOOKS.
An imprint of St. Martin's Press.

THE CASUALTIES. Copyright © 2015 by Nicholas Richard Francis Holdstock. All rights reserved. Printed in the United States of America. For information, address St. Martin's Press, 175 Fifth Avenue, New York, N.Y. 10010.

www.thomasdunnebooks.com
www.stmartins.com

Part of this book first appeared on the PEN Web site in 2013.

Designed by Anna Gorovoy

The Library of Congress Cataloging-in-Publication Data is available upon request.

ISBN 978-1-250-05951-2 (hardcover)
ISBN 978-1-4668-6459-7 (e-book)

St. Martin's Press books may be purchased for educational, business, or promotional use. For information on bulk purchases, please contact the Macmillan Corporate and Premium Sales Department at 1-800-221-7945, extension 5442, or write to specialmarkets@macmillan.com.

First Edition: August 2015

10 9 8 7 6 5 4 3 2 1

For all our outcry and struggle, we shall be for the next generation not the massive dung fallen from the dinosaur, but the little speck left of a humming-bird.

—Djuna Barnes, *Nightwood*

Prologue

AS WE APPROACH THE ANNIVERSARY, let us try to think back. Back through the bright lights, then through the darkness, to the start of this century.

At that time there was a small city called Edinburgh, which was the capital of what was then Scotland. It was a small city of half a million built between seven hills, one of which was an old volcano that was believed to be safe. Though its best days were past, the city was still thought of fondly.

However, the place of which I wish to speak played little part in either the city's past or present. It was an old cobblestoned street known as Comely Bank. Though no battles were fought there, and no kings were crowned, it was still an exceptional place.

The shops of Comely Bank sold food, clothes, books, music, alcohol, and medicine, plus many other things we would be familiar with (after all, it has been only sixty years). There were larger shops that were cheaper and had more products to choose from, but to reach them you had to drive to the edge of town. On the way the buildings shrank from high apartment buildings that contained hundreds of people to small, squat houses built of stone where only one family dwelt. After that the houses stopped and you were driving through an area of such desolation it seemed like a place and time before civilisation. There were no buildings or streetlights, just rocks and twisted trees. You wondered what would happen if your car broke down. You'd set off to find a house or shop, and at first you'd walk at a normal pace, maybe even whistle. But soon that blasted landscape would make you nervous and your heart would beat faster; you would walk more quickly, looking left and right, sometimes behind, telling yourself you were being stupid and there was nothing to fear. You'd laugh at your foolishness, and then a black shape would flicker at the edge of your vision and you would just *run*.

And so the residents of Comely Bank bought from the local shops. It was easier, and they enjoyed the predictability of the different shopkeepers: Mr. Asham was unfailingly civil; Mr. Campbell was snide. Sam was patient, always helpful; Caitlin avoided your eyes.

They were also familiar with their fellow shoppers, whom they smiled at, or even spoke to, whilst standing in a queue. This was far from common practice. If you did this in the supermarket at the end of the world, people looked startled or scared. It is true that some of Comely Bank's customers did not enjoy this kind of familiarity, and on the contrary, found being addressed by a stranger so rude and invasive it was like the glint of a knife. But these were sour, unpleasant people; most enjoyed the meetings. They produced a sense of community absent elsewhere in the city. People recognised each other; they knew each other's names, where they lived, what they did for a living, if they were married, if they had children. This alone made Comely Bank an unusual place. However, what made it truly remarkable was not how its residents interacted. Whilst most of its people were wholly of their time—in that they did not believe in God, had small families, took holidays to faraway places, enjoyed electrical consumer goods, believed in things like equality, democracy, and the worth of the individual—there were a few who stood out. This was partly due to the way they looked (their size, their face, the way they walked), but mostly because their ideas went against the grain. They worshipped God, wished for death, or were chaste. They refused to own property.

Yet for all their eccentricities, they had a place in Comely Bank. Most people saw them as quaint characters who added colour to daily life. They were the human equivalents of the commemorative plaques on the walls, the statues of great leaders, the dried-up wells into which people dropped coins in exchange for luck. They were relics of a long-past age that were worth preserving.

There have been many changes over the last sixty years. Our cities are cleaner; we commit less crime; we manage our desires. If there are no statues or plaques on our streets, it is because we prefer to look forward.

So if I speak of these characters fondly, it is not because I am nostalgic for that era. Quite the opposite. I just think we should remember the old world as it actually was. Not only the average, but also the exception.

Part I

1. A Curious Man

SAM (SHORT FOR "SAMUEL") CLARK, born 1988, was the only child of William and Rebecca Clark. Like most murderers, he was unexceptional. There were richer men, more intelligent men, men with more appealing faces, men who could tell a joke or funny story better (the same was true for women). He definitely was not one of Comely Bank's relics; no one thought him a "character." But to get to know the more interesting residents of Comely Bank, we must begin with him.

In 2016 Sam was twenty-eight and single. He worked in a secondhand bookshop whose profits went to the National Society for the Prevention of Cruelty to Children. This charity was founded in 1884, sixty years after the founding of the Royal Society for the Prevention of Cruelty to Animals. It is not just the order in which these charities were founded that is revealing. That both needed to exist had led some to suggest that hurting defenceless creatures was a part of British culture.

There was certainly no shortage of people who wanted to support Sam's charity by working in the shop for free. Without wishing to diminish the kindness and generosity of these volunteers, it must be said that most of them were deeply troubled. They were alcoholics, misfits, former criminals, or just very lonely, boring people who lived through their pets.

When these people told Sam their problems he listened closely and did not interrupt. He was flattered to be trusted with their secrets; it made him feel as if they shared a special bond. But he was mistaken. Their pain was so deep and abiding they would have told anyone.

It was from them that he learned about the jealousy, sadness, betrayal and longing that seethed beneath the visible life of the street. When Sam looked at the queue in the post office he did not just see strangers waiting. He saw a pulsing pink line of affection that jumped from the head of "Spooky" standing at the back; it leapfrogged the heads in front to reach the head of Indira, who never once turned round or gave any intimation that she felt herself being adored.

Sam's volunteers were not his only source of information about the residents of Comely Bank. Every day people brought him bags and boxes of books they no longer wanted. From these he could deduce the person's job, where they had been on holiday, their political views, what kind of food they liked, what their hobbies were, if they knew languages besides English (which was more the exception than the rule, English being a lingua franca at that time), if they had been learning to draw and paint, if they had physical or psychological problems, if they were interested in war, if they believed in God or gods or spiritual forces that lacked names and personalities but were still all-powerful.

Even the condition of the books was revealing. Their owners always left a trace of themselves in the pages. It is hard for most people today to understand how books could be so personal. What difference did it make that the texts of the past were written on pages? When people then read the works of Tagore or Lu Xun, their eyes were consuming the same words as those we see on our screens. As for the books themselves, they were mass produced, identical.

This changed as soon as a person began reading. Then they folded page corners over, opened the book so wide its front and back covers touched, turned pages with food-smeared hands, underlined passages, scribbled comments in margins, wrote thoughts or a phone number on its blank pages, forced it into a coat pocket, tore strips from a page to write on, rested a cup or mug on its cover, left it lying in direct sunlight, spilt water on it, took it into the bath, sat or slept on it, highlighted significant passages with fluorescent pens, drew smiling faces next to parts they liked, drew frowning ones next to parts they hated, tore out pages they thought offensive, tore out pages they thought brilliant, sprayed perfume or cologne on its pages, substituted their name for one of the characters, unstitched the binding then reordered the pages, crossed out every word containing the letter *T*, crossed out every female name and wrote *the bitch* in their place.

Of course, a maltreated book was not proof of its owner's bad qualities. It was merely suggestive. Someone who bent a book's cover and pages till it was folded double might not have been a callous, thoughtless person. They could still have believed that every book contained the potential to instil wonder, joy, sparks of enlightenment.

But Sam's favourite aspect of the books was the ephemera they contained. He found airline tickets, bank statements, receipts, birthday cards—best of all, a postcard, photo, or letter. Sam put these in a battered tin chest the size of a bathtub that had belonged to his grandfather, who had spent thirty-five years in the merchant navy and appeared at Sam's house only once a year, usually without warning. Dinner would be a slow and gruelling event during which his parents struggled to pass the baton of conversation, usually by speaking of what had happened since his grandfather's last visit. Unfortunately this was an event in which the old man refused to compete. He sat quietly, listening with a slight smile, speaking only when directly addressed. His only burst of loquaciousness was telling Sam a bedtime story, or rather stories, because they jumped between places and people. They were tales of boats, typhoons, and beautiful women who could throw knives. Fortunes were found, friends betrayed; men were tied to masts. His grandfather often got characters' names confused, or used two different ones for the same person, but Sam didn't mind. It was part of the telling. Sometimes the stories were just memories of people his grandfather had known—those he had sailed with or met in a port—and these often had no end. These were the stories young Sam had liked best, the ones he could finish himself.

He had been almost eleven when his father came into his room early one morning. His father did not turn on the light, so Sam could barely see his face when he said, "I have some sad news." His father didn't sound sad. The funeral was well attended, mostly by old men with beards who ignored Sam and his parents. In the will Sam's grandfather left him two hundred pounds and the trunk.

In March 2016, the chest was almost full. By then Sam had been working in the shop for eight years, opening ten to fifteen bags a day, dealing with more than a thousand books a week. He didn't keep most of what he found, but it had still accumulated. The top layer was composed of the most recent additions, plus a few letters and diaries he often reread, hoping to find a phrase he had overlooked, some name or event that had meant nothing before, the way that every piece put into a jigsaw makes another possible. Amongst these favourites were sixteen letters from "George" to "Iris," all ending with the phrase *Forgive me;* a Christmas list scrawled in green crayon, with *NO* written by each item in an adult hand; and a black leather-bound notebook in which someone had recorded everything they bought, where they had bought it, and its price, between June 2008 and August 2009. The notebook was titled *Book 29* and smelt strongly of smoke.

As for the rest of the chest's contents—perhaps five thousand items—they were mostly forgotten. Sam was more interested in finding out new things. During the rare moments when he was not in the shop, he wandered the streets of Comely Bank, glancing in windows, loitering in shops, sitting on benches, observing people and listening to conversations in which he took no part. He was like a ghost that everyone could see. If you had asked him why he did this, he would have shrugged, smiled, and said something about being interested in people. A few thought him a little strange. Nobody, including him, thought he could do harm.

2. Lost

COMELY BANK HAD AN OLD stone bridge that crossed the Water of Leith. Whenever Sam went over it he always paused to look down, partly to see the swift, brown river, but also in hopes of catching a glimpse of the man who lived beneath. Alasdair was first seen in Comely Bank at the start of spring 2015, and after a few nights of sleeping in the park he installed himself under the bridge. Though it was dark, cold, wet, and uncomfortable, Alasdair thought it an excellent place. He put great stock in the powers of water. The best kind was fast and north flowing, because this made the air magnetic. Magnetic air was good for the blood, because it made the iron in the blood more active, and what was good for the blood was good for the brain, because it used blood, and so the water was good for memory and thinking, and also for vision, because the eyes were part of the brain. On fine days Alasdair liked to stand on the pavement above while looking upstream. He took slow, deep breaths and thought of how his brain was getting stronger. Soon he would be able to remember his second name, where he was from, and what he had done for the first forty years of his life.

The other reason Alasdair liked the spot was that many people went by. Each of these was interesting and contained a lesson. He could immediately tell why someone's complexion was poor, why they wore glasses, why they looked depressed. He was constantly surprised that people did not want to hear that their spots were caused by fear, that their poor eyesight stemmed from eating cheese, that they masturbated too much. This was vital information; it was about their *health*.

But although many found Alasdair's opinions unpleasant, often embarrassing, they didn't walk away. It was rude to ignore someone, however crazy they sounded. As the passersby reluctantly paused to listen, they faced the dilemma of where to rest their eyes. Not because Alasdair was ugly or disfigured: If viewed in isolation his features were those of a handsome man. The problem was that they seemed disarranged. His ears were too far back. Though his brown eyes were appealing, they were so misaligned that he squinted. As for the long and shapely nose, it seemed entirely supported by the upper lip. Only the mouth, with its crown of dark bristles, looked properly placed. This was where people glared when Alasdair told them how to be happier, taller, grow back some of their hair.

It was usually at this point, when the person was scowling, that Alasdair asked to come home with them. Though living under the bridge had many advantages, it was hard to cook or take a bath, activities that were both important for a person's health.

But the only person who let him stay was old Mrs. Maclean. That night Alasdair slept well, except for the fact he woke up crying. The next morning, before he left, Mrs. Maclean offered him a large cut-crystal bowl on which was inscribed: *To Eileen, in gratitude for forty years of service.* When he hesitated, she said, "Go on, take it," in so desperate a tone he fled from her house. This was the problem with owning too many things: It drove people mad. The only items he owned were his bicycle, a penknife, a cigarette lighter, and a copper bracelet he wore for the good of his teeth.

He'd have taken the bowl if Mrs. Maclean had been less insistent. Not because he wanted it for himself, but so he could sell it. For Alasdair was something of an entrepreneur. His bicycle was always laden with things he found on the street. In addition to bags of books, clothes, ornaments, and plates, there would be a ripped lampshade, broken toys, electrical cables coiled round the frame like loving boa constrictors. His hunting grounds were the streets around Comely Bank, with the exception of a broad, tree-lined road at the edge of the park. The houses there were imposingly large and eerily deserted. There was too deep a hush, a sense of something awry. Even going near there made him so anxious he had to put his feet in the river and slowly count down from one hundred.

He sold the items he found in a small market that took place on weekends in the church car park. People brought their unwanted books, clothes, and household items and sold them for less than they usually cost. Alasdair saw most of the traders every week, but he had little contact with them. Although they were pleasant people, they made him sad. They came to get rid of their things, and usually succeeded—but then, often late in the day, some sort of panic began. They asked a friend, or their spouse, or a partner, to keep an eye on their stall so they could look round. Few came back empty-handed. They were excited, thrilled with discovery; they had finally solved the momentous question of what to put on the chest of drawers.

This was the problem with having a home: It asked to be filled. Each room had to be decorated, furnished, stocked with its proper objects. People spent all their time working to earn money to make their houses perfect. They thought that every lamp, rug, and cushion was a step towards peace. If they'd been told that it would be far better for them to sell their house and everything in it, and then leave the country, they would just have laughed.

Even Alasdair was not immune to the lure of ownership. Although he sold most of the things he found, there were some he wanted to keep. One morning he found a set of place mats that had been spattered with paint. On each were sailing ships that looked so full of speed and grace they threatened to glide off the mat. He stared at their masts, rigging, and sails while a light breeze rustled his bags. His nose filled with a stinging sensation. He thought of the sea.

He spent the afternoon scratching the paint off the mats. First from a clipper, then a schooner, then a galleon. He was halfway through a barque when the knife cut into his hand. The wound was not deep, and the river numbed it, but the interruption was enough. The mats were no good without a table, and once he had that he would need plates, cutlery, glasses, napkins, a tablecloth, chairs, a vase for beautiful flowers.

He broke the mats with a rock.

But he had more trouble getting rid of the photograph album he found in a stack of newspapers in early March 2016. The album was covered in shiny, scaled skin; its pages were made of thick card. The photos showed three generations of a family and were labelled with place names and dates. The earliest was titled *Porto-bello, 1925.*

The final picture was labelled *Aberfeldy, 1938.*

There were perhaps thirty pages in the album, each with two photos. Although the pictures were from long ago, little seemed to have changed. People had houses, and these houses had things, and this made people unhappy.

He saw the same crowds of people, desperate to buy more.

But although these pictures seemed to confirm his worst fears—
that the sickness of the present had its roots much further in the
past—he could not stop looking. This was the danger of pictures: they
contained so much. The more one looked, the less one knew. They

raised too many questions. For example: What was the relationship between these women? Were they neighbours, friends, or sisters? Which of the men behind the women (if any) were married to them? Was it fashion or coincidence that made the women carry their coats on their left arms? Were there really, as the sign claimed, *Dances Every Evening*? However much one studies the image, there can be no answers. In its absence, we supply it ourselves. We mistake a casual glance for devotion, think silence proof of a feud. As for Alasdair, when he looked at three of the pictures, he saw grounds for hope:

Whether dancing or posing by the edge of the field, these women were happy together. Their smiles stemmed from a love that did not depend on what they gave to each other, what they owned, what they hoped to acquire.

But although the album was important, Alasdair did not want to keep it. If he did, if it was *his*, then it would need a shelf. The shelf would need a wall, and thus a room, and then there would be carpet, chairs, pictures, curtains, a table, a rug. He would have a house, a home. It would be his tomb.

He knew he should destroy the album. Instead he placed it with the other things for sale. So long as someone bought it, the end result would be the same. That Saturday he sold a record player, a walking stick, a lion made of china. Then Mr. Campbell, who owned an antique shop on the street, asked to look at the album. His version of what happened appeared in the local newspaper several days later.

MARCH 25, 2016

As both a long-time resident of Comely Bank and the proprietor of a successful business, I am extremely concerned about the rise in street crime.

After listing various minor acts of vandalism—broken glass outside his shop, damage to his car—he implied that this was connected to the homeless.

What no one seems willing to admit is that most of these unfortunate creatures need psychiatric care. Most are confused and angry, many prone to violence. Only yesterday I was threatened by a man selling things at the car-boot sale. Although they were of no great value, I was concerned that they might have been stolen. One of the items, a photograph album, clearly did not belong to him. Rather than confront him about his theft, I decided to purchase it then try to locate its rightful owner. Before I gave him the money I took a moment to check through it.

This was when Alasdair saw the greed on Mr. Campbell's face. There was something obscene about the way he moistened his lips as he turned the pages.

I was shocked when he snatched the album from me then said it was not for sale. When I tried to reason with him, he began making offensive remarks. He berated me for wearing glasses and said I had eye cancer.

During the following weeks Alasdair was frequently seen staring at the album, even under a streetlamp at night. The pictures made him content. For he must have had a mother and father, who must themselves have had parents. The fact that he couldn't remember their names or faces didn't change that they too had worked, gotten married, raised children, gaily danced in their garden.

From then on, when he stood on the bridge, the water flowing fast beneath him, the iron pulsing in his blood, he no longer called out people's diagnoses. Instead of telling them to eat more carrots or wash their faces with urine, he held out the album and said, "This is my family."

People who had previously ignored him now began to stop. They wanted to see where he had come from, whether what was wrong with him had started early on. When they realised the pictures were too old to be of his immediate family, most were not disappointed. They inspected the album as avidly as they did shop windows. They liked to see the past: It was proof of progress.

Alasdair no longer questioned having the album. It wasn't something he *owned*. He was just looking after it.

He took care of it for two months. Then, on a warm night in May 2016, four men came under the bridge. All of them wore black masks. They did not speak when they pushed him to the ground, nor while they kicked him. They offered no explanation. It was as if he didn't deserve to know why.

Consciousness, when it returned, was like being slammed into the ground. First came an instant of numbness, then the impact of pain. He lay and listened to the river. He could open only one eye.

Light was bleeding into the dark by the time he could move. When he sat up he saw the wreck of his bicycle. The frame was buckled, the cables ripped; both its wheels were bent.

This was inconvenient, but it did not upset him. Unlike Sam, he didn't care about the history of things. A book's job was to give you knowledge. A knife was something you cut with. Objects were only a set of functions that could be replaced. If his bicycle could not be fixed, he would find another.

But the album was different. It was unique. It was a piece that had broken off the giant blank of his past.

And it was not on the path.

Not in the long grass.

Not further downstream.

Not in the rubbish bins on the street.

Not at the police station.

Not at the library.

Not in the paper recycling centre.

Not on the shelf of books in the pub.

Not in the rubbish bins by the park.

Still not at the police station.

Still not at the library.

Still taken from him.

3. The Lump

FOR A SMALL CITY, EDINBURGH was extremely cosmopolitan. There were people from every country and ethnic group, either as residents or tourists. Edinburgh's citizens did not usually stare at someone merely because they looked different. Something exceptional was required, such as the old man with an elderly dog he carried in a harness strapped to his back. The dog's paws rested on the man's shoulders; its snout nuzzled his neck. The sight of them inspired delight. People liked petting the dog.

Another person who reliably attracted attention was the woman who always wore a bridal veil. In itself this was not strange; back then there were plenty of women who covered their faces for religious reasons. What made people stare was what they saw beneath the veil. The woman's face was thickly covered with white paint. Whatever this concealed—some terrible skin condition or scars—was not the reason she wore the veil. The cause was a lump on her left cheek the size of a human eyeball. This lump was also painted white, perhaps in the hope of disguise. Unfortunately this had no effect: the bulge was obvious.

Though there were many different theories about the woman—she had been bereaved or jilted or it was performance art—no one knew for sure. Alasdair thought she needed to drink more water, but he never got a chance to tell her this, because she was rarely seen in Comely Bank. If she had spent more time there, someone would have learned who she was and why she kept the lump on her face when it could surely have been removed. As it was, she remained as elusive as a beast in a fable whose only function is to frighten a princess.

In this case, the princess was a young woman called Caitlin who worked in a charity clothes shop next to Sam's bookshop. Caitlin also hid her face, though not behind a veil. Hers was hidden under makeup applied so thickly it was like a mask. She did this because the skin on her face was constantly flaking; occasionally it sloughed off in sheets. She could wash only in tepid water. She dried her face by dabbing it with an especially soft towel. After this she applied thick ointment from a tub whose label warned that it should not be used for more than three months.

By spring 2016 she had been using the ointment for six years. Every morning her face drank it, but by evening it was thirsty again. Although the cream made her skin feel like wet paper, she couldn't stop using it. She had only done so once before, after losing the container while on holiday in what was then Spain. Within two days her cheeks had developed cracks no makeup could hide. She spent the next four days in her hotel room reading, then rereading *Tess of the d'Urbervilles.* By the end of her third reading, Caitlin had no sympathy left for Tess. At least she was pretty.

Caitlin's skin was not her only source of unhappiness. Her job was low status and poorly paid, with no chance of promotion. Her main task was sorting through bags of dirty, unwanted clothes. The trouser crotches were spotted with urine, the shirt collars speckled with blood. Every time she received a donation, she wondered who had died.

Her private life was no better. She had no boyfriend and never went on dates, but at least she was not a virgin. Her first sexual experience had been at university four years earlier. She had been at a party she hadn't wanted to go to because she saw no point. Most boys paid her no attention. She'd stand on her own and drink too fast, and there would be a boy she'd like, a boy who was handsome, friendly, funny, and nice, but even if they somehow got talking—at the kitchen sink, in the queue for the toilet—his eyes would soon skip from hers.

But she was no different from pretty, stupid Tess. She believed there had to be angels amongst the devils. And so when a girl from her tutorial group said she was having a party and Caitlin *had* to come, she could not resist. "I'd love to," she said, and two evenings later she was drinking cider in a hallway. The only person she knew was Emma, who'd squealed her name when she arrived and then forgot her quickly. Emma was too busy laughing and drinking with athletic boys who kept touching her arms. This was only to be expected. Good-looking people were like a fire at night. Caitlin wanted to stand on the edge of Emma's group, because if she was quiet and avoided eye contact, she might borrow their warmth. But she did not dare. She would laugh too loudly or, even worse, speak, and then they would fall silent. Their heads would turn; they'd coldly stare; she would be cast out.

Caitlin hated them for being shallow and stupid, but it wasn't entirely their fault. They had been taught to confuse beauty with virtue, as of course had she. For the rest of the evening she stood with groups of average-looking people, listening, sometimes risking a laugh, and nobody stared or looked disgusted, either because the lighting was dim or because they were too drunk to notice. One boy had terrible hair and crooked teeth and was certainly a virgin. His eyes followed the other girls. He didn't look at her.

By midnight he was drunk. By one o'clock, they were alone. Caitlin went up to him, and without speaking, kissed him on the mouth. This was a moment she often recalled. His half step back. His look of confusion. As his eyes focussed, his mouth got small. He was angry that someone so hideous had kissed him. He was going to push her away, spit in her face, hit her with a bottle.

Instead he kissed her back passionately, as if it was something he had been wanting for hours. Caitlin pulled him into a dark bedroom and there, atop a pile of coats, he pushed against her, and she pushed back, and in her mind this moment had always had more dialogue: the boy saying how much he liked her, she saying it was her first time.

They took off their trousers then pulled down their underwear. Soon he was moving and groaning, and it was fine but she could not relax. If someone turned on the light, he would see her face.

But no one did, and soon, he finished. He put his arm round her. As they lay in the dark, she felt the slow rise of hope. They had done it. He seemed pleased. Perhaps this could continue.

The next day they went to the cinema and watched a film about a man who could hear women's thoughts. The lights in the auditorium seemed too bright. At no point did the boy take Caitlin's hand or even lean against her. Instead he stared at the giant women on-screen who were all without blemish. Afterwards he kissed her cheek and said, "I'll call you." They never spoke again. She only saw him once more. Six months later she glimpsed him sitting in a café next to a Japanese girl who was so petite she seemed like a doll. Then the girl threw back her head and laughed so hard she appeared possessed.

Perhaps the boy had told the story of how he'd been raped by a monster.

Caitlin didn't go to parties during her final year. When people asked her to the cinema, she said she had to study. As the final exams approached, she started noticing how her classmates had changed. Beautiful girls were now beautiful women; even the plainest, dullest girls had an air of maturity, a confidence that they would find jobs and boyfriends or girlfriends that were perfect for them.

After graduation, she worked in a restaurant, then a bar. She got a job teaching French at an all-girls school. Though the girls were studious and called her Miss Matthews, she quit after a year. She hated their eyes on her face.

In July 2015 Caitlin began working in the charity shop. She was twenty-four. Soon after this her grandmother died and left her thirty thousand pounds. Though they had not been close—Caitlin had dismissed her grandmother as a racist when she was eighteen—the money made her feel bad for not trying harder. She used her inheritance to put a deposit on a small flat that was in poor condition. It would take a lot of time and effort, but it could be fixed.

For nine months she sanded, scrubbed, and painted. When she finished, in March 2016, every wall was cleanly painted; the wooden floors were smooth. She was pleased, but it was only a start. She would read more, eat better food, take regular exercise. Having terrible skin was no excuse for having a terrible life.

She also changed the way she worked. If the person who donated clothes was badly dressed, she threw the bag away. This meant that on days when she had a volunteer, she could sit and read in the back room for hours while Dee (Mondays and Thursdays), Janet (Wednesdays), or Karen (Fridays) watched the till. She finished the novels of Jane Austen, then those of the Brontë sisters. The pretty girls in these books got married; the rest bore their lot with grace.

She bought her books from Sam's shop. Every time she went in he asked about the one she'd just finished. What did she think of Mr. Bennet? Had she enjoyed the scene at the ball? He listened to her answers with interest, but offered few of his own. He did not seem cool or aloof—just very contained. When he looked at her face he never seemed horrified.

When did she fall in love with him? Perhaps it began then, but only partially, because there was something asexual about him. When Sam spoke to other girls, even beautiful girls, she never saw him flirt. She was also distracted by a man known as Charming Robert. In addition to being charming, Robert was clever, funny, handsome, and the boyfriend of one of her volunteers. He usually came to pick up Karen on Fridays, so naturally he and Caitlin talked, but never for long. She could not imagine being in bed with him, his flawless face near hers. It was too incredible to even be a fantasy.

But on a warm afternoon in late April 2016 Charming Robert strolled into the back room and said hello although it wasn't Friday. She said, "You've got the wrong day."

He laughed. "That depends." He brought his hand to her face. His lips to her mouth. It was like being kissed by someone famous whom everyone wanted to kiss. But even as he locked the door, she knew he was not to be trusted. Three of his ex-girlfriends had attempted suicide. Karen believed this wasn't his fault, just a case of lightning striking three times in the same place. Caitlin did not blame her for being so deluded. She would have believed anything in order to stay with him.

And they were not going to have *sex;* that would be stretching what was already impossible. But his hands were between her legs. He was pulling her trousers down.

He'd hurt her, or it was a trick, or Karen would walk in.

Charming Robert turned her round; then everything seemed to pause. He was no longer touching her. He did not seem to be there. Either he had regained his sanity, or he was stopped by disgust.

Then he was pushing hard into her without touching her anywhere else. This went on for several minutes, during which he made
no sound. It was as if he had gone but left his penis to finish, and her
body, for the first time in years, was not a lump of flesh. It permit-
ted, it *enjoyed*. The sex was like falling—no, like *running,* the almost frantic heat that stopped her sounds from being words.

Caitlin came, then he pulled out of her. He made a sound of such
relief it was at least part laugh.

When she turned and tried to kiss him, he was pulling up his
trousers. "Sorry," he said, then kissed her cheek. "I've got to meet
Karen."

Afterwards she sat on the floor and waited to wake up. The sex
had felt so intense, it still seemed to be happening. And so what if
it was just this once? Such are miracles. The rhythms of daily life
make us forget that anything can happen. The world could end
tomorrow. Skin that had been sick for years could heal in a night.

Caitlin needed to tell someone else so she could believe it. But it
was hard to keep a secret in Comely Bank. There was so much gossip, so many eyes and ears. Even if you told only one person, that
person could easily get drunk and tell someone else. And so Caitlin
went home and did not shower and had incredible dreams. When
Karen came into the shop next day, all she said was "Freak," and
then broke Caitlin's jaw.

Obviously Robert had told her. While the doctor was cutting her
face, inserting wires and pins, Caitlin had the distraction of wondering *why*. Had he done so from guilt or simply out of malice? Had
Karen suspected it, then forced the truth from him?

For a week Caitlin lay in a haze of painkillers, remembering Robert's lips, the rage in Karen's face. She deserved this. She was worth-
less. Tears burnt her cheeks.

Perhaps she too would have drunk bleach, cut her wrists, placed
a rope round her neck. But on the eighth day there was a knock at

the door. She did not want to see anyone (or more accurately, did not want to be seen *by* anyone), so she did not get up to answer.

She lay very still, as if the person might hear her moving. There was a second knock. Then the letterbox flapped, and she heard something thump onto the mat. When she went to look she found a thick brown parcel that had barely fit through the slot. There was no postmark, only her name. The letters were careful, properly formed, not a scrawl of lust or revenge. She almost opened it with her finger. She stopped. She took it to the kitchen and slit it open with a knife. There was no cloud of poisonous gas. No snake or broken glass. Just a copy of *Middlemarch* with a note from Sam. *Get well,* it said.

BY MAY 2016 Caitlin was back on solids. She felt beaten and humiliated, but she would carry on. She went back to work. She got another volunteer to replace Karen. She started planning a holiday. There were two, three weeks when she felt she'd gotten back to where she'd been before. Then the first crack appeared. It was a long thin cut to the left of her nose that was painfully deep. She did not know what had caused it. She had not been exposed to a cold wind or sat in a place that was too hot; all she had done was sit in bed and read *Netochka Nezvanova.*

That evening she settled on the sofa with a pile of clothes she had been meaning to mend. Some of the tears were probably too wide, but it didn't hurt to try. Slowly, patiently, she stitched till it was time for bed. She read for a while then turned out the light, hoping that, in the peace of sleep, healing might take place.

The next morning, the mirror showed a second crack on the other side of her nose. She gently smothered it in ointment. She tried not to worry.

After a week without improvement, she went to see her dermatologist. His practice was on the other side of the city, up the hill, then down grey streets where everyone looked sick. To get there she had to take a bus that left from near the bridge. She walked along the main street—past the bookshop, where Sam was not working, past Mr. Asham's, then the French delicatessen—until she reached the river. There she saw Alasdair leaning against a wall. His face was one great purple bruise; an eye was swollen shut. He was muttering about killers and thieves, but she did not feel sorry for him. He often yelled that her bad skin was caused by perverse thoughts.

She boarded the bus that parted the traffic like a whale amongst fish. She read her book. The bus ascended. At the crest of the hill, it stopped. She raised her head and saw a veiled girl standing at the traffic light. Although many pedestrians were crossing, she stood motionless, head slightly raised, as if, just like the cars, she was waiting for a signal. She was wearing a pretty lace dress that Caitlin soon realised was not a dress but many petticoats. They were a beautiful cream colour, probably silk, and looked very old.

The traffic lights changed; the bus moved forwards. The veiled girl, as if suddenly waking, stepped towards the kerb. Either she did not see the bus—which now blocked the crossing—or thought it presented no obstacle, because she continued towards it. Caitlin was glad to see her approaching. She wanted to see the lace up close; the veil looked antique.

As the girl came closer Caitlin saw the white glow of her face. It was like glimpsing a full, bright moon through the fabric of a tent. She felt a pulse of sympathy; the poor girl must also have terrible skin.

The veiled girl came to the edge of the pavement, but did not stop there. She stepped off the kerb, and then her face was an arm's length from Caitlin's. She could see her fellow passengers nudging each other, saying *What is that?*

Caitlin turned away. She stared out the windows on the other side of the bus. The girl would step either left or right, then go around the bus.

When she looked back the girl was standing so close the window seemed not to be there. Slowly she lifted her veil. Even Caitlin was appalled by the lump. It was more than disgusting; it was malevolent. For a few seconds she found this comforting. Someone looked worse than her. This gave way to a burning in her stomach, a tightness in her throat. It must be how she made others feel.

The lump was pressed against the glass; still the bus did not move. There was a brief flurry of phones, some satisfied clicks.

When Caitlin told Sam about it, she said the moment felt strange.

"How?" he asked, and though she answered, it took her some time. "Because I thought she was going to come onto the bus. Either through the window, or at the next stop."

"Through the window? No, you didn't."

"I didn't say I believed it, that's just what I thought. Anyway, that was when the bus began to move."

As the street slid by, Caitlin felt herself pulled backwards. It felt like some part of herself had been tied to a lamppost. Something was holding on to her and would not let go.

She was stretching.

She was cracking.

She would fray, then snap.

Then the bus was moving faster, and she was released. She forced her eyes back to the page. She read without thinking the words.

The dermatologist tested her skin. He said its pH had changed. He asked about her washing habits and diet and did not believe her answers.

He said, "You need to be honest. If you don't, I can't help you. If this goes on any longer, there's sure to be scarring."

It was like having to go through puberty again, but without the consolation that everyone else was a mess. Then, there had been the prospect of worthwhile transformation. Now there was no such comfort. Her skin would split into ravines that would become canyons. Her face would be a cratered landscape. There would be a lump.

That night Caitlin took her mirrors down. The next day she put them back up. She had no reason to be ashamed: Her skin had broken the ceasefire. It had launched these crimson flares, drawn the battle lines. And although she had been unprepared, perhaps even complacent, she would fight with every weapon she had. If herbal baths and face packs failed, she would deploy moisturiser, powder, and foundation in a holding action. Under their covering fire she'd launch volleys of cortisone.

But all these strategies failed. Her forces were routed. As soon as a red line healed, two more took its place. Caitlin plastered her face with foundation and powder but to no avail. People stared. Children pointed. Blood was always of interest.

I suppose this has been the case throughout human history. When the first hut caught fire or collapsed, although there were those who turned away quite leisurely from the disaster, most pointed and laughed.

But the people of Comely Bank did more than mock the afflicted: They consumed their lives. The bookshops were full of "true" stories of illness, abuse, and bad luck; every month a new magazine devoted to others' misery appeared on Mr. Asham's shelves. People liked these stories because they were reminders that their lives could be much worse. So what if they did not like their job or love their husband, or their children seemed boring and average? Their lives were imperfect and they were unhappy, but things weren't that bad.

We do not read such books today. We do not need reminders.

4. More

BY THE START OF JUNE it was warm enough for Sam to eat lunch in the park. He usually bought a delicious but expensive sandwich from the French delicatessen next to Mr. Asham's shop. The staff in the delicatessen were incredibly dismissive; either they thought him socially inferior because he was only buying a single overpriced item, or that was how they spoke to everyone. Most likely, they were just following the lead of the owner, a middle-aged man with floppy brown hair whose attitude seemed to be that he was doing people a huge favour by selling them meats and cheeses at grossly inflated prices. Though he was a condescending, pompous fool, in his defence it must be said that the produce was excellent. There was a soft cheese called Explorateur you wanted to keep in your mouth for hours, and a sausage made with fennel that was too exquisite to eat with anything else. It is hard to accept that no one will ever taste these things again.

Sam's favourite place in the park was a bench under an ash tree by the man-made lake. It was a relaxing spot. He could read while ducks and swans swam smoothly before him. But even in the quiet of the park there was always some distraction, some human question mark. A man wearing a balaclava on a sunny day; a very short woman walking backwards; a couple walking hand in hand, their wrists tied together with string. Some of these mysteries were easily solved. He had often seen the short woman in the company of several elderly Chinese women, who sometimes liked to walk backwards during their morning exercise. They did this to stretch different muscles and shift the point of impact, and it made perfect sense, just as it does to the aged men and women I see doing it outside my building every day.

Sam's main distraction was a little man with a closely trimmed black beard who was usually accompanied by a younger man of elephantine proportions. The latter was so huge there was barely room for the little man on the bench. The two seldom spoke; the little man was usually preoccupied with a novel written in German or French. The only attention he paid to the younger man during the hour they spent sitting together was in the form of a chocolate-covered raisin he dispensed at ten-minute intervals. This seemed like a longstanding pact, one that involved a reward in exchange for silence.

Though this scene demanded explanation, Sam knew little about the pair. The bearded man's name was Mortimer, and he was an occasional customer in the bookshop. Whenever he came to the till he did little more than blink. As for the younger man, his name was Toby, and he was well known in Comely Bank—in every town and village there used to be a person whose body commanded attention because of its great size. Given that Toby was four times larger than average, he was as familiar a landmark as any statue or tree. Lest there be any doubt that he was this large—because people change in one's memory, become simpler, more consistent—here are his measurements, as recorded by Mortimer.

The subject was a Caucasian male, aged 29, weight 164 kg., with a Body Mass Index of 45. Though there was no definitive evidence of mental retardation (as measured by a battery of standardised tests), the subject performed badly on various tests of cognitive function, and was, in the opinion of the experimenter, incredibly stupid.

This was all true, even the last part (though one could put it more kindly). Toby was a gentle, trusting creature, more a swollen boy than a man. He lived with his mother, Evelyn; his father was dead, and he had no brothers or sisters. It was not his fault he liked eating so much: One could no more blame him than one would blame a balloon that was overinflated. He was surrounded by temptation. In addition to the street's two cafés and restaurant, there was Mr. Asham's, which sold most kinds of food. But his favourite was the delicatessen. Toby pressed his nose against its windows; his breath fogged the glass. Though he loved the sight of the food—in packets, on plates, under glass counters—his real hope was that someone would share what they had bought. He couldn't buy food for himself, as his mother didn't trust him with money. But just as the streets gave Alasdair the things he needed, so Toby was able to find small brown coins on the ground. Everyone saw these coins, but because they were so low in value they were not worth the effort to bend. Yet even one of them was enough to buy Toby a sweet.

Unhappily, they were not enough for the pies, sandwiches, chips, and burgers that were so painfully close. No matter how long he stood outside cafés and shops, his eyes wide with hunger, pleading, crying, no one fed him even when they had spare food. Toby did not understand. According to his mother, it was good to share. It was one of her rules. There were rules about bottles he must not touch, rules about the television, rules about the old green parrot that lived in a cage in the lounge. He did not understand these rules. Whenever he asked her why, she said, "It's because I love you." She loved him, and he loved her, except for when he hated her. Like when she stopped him from going through rubbish then put soap in his mouth. Or when he pulled on the fridge or cupboard doors because, although she always remembered to lock them, even to go to the toilet or answer the phone, it was possible she might forget. This had happened only once, when they heard a woman screaming from the flat next door. It was a frightened sound of pain that made Toby put his fingers in his ears. His mother had rushed out and started screaming at the woman's husband, who had shouted back, and although all this screaming and shouting took little time, it was still enough for Toby to eat most of the food in the fridge. He had his hand in a jar when his mother came back. She grabbed his wrist and shook it till the jar came off and hit the wall. The glass cut his face and her hand; when she forced her fingers into his mouth and down his throat, her blood was a smear of salt. It was the taste of this, as well as her fingers, that made Toby throw up.

Looking after Toby put a great strain on Evelyn. Mercifully she was given money by the government to hire someone to help. She put an ad in the local paper.

> Responsible person required to look
> after large but lovable young man.
> Must be kind but VERY strict. Lunch
> and Dinner provided.

When Mortimer took the job in 2013 he was the twenty-seventh person to hold the position. Despite the fact he had no experience in care work, he would last three years, far longer than anyone else. This can only be explained by the fact that he, like Sam, had a curiosity that was hard to satisfy. But Mortimer's interests were more scientific. Despite having no formal credentials or training, he had published several articles whose titles included "How to Confuse Pilot Fish," "When Big Dogs Are Small," and "A Personal History of Horse Contraception." These appeared in a magazine called *The Journal of Scientific Investigation,* a publication that, despite its name, was not scientifically legitimate. Its articles were not peer reviewed; anyone could have their study published so long as they paid.

Though Toby might seem like an obvious subject of study, it took Mortimer a long time to become interested. Until spring 2016, his only concern was to make sure Toby didn't swallow glass or get hit by a car. The raisins in the park were not part of some experiment on conditioning techniques in the lower primates; Mortimer just wanted Toby to stop whining so he could read. He once boasted to a woman called Trudy (whom he paid for sex every Wednesday evening) that during these outings he had completed the reading lists for six university degrees.

But Mortimer was no scholar. A truly analytical mind would not have taken three years to find Toby interesting. If you wanted to know about unfettered desire, or monstrous greed, you needed look no further.

Mortimer's curiosity was finally piqued when a series of storms disrupted the television signal. Toby usually watched cooking programmes every afternoon in which people competed to make the best-tasting food. In one, the judges were other cooks; in the other, the judges were members of the television studio audience. Toby liked both programmes, because they showed so much food. Unfortunately, they were on different channels at the same time. No matter how delicious the food in one programme looked, there was always the possibility that the other was showing something better. At the start of the programme, when there was just talking, he switched channels only a few times a minute. Once they showed the ingredients, he began switching faster, and when the actual cooking began he lingered only a few seconds before changing channels. By the time the food was ready Toby would be sitting so close to the screen that all Mortimer could see was the back of his head, nodding and twitching with joy.

Toby missed some of these programmes on the first and second day of the storm. He whined, pawed the static-filled screen, and put his hand in his mouth. After missing the entirety of both on the third day, he screamed so loudly it took a whole pack of raisins to calm him down.

Mortimer would probably have dismissed this as a tantrum but for Toby's eating behaviour that week. He usually finished his meal within two or three minutes, then scraped and licked the plate. After missing his programmes his hunger verged on the bestial. Even his mother, who had witnessed three decades of his gluttony, was taken aback. One hand fed his mouth with a fork while the other took food from the plate. The result was a constant delivery of food; scarcely chewed, it bulged like a fist as it pushed down his gullet.

For Mortimer, this obscene display was clearly asking a question, one he resolved to answer. Over the following two weeks he surreptitiously measured the time his subject took to complete his meal (a meal began when "the food first entered the subject's mouth," and finished "when the subject's jaws ceased moving").

Having established his subject's average Meal Completion Time (MCT), Mortimer began his experiment. For the next six weeks, he pretended that the television had an intermittent fault. This allowed him to control how much of the cooking programme Toby missed, a manipulation that made his unsuspecting subject "impatient, agitated, very often in tears." The effects of these disruptions on eating rate are shown in Figure 1.

Figure 1 *Effects of viewing disruption on meal-completion rate* (adapted from Skelton: 2016)

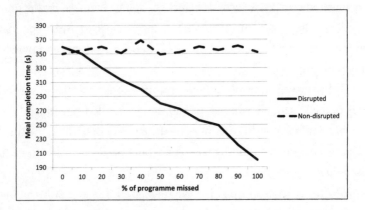

Just as Mortimer had predicted, there was a strong correlation between the amount of programme missed and the speed with which Toby ate. Though this caused Toby considerable distress—screaming and one minor fit—Mortimer saw no reason to stop the experiment.

The next question Mortimer tackled was the content of the programme. Did it have to be about food? Would an equivalent amount of some other programme produce the same effect? In order to investigate this, Mortimer (after allowing Toby a week of uninterrupted viewing, during which time his eating rate returned to normal and his mood stabilised) tuned all the television channels to a programme about a group of teenagers who lived in a low-income housing development (the likes of which were nowhere near the sedate Comely Bank). The results of this change in programme content are shown in Figure 2.

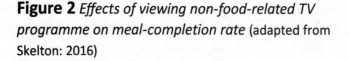

Figure 2 *Effects of viewing non-food-related TV programme on meal-completion rate* (adapted from Skelton: 2016)

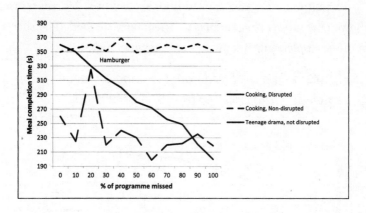

The effect of watching the teenage drama was not significantly different from that of watching no television. Though there was a slight reduction in MCT after the initial viewing, this was attributed to expectation on Toby's part. The other point that deserved explanation was the single occasion when viewing the teenage drama caused a significant reduction in MCT, comparable to that of the Cooking, Non-disrupted condition. Mortimer attributed this to "a scene in a fast-food restaurant involving hamburgers." Both this, and the trend it contradicted, supported the notion that the presence of food in the programme was the crucial factor in television's ability to reduce Toby's rate of eating.

By this point the subject was showing other behavioural changes. In addition to erratic eating behaviour, he showed "signs of insomnia, depression, and a general listlessness." He was also wetting the bed.

Mortimer waited a month before his next experiment. Not from squeamishness or guilt, but so that his subject's behaviour could return to "normal." The purpose of this third experiment was to determine the extent to which watching food-related programmes could reduce the subject's eating rate. In addition to the usual thirty minutes, Mortimer showed Toby an additional fifteen, thirty, forty-five, or sixty minutes of cooking programmes.

To control for the effects of additional television, Mortimer also showed his subject programmes that contained no food. The effects of these supplementary viewings are shown in Figure 3.

Figure 3 *Effects of additional viewing on meal-completion rate* (adapted from Skelton: 2016)

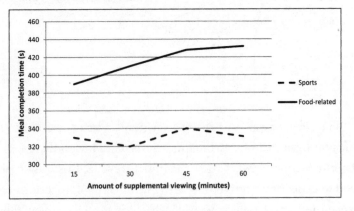

Supplemental viewing of food-related programmes significantly increased MCT in all conditions. There was, however, no significant difference between the effects of forty-five and sixty minutes of supplementary viewing on MCT. From this, it was concluded that the limit to which MCT could be increased by exposure to food images lay within this range.

Needless to say, this change in Toby's eating behaviour greatly pleased his mother. Mortimer could probably have carried out several more experiments before she became suspicious. In his article he put forth many intriguing ideas: that the subject be shown only photographs of food; that the subject be shown video footage of himself eating; that he be shown images and/or footage of those few foods he refused to eat (sweet corn, lamb's liver, anything pink); that he be "given a nausea-inducing substance before watching the cooking programme" (Skelton: 2016). But he decided not to. After this experiment he went to Italy to live with an elderly woman he met through an Internet-dating site. Perhaps they had a happy year together. Perhaps they held hands so tightly it was as if they were bound. I would like to think so, but then I am something of a romantic when it comes to filling such temporal gaps.

As for the reason for his abrupt departure, there are two possibilities. One is the reason he gave to Toby's mother: that he was sick of living in Comely Bank and looking after her monstrous son (they did not part on good terms). The other we must infer from a story he told Trudy shortly after the end of his last experiment. It was the third evening in a row that Toby had eaten at almost a normal rate. While he masticated his mother tried to shake off her wonder. "Did anything . . . *different* happen today?" she asked in a plaintive voice.

Mortimer did not dignify this with more than a "No." But a short while later, as he stood at the sink, he said, "It's just an idea, but—"

"What?" she said, her voice unsteady.

"His cooking programme was longer today. It was some sort of special."

"And?"

"Well, I think it affects him in some way. It's like when we had those power cuts and he ate incredibly fast."

He shrugged and waited a moment, so the thought could fester in her.

"I don't know how. But I think it makes him less hungry. As if he's eating the food he sees."

He reached for a plate and washed it. He slotted it into the rack and turned. Toby sat at the table, head resting on his hands like a dog with its paws.

His mother stood a few steps behind. Instead of looking pleased, her eyes were sunken and her mouth was small. She was turning the tea towel in her hands, twisting the cloth till it was taut. Then she came forward and slipped it round the trunk of her son's neck.

"So you like the pictures?" she said.

"Yes," he said. "Delicious."

She tightened the cloth.

"Does this mean you're going to be a good boy?"

"I'm a good boy," he said.

"Are you?" she asked in a tone so weary it spoke of decades spent pushing a boulder up a hill, only to watch it roll back down. Years of patience, love, and sorrow; time that had been wasted.

5. Mrs. Maclean

THE RESIDENTS OF COMELY BANK were bound in many ways. In addition to the daily rituals—buying a newspaper or a coffee, taking the same bus—that made them familiar with each other, they shared a history that sometimes went back as far as childhood. The school at the end of the street had been educating the boys and girls of Comely Bank since 1885. The original building was two storeys of dark grey stone with high, diagonally muntined windows and a steeply sloping state roof topped with a weathervane. This solid, imposing building remained the school's heart even when other structures were added. It was here that the children learnt history, maths, and English.

It was where they learnt about our galaxy and its planets, how space is busy with stars and comets that burn a trail through the dark.

The old building contained a large, wooden-floored hall where morning assembly was held. This consisted of prayers, school announcements, and the singing of a Christian song. When Mrs. Maclean first started teaching at the school in 1965, there were still few enough pupils for the headmaster to call out their names at assembly to check if they were present. As a child, this made me anxious; if someone did not answer I worried that something terrible might have happened. Sometimes I dreamed that the whole class list was read out and no one answered.

Though my reaction was unusual, I doubt anyone enjoyed morning assembly. This is how one former pupil described it in his memoirs.

We waited in silence, without expectation, for the stalk of the headmistress, Mrs. Maclean, across the stage. In this movement, as in all others—the jerk of her head, the point of her nose—she resembled a raven, though not of the kind described by Poe. There was nothing foreboding or ominous about her, no suggestion she was anything but a grey woman in her grey fifties. Her faith was of a similar colour. She sang the hymns and read the prayers with little trace of fervour. I have no doubt that Mrs. Maclean believed in God. But did He believe in her? She was of so little substance, so scarcely present, that even He, who had created her, might have doubted her existence.

Despite the author's facetious tone, Mrs. Maclean was one of the pillars of Comely Bank. Not only had she taught at its school for forty-five years (both Alasdair and Mortimer were among her pupils), she was also its longest resident. She had been born in 1936 in a terraced house with a crooked chimney and a privet hedge. Her father worked in a steel factory; her mother was a seamstress. She had an older sister named Susan, and a baby brother named Albert who was killed by a runaway horse. Though this was a terrible tragedy, the 1930s and '40s were otherwise an excellent time to be a child in Scotland. Her father had regular work, so there were shiny bicycles to ride, dollhouses and tea sets to play with, fish and chips on a Friday. As for what happened in those distant countries coloured red in the atlas, whose children did not have dollhouses or train sets, but other, less pleasant products of Empire, this was not a subject that darkened young minds.

After her parents died in the early 1960s, she did not even consider selling the house. It was the only home she'd known, the only one she could imagine. The longest she ever spent away from Comely Bank was a week in 1974, when she took a bus that crawled from town to town till it reached the west coast of Scotland. There she took a boat, and since the weather was fine, she sat out on deck. The water was like glass through which she could look down, down, through the seaweed, to the depths below.

As she neared the Isle of Mull, she must have thought of her sister. They had quarrelled five years previously and had not spoken since. Though their actual words have not been preserved, their substance can be guessed. In a letter Mrs. Maclean accuses her sister of "wanton behaviour" with a man "who was as good as married." Susan's answering accusation, which seems to have particularly upset Mrs. Maclean (she refers to it as "inexcusable"), was that she was jealous.

The identity of the "as good as married" man (and what took place between him and Susan) must remain unknown. Neither Susan nor Mrs. Maclean ever used his name. As for why Susan put stones in her pockets then stepped off a cliff, we can only surmise that something went awry. The man must have chosen to stay with the person he was almost married to. What is beyond doubt is how much her sister's death hurt Mrs. Maclean. If Susan had died in an accident, it would have been painful, the shock compounded by the knowledge that there could be no reconciliation. That Susan had committed suicide was worse, not just for the usual reasons—the feeling of guilt, the sense that one has failed to prevent it—but because Mrs. Maclean was a devout Catholic. She believed, as people used to, that all life was sacred. However much pain a person was in, there could be no excuse for taking one's own life. It was up to God in the heavens to dispense mercy, Him and no one else. For anyone who chose to end their own lives, there was only hell.

Mrs. Maclean found it hard to live with this belief. She sought solace in work. As a teacher, there is always something to do, whether it be a lesson to prepare, homework to grade, or a student's failings to consider. During my first few years on the job I slept only four hours during the week. On Saturdays and Sundays I struggled to leave my apartment for anything other than to buy essentials. I certainly never subjected my three rooms to the assault of cleaning that Mrs. Maclean unleashed on her house every Saturday morning. Outside of work, the only person she saw was Mrs. Wallace, whom she called for on her way to church on Sundays. She spent the rest of her time preparing lessons, attending staff meetings, or visiting patients at a local hospice. She did not socialise with colleagues, and she was seldom seen in male company, married or otherwise. Even after she became headmistress in 1986, the increase in status and salary did not alter her habits. She did not take holidays, buy better clothes, or redecorate her house. She did not go to the cinema or theatre. Though respected by most people in Comely Bank, many of them her former students, she did not have friends. Although she was neither cold nor aloof, there was something in her manner that discouraged familiarity—people addressed her as "Mrs. Maclean," almost never "Eileen." Hers was not only an emotional distance; even when standing in front of you, she did not seem fully present. She was like a ghost who had come to smile and comment on the weather.

Most thought her reserve was a shield she'd acquired during her years as a teacher, a way of defending herself from the stresses of school life. They thought that, even after retirement, she could not lower her guard.

A glimpse at any of her early letters shows how wrong these people were. Sam found one in an old atlas she donated to his shop.

May 15, 1979

Today I was on playground duty because Mr. Bethune is sick. The sun was warm and there was a breeze, and I thought of when we walked by the river. I stood by the oak tree, half in its shade, while the girls ran round and round, calling out each other's names, screaming in delighted fear when they thought they were caught. Their voices were shrill and loud, and they did not look at me as they turned in their circles, spinning faster and faster, till their faces blurred and instead of features there were only eyes that stared. And then they seemed like wild things that had been tamed but could at any second revert. The tree trunk pushed into my back. I felt lightheaded, dizzy, as if I were the one who was spinning. I closed my eyes and slowly breathed, and then your hand was in mine. We were walking by the river while birds sang in the trees. At the bridge, we picked up sticks and dropped them into the water. When we went to the other side I saw mine emerge but before I could say "Pooh sticks," you said, "What is that?" I looked downstream and saw a grey blur that was distant, coming closer, still grey but no longer a smudge; now it was two arches that rose and fell, pushing air down, but slowly, too slowly to keep the bird in flight, and yet it came towards us. We stood and watched, my hand in yours, and then, above the rush of the river, we heard the beat of its wings. The heavy flap of a sheet being shaken. A flag fighting the wind. For a moment, we saw the heron entire: the hooded lids, the pointed beak, the speed and line of it. Then it had moved the air beneath and was fast becoming distant. We watched it dwindle, resume its blur, and then you said, "Eileen," and put your lips to mine. And although you had kissed me before—after our walk up Arthur's Seat, and while we sat on the tram—I still think of this as our first time.

Sam had many questions after reading this, not least about the identity of the man. But at that time he knew no more about Mrs. Maclean than anyone else, and although it was a mystery, there were many others. Two years would pass before he saw the remainder of the letters. There were hundreds, the earliest from 1956, the last from 2016. Though they varied in tone and length, all addressed the same person, though never by name. All of them were unsent.

The obvious conclusion was that Mrs. Maclean had been involved in a secret love affair. But if she regularly saw this man, why did she write to him? And if he was often absent, why didn't she send the letters? There is also the matter of her religious beliefs. It seems unlikely that a woman so outwardly devout could be involved in what to her would seem immoral.

These are not the only mysteries. Apart from the day at the river, there are only six, at most seven, occasions she refers to: a walk on the beach; two trips to the cinema; a drive in the country, then a picnic (though these may have been separate occasions); a rainy afternoon spent playing cards; climbing a nearby hill. In hundreds of letters, written over six decades, she returns to these events. By the mid-1970s, the recollections have ceased to differ in detail; by the 1980s they have become a liturgy.

It is only in her later letters that things become clear. The following is from a letter written when she was seventy-nine. The opening, though apparently plain, is uncharacteristic. Instead of reciting the hallowed event—*Our father, who art in heaven, that day we walked on the beach*—it begins by describing the weather.

February 12, 2015
A cold morning. The pavements were icy. Although there was grit on the road, they had only done the pavement at the crossing place.

On the surface, this is a legitimate complaint for someone Mrs. Maclean's age. However, she continues:

I put on my black shoes that had better soles, then went out to buy milk. After ten steps I slipped, but kept my balance, which made me cry out, and then some people turned round. On seeing I was still upright, they smiled and walked on. But I was too shocked to move; I stood and stared at the ground. Not because I was afraid of falling. I could imagine breaking my hip, my leg, the back of my head; me lying there and growing cold, the wail of sirens, too late.

It was not this thought that upset me. On the contrary, the reason I was shocked was because the thought did not upset me at all.

There are many similar entries over the following months. She writes of being unwilling to drive, cross busy roads, or go down steep stairs. She confesses to feeling "impatient," of "wanting what is due." The tone of her letters becomes desperate. Finally, she speaks to her priest.

July 25, 2015

After the service, I asked Father Robert to hear my confession. We went in a booth that smelt of polish and needed a new cushion. He asked how long it had been since my last confession. "Six years," I said, and I am sure he was pleased: He has had to listen to so much about Father McCabe, how kind and holy and patient he was. To hear that I had not confessed to him in his last four years (as I have not confessed to Father Robert in his first two) must have been welcome news. I could see his small head nod behind the screen. Then I heard the steps of a woman in heels—they were distant, from the other end of the church, but even if they had been close, just outside the confessional, it would have made no difference. Who cares what an old woman says?

Father Robert asked what I wished to confess. I said I was tired of waiting. At first, this confused him (impatience not usually being thought a sin). He began to apologise for keeping me waiting, but he stopped when I said that every night I prayed I would not wake up next day. Then he breathed out through his mouth, and perhaps it was a sigh. The wish for death by the old is probably something priests are told to expect. They must be bored and relieved to know what to say.

He said what I had expected, what I had said to myself. "It is not for us to decide. It is only God who can choose because He knows all things. He understands when a person is ready and when they need more time." Father Robert paused, pleased by his rhetoric. Or the pause was intended for me, so I could appreciate such wisdom.

"You must be patient," he continued. He managed to say, "God will—" before I cut him off.

"I have been patient for over fifty years. I cannot wait any longer."

The woman outside must have been standing still, because it was only after I'd spoken, in the quiet that followed, that her steps resumed. They approached, passed close by us, then quickly died away.

When Father Robert spoke, he sounded uncertain. "Is there a problem with your health? Are you in pain?" he asked, and even this solicitous enquiry was somehow unconvincing. As if he, in his early forties (and presumably good health), could not yet fully believe in the idea of sickness. It was probably the same with old age: Although he saw it every day, because it had not yet happened to him, it was still as abstract a notion as grace is to most of us.

I said that I was in good health.

He coughed, then said, "You have worked hard. You

should enjoy your retirement. You can learn new things, spend time with your friends."

I told him I did not have any.

"What about your family?"

"All dead."

"Look," he said, and sounded annoyed, but for only an instant. The rest of his sentence—something about it being hard to adjust to retirement—had a be-reasonable tone. As if it were only obtuseness that kept me from agreeing.

By then I was certain Father Robert could not help me. He was a man who was too far from death, who had probably never known love. And this made me angry. I said, "What do you think heaven is like? Every day you read about it, every day you speak about it. Is it clouds and angels sitting on thrones? Is it—?"

"I do not know," he said. And for the first time, he sounded genuine. As if heaven—unlike old age—was something he did not presume to know.

He cleared his throat. "No one who is living does. Even if God told us, we probably wouldn't understand. What heaven is like should not concern us. We must concentrate on the good we can do now."

"But how can we not think about it? Isn't it what we live for? So we can be in a place with people we love for all eternity."

The shriek of an ambulance broke into the church. I thought of being hit by a car.

"Perhaps," he said, then stopped. As if, having thought the sentence, he was no longer sure. I did not mind: better he said nothing than more platitudes.

But his final words were spoken in a different voice. His tone was surer when he said, "God loves us. All of us. He gives us our lives and so we must be grateful. Not just in our hearts, but in our actions. Maybe you are not the only one waiting. Maybe He is also waiting."

"For what?" I said, and my voice leapt, too fast and too eager.

"I don't know," said Father Robert. "But you must be patient."

At the time, this seemed no answer. Afterwards I stood by the side of the road, watching the cars pass.

Poor Mrs. Maclean's love letters were written to a dead man. It is possible he was still living when she began their "correspondence," and there was some other reason she did not send the letters—perhaps she lacked the courage, or, as in her sister's case, the man was already married. However, her mention of having "been patient for fifty years" suggests he had been dead that long. Sam was of the opinion that the man had died in a plane crash. He based this conclusion on a photo he found in one of Mrs. Maclean's bedroom drawers that pictured a man in an airman's uniform standing by a row of planes. On the back of it was written, *To Eileen, with love from Stanley, September 1954.*

Whether it was this man or someone else whom Mrs. Maclean was waiting for, what is certain is that she believed they would be reunited in heaven. This was the hope that made her live like a book with its pages shut.

In the months that followed her confession to Father Robert, Mrs. Maclean began to act strangely. Whenever she met someone she knew, she always stopped to ask how they were. In itself, this was nothing new; she had always been polite. What pleased some, but unnerved most, was the intensity with which she asked. She seemed to care too much. They felt as if she were privy to some secret and terrible information regarding their fate.

The other great change in her character was the compulsive way she tried to be kind. She gave up her place in queues for people in a hurry. If she got in someone's way—in a shop entrance, or on a narrow stretch of pavement—she would insist that the other person go first, which usually led to the person insisting that *she* go first (partly because this was general etiquette, but also because she was an elderly woman), to which Mrs. Maclean would again insist they step through first, and perhaps this seemed comic the first time it happened, but soon people dreaded meeting her. It was easier to just push past her.

There were other, more dramatic manifestations of her wish to be charitable. During the freezing winter of 2015, she called out to Alasdair when he was shivering under the bridge. At first he did not hear her faint voice above the sound of the river, but when a series of stones hit the water, he looked up. If he gave little thought to why an old woman who used to ignore him should now offer him shelter, it was because he did not regard it as any great favour, merely his due.

For her part, Mrs. Maclean offered no explanation. All she said was "It's not far." Then she set off along the icy pavement, perhaps too quickly for safety. During the short journey he repeated what he always told her, that she should eat more seeds for her bones. But she was not listening.

At home she led him upstairs to a room with a bed whose sheets were printed with roses. There she turned to him, as if to speak, but her mouth stayed closed. Only after a great effort did she say, "I hope you'll be comfortable." She left him, and after a moment he began to undress.

He was about to get into bed when she returned. She did not seem to notice, or mind, that Alasdair was naked. She put down a mug and said, "I've brought you a hot drink." From under the blankets he watched her staring past him, and he—who was often oblivious to the feelings of others—could not help noticing the pain on her face, its wrinkles merging into folds, her eyes like coloured glass. She brought her hand to her brow, then smoothed it down to her nose, as if shutting the eyes of a corpse.

Given her obvious reluctance, why did Mrs. Maclean invite Alasdair into her house? Why did she pamper him? Not only with the hot drink, but also with breakfast, and then, when he was leaving, by offering him the crystal bowl she had been given as a retirement present?

The answer was that poor Mrs. Maclean, in her desperation, had interpreted Father Robert's suggestion that God was "waiting" as a kind of pact. She believed these acts of charity would encourage God to grant the mercy He had been withholding. She may also have been hoping that Alasdair would kill her in her sleep.

The idea that she was trying to petition God is supported by her actions over the following months. She donated many valuable items to the charity shops on the street. And it was not just her possessions, but her time as well. In the late spring of 2016 she began volunteering in Sam's bookshop, twice a week, for three hours at a time. She sat at the till while he worked in the office, but unlike other volunteers she did not read or even glance at the books. All she did was gaze straight ahead. Sam thought her expression was one of calm expectancy. Like that of a person waiting at a railway station who constantly sees trains go by but knows that someday one must stop. This was how she remained during those final months, right until the clear morning the following August when everyone's train arrived. On that day, when she looked up, Mrs. Maclean must have smiled.

6. The Ballad of Rita and Sean

WHENEVER I DREAM OF COMELY Bank I am looking down from above. The roofs of the shops flow in a straight line until the road bends. Then there is the bridge, the river rushing beneath, and as my mind's eye travels it names the streets, sees cracks in the pavement, holes in the road, so much detail it almost feels real. But because it is gone (which cannot be forgotten, even by my imagination), what I see is more like a stage. In this real-but-not-real place all the people I remember are always in the same spot, like actors on their marks. Alasdair is on the bridge, Mr. Asham is behind his shop counter, Toby is at the window of the delicatessen. So rooted are they in these locations that it is hard to remember them elsewhere. Only with great effort can I shift Mr. Asham to Trudy's house, put Sam in Sinead's flat.

This is also true of Sean and Rita, though they were late arrivals to the street. After April 2016 they were always, weather permitting, on the wooden bench at the entrance to the park. Even during that final winter they sat there under blankets, warmly dressed, like those people who queued outside shops for hours, days, in the hope of paying a reduced price for yet another object. But Sean and Rita wanted nothing except to stay as drunk as possible.

Sean was tall with thick hair greying at his temples. His brown eyes were flecked with orange and seemed large in his face, like those of an owl, an impression strengthened by the way they held you even when he was slurring his words. His was an unpleasant gaze. It was a blade hovering over a cake, looking for where to cut. Sean could be so charming and funny that even after a few minutes of conversation you felt he was your friend. A day or week later, as you headed for the park, you would find yourself smiling in anticipation. But as you neared the bench, hand raised in greeting, you'd see his disdain. As you hurried past he'd say "Is it a race? Don't fall and hurt yourself." At his worst he spat at people, and once he threw a bottle at Alasdair. Sean did not like homeless people; nothing enraged him more than someone thinking that he spent all day drinking on a bench because he had nowhere to live.

Sean was the reason most people avoided the couple. That they did so with regret was entirely due to Rita. She was short, very pale, at least a decade younger than Sean. Her hair was straw-coloured and wispy and piled on top of her head with such care that it was as if two birds had prepared it for their chicks. Though they had woven it with love—thinking of pale blue eggs that had to be kept safe, of nestlings with still-closed eyes and fluffy, useless wings— the nest they had fashioned seemed as fragile as the little birds' heads. A gust of wind, the paw of a cat, and everything would be lost.

Rita's mood was harder to gauge than Sean's. Whilst her face was not quite a blank canvas, the lines drawn there were faint. A mouth corner turned up or a tightness of the jaw was all you had to go on. Only at her drunkest was there more than a sketch. Then she had a wonderful, terrible smile that suggested something impossible had been achieved at monstrous cost. The smile stayed fixed for several minutes, till it no longer seemed a mark of pleasure, more a sign of agony, as if her lips were frozen in the rictus caused by certain poisons. It was a horrible expression that made any witness want to offer help.

Sean and Rita rarely fought. He might raise his voice at her, but it never went further. Yet when Rita had a large purple bruise on her cheek he was immediately blamed. "The man's a brute," said Mr. Campbell. "That poor girl," said Mr. Asham. "I hadn't noticed," said Caitlin. The matter was settled only when Sam said he'd seen her fall over.

Sometimes Sean had good reason to be angry, because although Rita was a poor, pale angel, she was also clumsy. She was always spilling wine on his clothes or blanket, which was both uncomfortable and wasteful. She was also careless with matches. She liked to strike them slowly to see the lazy way the head of the match caught. She enjoyed all kinds, but her favourite were the long, thick ones used for lighting fires. There was plenty of time to watch the flame's progress from initial flare to unsteady beginning; its calm maturity as it crept along. As the flame grew old it slowed till there was only a blue flicker at the end of a blackened line, and after that, just smoke. Sometimes she grew bored of one flame and dropped the match so she could light another. This was what led to burn marks on the blanket and, on several occasions, a fire.

When Sean got angry with Rita, she would answer, in a very small voice, "But you gave them to me." That this was true only made him angrier. He gave her a new box of matches every morning, one of several presents. The others varied, but always included a bottle of white wine, a mango or guava, and some chewing gum. Such casual, minor gestures proved he was in love. How she felt was hard to say. They were not a demonstrative couple. They never kissed, held hands, or said anything affectionate when others were around. There is no way to know how they acted when alone; whether they had a sexual relationship; if she thought of him as a life partner, a soul mate, or just a man she was fond of.

Sam thought there was something special about Sean and Rita. They formed a unit so hermetic it was their own universe. They had no other friends, nor appeared to want them. They acted as if they were the last people on earth. Their love seemed to be the kind of all-consuming feeling that made people so selfish they forgot their friends and relatives, perhaps even their children. Was this potential inherent in all kinds of love, or did it spring only from people with a certain emotional history? Sam felt their relationship could help him with such questions.

Unfortunately, Sean and Rita's lives remained hidden in fog, like the special kind we called the *harr* that rolled in from the sea and stayed in the city for hours. This fog was thick, unmoving, above all capricious: one street might be submerged while its neighbour was clear. Though Sam was usually good at dispelling such fog, in Sean and Rita's case he struggled. They never bought or donated books. None of his volunteers knew anything. Throughout May and June he tried to find out more, but with no success.

It was desperation that made him approach them directly. His initial plan was to pretend to be a journalist interested in alcoholism. After asking a series of questions about their drinking habits, he would ask his actual questions under the guise of needing "background." But this seemed too convoluted, too implausible. Instead he did what anyone did back then when they wanted someone to do something for them, or to them, that the person did not want to do. On a bright July morning in 2016 he crossed the bridge, walked the length of the street, and turned down the lane that led to the park. Sean and Rita were on their bench, both beneath the blanket, each wearing a hat and a scarf. Sean was drinking from a tarnished hip flask, Rita from a mug.

"Excuse me," he said. They looked up, and Rita had a sweet expression, as if she were waking from a dream in which rabbits hopped through a sun-dappled glade where bluebirds sang for joy. Sean's face was less encouraging, but it did not seem hostile. He produced a slow yawn he covered with his hand. The sound seemed to surprise him. "Excuse *me*," he said.

Sam blurted his offer.

"I'll pay you if you answer some questions. Just a few."

The silence that followed was caused by neither shock nor dismay. It was the pause of a ruler who knows they do not need to reply. Though Sean and Alasdair disliked each other, they were alike in thinking of themselves as people of great worth. They spent more time on the street—sitting on benches and walls, leaning against fences and lampposts—than anyone else, and as a result they felt seigneurial, especially in their habitual spots. It was why Alasdair felt able to issue proclamations on people's health. It was why Sam received no answer for ten seconds.

Rita was the one who deigned to respond. She brought her hand to her cheek with a look of amazement, as if she thought his proposal a kind offer that made her heart beat faster. He wondered whether she had heard him correctly. She looked overwhelmed.

"No," she said, and her voice was hard. "We won't. We don't want to—"

"Hang on," said Sean. "What questions? How much?"

"Just some questions about your childhoods. I'll pay you a hundred pounds."

This sum of money would have bought twenty bottles of wine. But she shook her head. "It doesn't matter," she said, and seemed very sober.

"Why not?" said Sean. "If he wants to waste his money, let him."

"Because it's none of his business."

"It's a hundred quid."

"It doesn't matter. We don't need it."

"Please," said Sean. He seemed close to tears.

Rita sighed. "Fuck. All right."

"Thank you," said Sam, but she cut him off.

"I don't want to talk to you. Tell us your questions and we'll write our answers down. Come back tomorrow with the money."

Sam did as he was told. This is what Sean wrote.

Dad worked in a factory and Mum worked in a sweet shop. I had a dog called Goldie who had a red ball and we used to play until one day she could not get up because she had been poisoned. At school I was good at running and history. My best friend was a kid called Darren who other kids said was a bastard. He was the first person I kissed. The first girl was Susie Greene who lived next door and there was something wrong with her eyes. I've been with Rita for six years and she's all I want.

This was Rita's answer.

Mum and dad beat me every day and sometimes they made me get in bed with them and when I went to school the teacher made me stay late and what we did was our secret and on Sundays before Mass and sometimes after the priest would ask to see me in his office and I would smell the communion wine on his breath and every night I cried myself to sleep and finally when I was ten I went to the police and they took me in a room without windows and said do for us what you do for them and so I drank bleach and jumped out of windows and tried to chop off my head with an axe and finally got eaten by wolves. Then I went to heaven where Jesus healed me and gave me peace and I was looking forward to eternal life because heaven was really beautiful. It was this grassy meadow with a stream and everyone lived in tree houses and I knew that in heaven I would finally be safe, forever, and so I went and found Jesus and knelt down before him and thanked him and he put his hand on my head and said I bless you and I tried to say thank you again but then he put his dick in my mouth and said as it is on earth so shall it be in heaven and then my dad and my mum and all the teachers and priests and police and social workers were there and so I ran away from heaven I came back to earth and from then on I knew there was no escape and this is what my childhood was like and this is why I am a drunk. The End.

Younger readers may find Sam's need to know the past of two strangers somewhat puzzling. This urge to know other people's pasts, especially their childhoods, was endemic then. When two people met, they would ask each other where they had grown up and gone to school, their parents' occupations. Similarly, in their novels and films, the past of the main character was usually described at length. Whether in art or in life, the reason was the same: They believed that knowing about someone's childhood was essential to understanding them as an adult. And perhaps I should not say "they." In this respect (and no doubt others) I am still no different. I could have written simpler portraits of the people of Comely Bank. I could have just described how they looked and acted in those final years. Instead I have tried to explain them. I told myself that otherwise they would seem too odd, too freakish.

If we no longer dwell on the past, it is not because we think it unimportant. Everything is determined by what came before. This has been true of every society and culture that has existed; ours is no different. Given how momentous our recent history has been— the almost total loss of life on three continents in less than a day— you might expect this to be all we talk about.

There are, I think, two reasons why this isn't so. If we seldom ask about people's histories, or talk about our own, it is because they are, for the first time, ultimately the same. Nothing else, no war or plague, has been so global in its effects. It happened to us all. Not as a country or a people, but as a species. It is what brought us together.

Even to call it the past is misleading. The events of August 2017 remain a part of the present. Every building, every child, every grain of rice: Each is possible only because of what happened. Just because it is not our custom to build statues, chisel letters in stone, recreate that day with actors, relive it in prose or verse, there's no doubt how people feel. As they hold their children, kiss their loved ones, they think of how things might have been. They imagine the wars, the climate change and overpopulation. When they think of life Before, most of them are grateful.

7. Sinead

THE SUMMER OF 2016 WAS one of the hottest on record. Rain was scarce and fell at night. The dawns were pale and cool. The sun shone without interruption, scorching and relentless. It burned like a ball of fire that seemed to want to drop.

How to describe the light of those endless days? Heavy? Golden? It was both of those things, but also with a quality I have not seen since. It did not simply lie on things—leaves, hair, and pools of water—it went *into* them. Every shop in Comely Bank had a prosperous glow. The fruit in Mr. Asham's was perfectly ripe. The old clothes in Caitlin's shop were mistaken for new. In Mr. Campbell's shop the coal scuttles and chairs were no longer the contents of dead people's attics; instead they were already precious relics of some ancient, vanished time. Even the river seemed brighter, faster, rushing like a shining arrow pointed at the future.

And perhaps this is the effect of hindsight: The light before a shadow falls seems brighter in memory. But even allowing for minor exaggeration, these were halcyon days for Comely Bank. You could see it in people's faces. Whatever else was wrong with their lives, at least they were no longer living beneath clouds. The sky was not a depressing grey. The wind was not a hand that shoved them. For several weeks they spent their free time in their gardens or the park. Their minds were as the sky above: calm, untroubled, clear.

Unfortunately the same was not true for our human antiquities. It was certainly not a time of joy for Toby. During that summer his mother fed him mostly vegetables, which, though they took up the same space on his plate, made him feel only half as full. In compensation, he was allowed to watch more cooking programmes, but these failed to reduce his hunger. He rattled the locks of the kitchen cupboards with such violence that Evelyn had to buy three different kinds of lock before she found one strong enough.

Mrs. Maclean did not enjoy the heat. It made her long for winter.

The good weather also made Caitlin unhappy. It upset her to see so many bare arms and legs, so much undamaged skin.

The sight of so much flesh was also difficult for a young woman called Sinead, who had replaced Mortimer as Toby's carer. Sinead was tall with dark brown hair and always wore black clothes. There were holes in her ears, lips, and nose through which she sometimes put pieces of metal.

Her problem with so much seminudity was that it made her want to have sex. As an attractive young woman with excellent skin this should have been easy. She could have approached almost any of the men lying on the grass in the park and been sure of success. But she was like one of those strange birds that refuses to fly. She was determined not to have sex; it had been almost a year since her last time.

Why did she deny this healthy impulse? It was certainly not because she felt, as did Mrs. Maclean, that unmarried sex was a sin. By the time she was twenty-nine, Sinead had slept with more than a hundred men, the first when she was fourteen in a classroom at school, the last the summer of 2015. Nor was it because this last experience had been traumatic. In her diary entry for September 2015 she described it as "my most amazing fuck since that time with Pepé behind the funfair." The problem was that it made her pregnant.

The abortion was unpleasant, but not her first. Perhaps this was why she bled so heavily. They kept her in the hospital for several days, and it was there that she contracted an infection that resisted three courses of antibiotics. During the next three weeks she was so feverish and nauseous she ate almost nothing. She became so weak that there was a morning when she could not get up to go to the toilet. The thought of swinging her legs out of bed, pushing herself up, having to cross the vast expanse of carpet that lay between her and the bathroom: Each seemed a Herculean labour. And so she lay there till her bladder was painful, till it was agony, trying to find the strength to make that impossible journey.

She lay in her sodden bed for hours, smelling the acrid scent of her urine, sobbing her throat raw. Her legs stung. She wanted to die. She would never have unsafe sex again.

By the time she was well, she had lost two and half stone. She had also come to a decision. It was not enough to have "safe sex." There was no such thing, not completely. Condoms broke, vasectomies failed, the pills could be fakes made in the Philippines. The only way to be sure was not to sleep with a man, not unless it meant something, not unless they were in love. And not in the casual, often drunken, way that made her think she adored, and was adored by, a man she had barely spoken to. Though this might seem an implausible volte-face for someone as promiscuous as Sinead, in her case it can be explained by the fact that almost no one was immune to the idea of true love. Like Mrs. Maclean, she believed that there was someone, somewhere, who was perfect for her.

Her celibacy proved difficult. Within weeks her desire grew to such threatening levels that she was forced to masturbate three or four times a day, always before she left the house. This was a sensible precaution, because during even the briefest outing she was sure to encounter a man who found her attractive. Though she had once welcomed such attention, it was now irksome, invasive, and, most of all, too tempting. Sometimes she dreamed of going under the bridge at night; pushing her mouth against Alasdair's; feeling the crush of his body on her, the rocks hurting her back.

By the end of 2015 Sinead was leaving her flat only to buy food or go to work. In November of that year she had started working part-time in a small shop next to the delicatessen. The shop was owned by Mr. Campbell's ex-wife, Stephanie, and sold ceramics, ornaments, polished stones, and jewellery. These items were the result of the "creative flowering" that followed her divorce. Though Stephanie had never previously done any arts or crafts, or expressed a wish to do so, she claimed this was due to the oppressive influence of her former husband. She immediately signed up for classes in pottery, painting, life drawing, jewellery, and sculpture. "It was a wonderful time," she said to Sinead during her interview. "My teachers were brilliant. They saw what was inside me and helped me get it out."

Sinead hoped this wasn't true. The jewellery was ugly. The pots and vases were crooked and squat, the efforts of a child.

Stephanie told her to think of the space as both an art gallery and a shop, "a place to sell things and also to share." In addition to taking money, Sinead had to act in a curatorial role. To test her ability to do so, Stephanie asked Sinead to pick her favourite piece.

"That's hard," she said, then prepared to explain precisely, cruelly *why*. She definitely did not want to spend days in that tiny room with its orange walls and objects that looked like they'd been made by people with head injuries. It would be fun to see the look on Stephanie's face, her shock and hurt.

But then Stephanie said, "In what way?" and there was dread in her voice. Obviously some people had already been honest with her.

"Oh, I mean, I just like so much of it. Especially this," said Sinead, and picked up a ball of lime *papier mâché* that could only be a paperweight. "It feels so solid. You know it's really there."

Stephanie nodded vigorously. "That's why it's perfect for dogs."

The job was better than she expected. There were almost no customers, so there was no temptation. Though the pay was poor, she was free to sit and listen to music or play games on her phone. But after a week of this she was bored and hated all her music. There was nothing to do but stare out the window, and that meant looking at men.

It was only a matter of time before someone caught her masturbating. If it had been a man, this might not have been a problem. He would have probably gotten to have sex with her. Unfortunately, it was Mrs. Maclean, who shut her eyes, then slowly backed out of the shop.

Sinead's next job was in a coffee shop, where she lasted two weeks, then in a restaurant, where she lasted four days. Her need to spend so much time in the toilet aroused the suspicion of the management, who accused her of avoiding work, and then, when her behaviour worsened (during a seven-hour shift, she had to masturbate four times), of taking drugs.

This was her situation when she saw Toby's mother's ad for a carer in June 2016. She had lost three jobs that month. Her groin was constantly sore. She knew she could not keep any job that required her to interact with the public. Which is not to say she had high hopes for this new job: prolonged contact with any male could have only one outcome.

Her first sight of Toby was in his mother's kitchen. Grotesque, looming, he shambled in, sniffing at the air. She watched him rattle the fridge and cupboard doors, then look in the sink. He was about to plunge his hand into the rubbish when his mother spoke to him sharply. Guiltily, he straightened, looked at the rubbish, then back at her, and only then noticed the dark-haired girl sitting next to his mother.

"This is my son," she said. Sinead extended her hand. "Nice to meet you," she said. She did not flinch when he threw open his arms (perhaps confusing *meet* with its homonym), nor when he threw his arms around her. He held her as tightly as if she'd been a slab of beef.

Their bodies pressed together.

She smelt his sweat.

His groin pushed against hers.

And yet, she felt nothing.

Toby stepped back and smiled. "Very nice," he said.

"Do you think so?" his mother said, and looked at Sinead, who was trying not to grin. Suddenly even the idea of sex seemed implausible.

"Do you want her to come back?"

"Yes," said Toby.

"Then she will," she said.

At first Sinead was not allowed to take Toby out of the house; his mother did not trust a girl who dressed as if she were in mourning. Instead they spent their mornings drawing or painting (his pictures were always of food) or she read to him. She brought a different book each day, but his favourite, which she read many times, was the story of the worm that ate and ate till it was able to fly. Toby did not mind having to stay home. Sinead was pretty and smelt very nice. Sometimes she gave him pieces of paper that had secret pictures. The paper was completely blank till he put paint on it. Then he saw a ship, a dog, an aeroplane, or, best of all, a cake.

Those six weeks were a happy time for Sinead. So long as she was in the house, with Toby, she was safe from temptation, even after seeing him naked. She had been on the toilet when Toby came in. When she yelled at him to get out he said he had to go. As proof of this, he took out his penis. It swayed before her face like some inquisitive snake, and if it had been attached to anyone else (or even to nothing), she would have grasped it. Instead she pointed to the basin then turned on the tap.

Sinead grew fond of Toby. When she stroked his back or rubbed his ears there was nothing sexual about it. There was something remarkable about his dedication to food. It was the source of all his emotions, his happiness and despair. Though she too was consumed by a single impulse that overrode all else, at least she had a degree of control. Toby did not even have that. He was dependent on other people's decisions about what he could eat. This was certainly for his own good, but it also seemed wrong. Why shouldn't he be allowed to have what he wanted most? So what if it was going to ruin his health? Maybe it was better for him to be intensely happy for a short time than miserable for years.

Though Toby begged and cried, she didn't give him extra food. If she did and his mother found out, she'd be fired and end up roaming the streets like a creature in heat. There was also something frightening about the old woman. Sinead could imagine her living in the forest in a cottage made of biscuits and cake. Her son was like a lost child she had overfed.

But there was no question that Toby needed to lose weight. The question was how. Though it was important for him to take walks and be kept away from food, the better method would be to reduce his appetite. The cooking programmes had proved this was possible, but their effects were temporary. What she needed was a way to make him less interested in food. If it had been Mortimer trying to do this, many of Toby's favourite foods would have suddenly tasted bitter or sour, or Toby would have inexplicably started getting regular attacks of food poisoning. But Sinead genuinely wanted what was best for Toby. As the months passed, and he got fatter and fatter, she began to worry that his heart would burst from having to work so hard.

How different things might have been if Toby's mother had trusted her less. If Sinead had been forced to spend her days with Toby, at home, until at least the start of 2017, she could have Survived. She might have met some handsome Japanese man. They might have gone to Kyoto that summer.

When Evelyn told Sinead she could take her little boy out of the house, Sinead said she was flattered, very pleased, but perhaps it was too soon. Perhaps Toby wasn't ready.

"Nonsense," his mother said. "The fresh air will do you both good. You're looking a bit pale."

And so, on a mild morning in July 2016, with the taste of fresh vomit in her mouth—such were her nerves—Sinead and Toby went forth. She was terrified. Her only hope was to get to the park and stay away from men.

Yet within moments of stepping outside she was approached by a man in his sixties who asked what time it was. His name was Lonnie, and he was the father of "Spooky," one of Sam's volunteers. Lonnie was not a handsome man. His battered face was the result of many years of heavy drinking and fighting. He was also not to be trusted. When she told him the time he thanked her and lifted his hand to his face so that she saw his watch. She didn't know if this was an accident, or on purpose, but it didn't matter. She thought his eyes were very nice, brown and really quite young. She watched his lips curve into a smile. She saw them slowly part. Without thinking, she leant closer, because she wanted to hear what he said. She was certain he was going to say something important, something that showed his interest in not just her face and breasts but also the person she was. Though only a simple utterance, it would be the start of a conversation they would continue for the rest of their lives.

She was about to kiss him when Toby's throat bulged then loudly delivered gas into her face. And this was not a small detonation. It burst with conviction. After travelling down so many kilometres of intestine, pushing past great boulders of fat, it could not be blamed for announcing its presence. When Sinead looked at Toby's mouth, his jaw was working, chewing air, his lips flecked with saliva. And though Lonnie's mouth was ready, it too had saliva, lips, teeth that didn't look clean. He didn't want *her* mouth, just as Toby didn't want a particular cake but would have settled for any.

And so she stepped away. Lonnie stared in disappointment, then called her a cocktease.

After this she had no problems being out. However inviting the mouth, chest, or buttocks, she only needed glance at Toby to regain control.

The summer of 2016 ended on August 19. On that day the sky dropped so much water it seemed an attack. Toby and Sinead were caught in the rain coming out of the park and ran to find shelter. The first shop was a Chinese restaurant, which was out of the question: The last time Toby had been in a restaurant he had grabbed food from diners' plates. The next shop was a place that did laundry, but it was closed, so they went into the third. When they wiped their eyes, this is what they saw:

These were the overburdened shelves of Sam's bookshop, which had many customers, even though there was a library at the other end of the street. The people of Comely Bank were not satisfied with borrowing a book: They wanted to *own* it.

Sinead and Toby had never been inside; neither was a great reader. After taking a few steps, they paused. Relief gave way to awkwardness. Toby shook himself. Sinead put her hand to her hair. As for what followed, here is Sam's account.

August 19, 2016

A long, wet day with few rewards, the only exception being two photos in a copy of Macbeth. Both showed a group of young men struggling to bring a small boat in from a rough sea. Despite their difficulties, all appear cheerful. From this I deduce that they were not usually engaged in any kind of manual labour—what made them enjoy the difficult task was its novelty. There are no names or dates on the photos—at a guess I would say they are from the 1930s.

Other than this it was just damp paperbacks with airline tickets as bookmarks. The only diversion was when Toby came in. He wasn't with

Mortimer; he was with a goth girl I haven't seen before. She had a broken look about her, as if she got slapped awake every morning. I figured they had only come in because of the rain, because at first neither made any effort to inspect the shelves. He stood there like a boulder; her teeth worried her lip. I asked if they needed any help, and this made her smile the way pretty girls smile when they receive the attention that is merely what they deserve. "We're just browsing." she said, although they weren't, and even after saying this she made no move toward the shelves. Instead she stared at my face as if it were hung on a gallery wall. She took a small step towards me, stopped, looked at Toby, and said, "Thanks." She turned and picked up a book about Japanese swords, leafed through it in a distracted manner, then put it quickly down. "Come on, Toby," she said. "Let's find the children's books."

She moved down the aisle, past history, past travel, till she reached the kids' section. I only glanced at her a few times during the next ten minutes, but each time I did, she was looking in my direction, probably to check if it was still raining, which it was. So large was the puddle formed at the crossing that every time a car went through at speed a sheet of water sprayed onto the pavement; two parents with a pushchair got completely drenched.

Though Toby had been well behaved, each time I looked over he seemed agitated. His hands were pressed against his stomach; he opened and closed his mouth while rolling his eyes at her. But the girl ignored him until Toby wailed horribly. He swung his arms like two elephants' trunks and knocked a pile of books from the shelf. In falling they struck another pile of books on the shelf beneath, which, in vertical domino fashion, brought down yet another pile. Books were all over the floor. "Sorry," she said, and bent, which threw the male customers into confusion. The two with girlfriends had to pretend to ignore the spectacle of her upturned bottom, the inch of skin above her waist. The other men took quick visual bites, flicking their gaze away when she straightened. The only one to properly stare was Raymond, who was standing on the kick stool, looking at *the erotica section. After the girl had put the books back on the shelf, she led Toby to the cookery section. "Maybe this will make you feel better," she said, and opened a book.*

Slowly the great head turned; for the first time I heard words emerge. "Sausages," said a high, girlish voice (or perhaps a normal male voice with a liking for helium). "That's right," the girl said, and swallowed, and then Toby took the book from her and slowly turned its pages. As he did a light grew in his face, a glow that you see in the faces of child actors in commercials when adult actors pretending to be their parents give them a toy or fizzy drink, and all of them pretend it's a surprise and that they love each other. The difference was that the light in the elephant's face was real. I could see this, and so could the girl, who looked at me and smiled, and then her face was more than a mask on which dark makeup had been smeared. The eyeliner and lipstick faded, and I could see that though she was what most guys call "hot," her face was a palimpsest. Beneath the lips she pushed into a pout, the jaw that seemed clenched, there was someone else. This girl looked out of the goth girl's eyes like they were holes in a fence. I do not think this girl would have spoken to me, or shown herself, and probably did not know I could see her. But maybe, when she came to the till, she might have taken that chance.

But then Raymond fell from the stool and hit his head, and the girl and Toby just went. Who would have thought the old pervert had so much blood in him?

When I read this, more than sixty years later, what strikes me is not so much his sarcasm, his general lack of compassion, but the way that, for all his intelligence, he had no inkling of how significant this moment was for Toby and Sinead. He can be forgiven for not realising the former; even Sinead, who was usually so sensitive to Toby's shifts in appetite (which was admittedly a fairly narrow range, consisting as it did of variations of ravenous) was too preoccupied to notice that Toby did not mention food for the next hour.

Instead he slowly turned the pages of the cookbook, his eyes consuming each picture.

But Sam also didn't notice how she looked at him. She wasn't looking out the shop window. She didn't care about rain. She was staring at him with an emotion that should have been unmistakable.

That night she wrote in her diary:

August 19, 2016
Could not sleep for thinking about bookshop man. The more I came, the worse it got; I couldn't stop my hands. After the third time it wasn't even about the thought of us fucking. It was about us lying together after we'd finished, his head on my breasts. I wanted to stay in this thought forever, to go to sleep with it, but pretty soon it started to fade and the only way to get it back was to imagine us fucking. And I should know better. Perhaps he is married or gay or has a girlfriend or only likes black girls. But I have a good feeling about him.

After this she took Toby to the bookshop every time they went for a walk. As the days shortened and the temperature dropped, she found herself walking past whenever she could—just to glimpse the back of him, sometimes to take a photo with her phone. Though she tried to be patient, to let things build, it was often a struggle.

September 10, 2016
What is the matter with him? He hadn't seen me for almost a week, but all he said was "Hi." Didn't ask where I've been or what I've been doing. Instead he went into the back room and didn't come out for ten minutes. I had to buy a book to make him talk to me. I was wearing a black mesh top over a black bikini and although the holes

are pretty wide he didn't glance at my chest once. All he said was
"How's it going?" to which I said OK but that I was really pissed off
because I wanted to go and see Damson play in Glasgow but had
no one to go with. It was a totally obvious cue, but instead of saying
he also wanted to go he started asking about Toby. I told him Toby
was fine, that he'd just been to the hospital for some tests, and then
I made myself shut up. All we do is talk. Instead I did what I've
been trying not to. I moved round the counter, not all the way, but
far enough so that it was no longer between us. I stared at him. I
bit my lip. I could see his eyes through his glasses. Although he must
have known that I meant to do or say something, he didn't seem
worried or nervous, and this was very bad. It meant he hadn't been
hoping something like this would happen. It meant he wasn't one of
those guys who pretend they don't want to have sex because they're
frightened of being rejected. With them you have to do all the work.
You have to do the kissing, the asking them back, you have to take
off your clothes, and sometimes theirs, before they relax. But all
Sam did was look at me in a neutral way.

The next few entries had an uneven tone. Frustration alternated
with desire; tenderness gave way to rage. Sinead became convinced
that Sam was involved with someone else. Then the journal entries
stopped for ten days. When they resumed, it was clear that Sinead
had crossed a line.

September 14, 2016
He lives on Royal Circus. No. 24. I don't know which flat. Either
5 or 6.

September 15, 2016
Definitely no. 5. His name is on the door.

His routine became her routine. She expected to catch him with someone, but he was always alone. But the absence of proof only made her more suspicious.

September 19, 2016
The girl with the fucked-up face was in the shop again. Maybe she does only work next door—but what reason is that to go into the same bookshop twice in one week? She barely looked at the shelves. She talked to him for ages.

Soon she was following Caitlin as well as Sam. She saw her go to the doctor and chemist; she followed him to car-boot sales. But in several weeks of surveillance she never saw them together outside his shop. Though it was obvious to her that Caitlin treasured every second with him—in his presence her face alternated between disbelief and gratitude—her adoration was clearly not requited. He kept her at the same distance that he kept Sinead.

8. Fahad

The Lahore Review
AUGUST 2047

The Peacock's Eyes

FAHAD HAS LIVED IN LAHORE with his niece Laila, her husband, Jaleel, and their two teenage sons for the last thirty years. They live in a modest but comfortable house in Allama Iqbal Town, close to many of their relatives. On Sundays they go to Gulshan Park, where they picnic by the waterfall. On Mondays Fahad goes with his niece to Kareem Block Market, where he is friends with many of the traders. When he is talking to Suleman, who sells shoes, or sitting with Bashir at his vegetable stall, Fahad seems wholly at ease. At home, he gets on well with the two boys, Hasan and Ismail, who call him grandfather (neither remembers Laila's and Jaleel's fathers, who died when the boys were young). Laila and her husband have a great affection for him, as do all of their neighbours. Yet every morning there is a reminder that Fahad is not entirely content. While Jaleel, Hasan, and Ismail are praying, Fahad goes to the park. And this is not a recent change: In the thirty years since Fahad came to Lahore, he has never been to the temple. In some respects, this is unremarkable—just because he is living in a predominantly Hindu part of Lahore does not mean he must be Hindu too. But Fahad used to be; in his youth he was devout. Given that people tend to become more, not less religious, as they get older, this loss of faith seems to demand explanation. Surely it concerns his friends and relatives.

But Fahad never has to explain. Everyone in Allama Iqbal knows that thirty years ago Fahad got on a plane in Edinburgh, when there was still a place called Edinburgh, still a country called Scotland. Many people don't know Fahad's name, but when you show them his photo they say, "Oh yes, the Survivor."

And if my withholding of this crucial piece of biography seems a prime example of journalistic coyness, consider how you would have felt about Fahad if this had been the first thing you knew. You would not have cared about his friendships, his niece's sons, his lack of submission to God. There would just have been the fact that he Survived.

Unsurprisingly, some people have interpreted Fahad's near miss—he left on August 1, 2017—as more than just good fortune. He frequently gets messages telling him he was chosen by a higher power. There are Web sites devoted to "his incredible story," some of which claim he has magical powers. A few say he is immortal; one says he can fly. Similar claims have been made for others who left the impact zone in time. Such people were "saved" or "special."

It is certainly true that many Survivors have done well. The current *Forbes* list has fifteen people who call themselves Survivors; three prime ministers and two presidents make a similar claim. A more prosaic explanation for their success is that almost dying is incredibly motivating.

When I mentioned the idea of him being special, Fahad shook his head.

"I had no plans to leave Scotland, but then one of my customers asked if I was going on holiday, and I decided I would. I hadn't had a holiday for almost ten years! At first I was thinking of Paris, because it was so close and I had never been. Then I heard there were cheap flights to Pakistan, so I went to visit my brother. If I hadn't known about those flights, I would have been in France."

He could have been eating dinner in the Marais when the first meteorites hit. And this thought was enough to make me pause, to make me have one of those flashes of empathy, which if they happened more often, would make life unbearable. I remembered what he surely never forgets: He had a wife, two sons, and a daughter who did not get on the plane to Lahore.

But Fahad's thoughts seemed lighter. As we passed the peacock enclosure he said, "Beautiful." The birds were showing their tails.

Fahad led us to a bench near the waterfall and without prompting began to speak.

"Before I went to Scotland, I lived with my parents in Bradford [a town in the north of England], where my father had a small newsagent. After I left school at seventeen, I worked with him for five years. Every morning, I got up at four thirty to deliver papers, then I opened the shop at six thirty, worked until three, then went home and slept for three hours. Most weeknights I went to evening school to learn bookkeeping and finance. I was too tired and busy to think about whether this was what I wanted. My father's health was bad, and so he needed a lot of help, and my other brothers were still in school. As the oldest son, it was my duty, so I didn't feel I had a choice. When I had free time, I spent it helping at the community association that was part of our temple. Sometimes I

was so tired that I fell asleep when the pundit was speaking."

At twenty-two, Fahad was, by his own admission, an overly serious young man. "I just worked and worried about the business. I did not like to go to the cinema or watch television; it seemed a waste of time. I never had a girlfriend because I told myself I was too busy. Then one day I came home and my mother said we would have guests. That was the evening I met Rabia, who came with her parents and only said 'Yes' or 'Thank you' during the whole evening."

He smiled, and his eyes disappeared. A peacock cried. Another answered. Then Fahad stood, and I did too, and I thought he had had enough. But he did not say he was tired (though he looked it) or that he had to be somewhere else. He said, "We got married three months later, and it made me very happy. I did not mind having to work so hard when there was someone to come home to. The business did well, and we had a daughter, and then in 1986, a son. Shortly afterwards Rabia's father asked me if I had ever been to Scotland. He said he knew of a good opportunity."

Fahad did not like leaving Bradford, but he could not turn down the offer of his own shop. It was in a town called Edinburgh. At first it just sold bread, fruit, milk, newspapers, cigarettes, and other essential items. But although these were things everyone needed, Fahad's store received little business at first.

"I could not understand it. I saw people

walk past, then, after five minutes, they came back with milk and newspapers they had bought in another shop. I did not understand why they had gone so far, because I knew that our prices were cheaper than the other shop. And you know what it was?" he says, and jabbed his finger at me. "It was because I was Asian. That was why. There were not many African or Asian people living there, and none who had a shop. I told myself it would take a little more time for them to get used to me, but after three months, business was still bad. It was a shock to me, because in Bradford the white people didn't care if you were Indian or Chinese or black, only that the things were cheap. Sometimes there were problems, but it was never serious. We had good relations."

Fahad seemed genuinely regretful. But then his tone shifted, and as he spoke, he poked the air with his finger.

"And you know what, it got worse. One night someone broke the window, and it cost a lot to fix. Two weeks later, someone broke it again, and the police did nothing. There was something wrong with those people. They could not accept a man who wanted to make a living for his family, who worked very hard, just because he was a Pakistani. If it hadn't been my shop,

and my father-in-law's money, I would have gone back to Bradford."

By this point, Fahad was shaking.

"Those were ignorant people; they were racists. They hated me because my skin was different, because my mother and father came from a different place. Why could they not accept me?"

This was not a remembered anger; it seemed fresher, more dangerous.

"And it wasn't only a few people, it was most of them. They could not look me in the eye, they would come in and buy something, and if they said 'please' or 'thank you' you could see they did not mean it."

Fahad was almost shouting. Someone, or something, had to be blamed, and perhaps it was safer not to be angry with God.

In this belief, Fahad is not alone. There are still people who think the destruction was anything but random. They say it cannot be a coincidence that the worst affected countries were former imperial powers. They say it was punishment, or karma, for all the murders, wars, and exploitation, the lines they drew on maps.

"But they weren't all like that," I said, and Fahad looked at me. He stared until I was frightened of that eighty-six-year-old man.

I didn't find this article until a year ago, and it was more than a surprise; it was a massive shock. It never occurred to me that Mr.

Asham might have Survived. The strange thing was that when I pictured him in that park in Lahore, he was still wearing the blue shop coat he always wore at work. It made no difference that I often saw him on the street, wearing a tweed jacket, looking very smart. Without that shop coat he was someone else.

This was one of the unfortunate consequences of Comely Bank being such a close community. People's ideas about each other quickly became fixed. For many people, Mr. Asham was just the man who sold them milk, eggs, and newspapers. The most they knew about him was that he was married and had children. In some ways, this was due to the nature of Mr. Asham's shop, which was not a place where people browsed. It was certainly not due to any unfriendliness on Mr. Asham's part. Of all the shopkeepers of Comely Bank, he was the one who tried hardest to make every transaction seem like a friendly exchange (something that is far from easy, as anyone who has worked in a shop knows).

But perhaps this level of customer service was part of the problem. It was so professionally pleasant it gave away nothing, did not remind people that Fahad Asham was a man who sometimes wore tweed suits. Which is not to say that the colour of his skin made no difference to the mostly Caucasian people of Comely Bank. Though it had been a long time since a brick had been thrown through his window, there were still all kinds of subtle (and not-so-subtle) moments when people slighted him or treated him without sufficient respect because his skin was darker than theirs. Most didn't realise they were doing it, and would have been troubled if they did. Though much has been written about the iniquities of people back then, in their defence it must be said that most were less prejudiced than their parents and grandparents had been. Unfortunately, they were still cruel in many other ways. Sam recorded this conversation on his phone on July 11, 2016.

Mr. Campbell: A packet of Drum tobacco, please.

Mr. Asham: There you are. That's five-sixteen, please.

Mr. C: Here's twenty.

Mr. A: Thank you [pause]. Wonderful weather.

C: Lovely.

A: Will you be out in the garden?

C: Probably.

A: Good weather for a party. Or a barbecue.

C: Maybe.

A: Saturday will be good. Very hot. Very good for a barbecue.

C: Yes, it will.

A: My son will be working on Saturday afternoon. I will not, I will be free.

C: Really?

A: Yes, I hope I will be out with some friends.

C: Do you?

A: Yes. Maybe we will go to a barbecue at the house of a friend!

C: So you *like* barbecues?

A: Very much.

C: What's your favourite thing about barbecues?

A: The food. Especially the chicken. That is very good.

C: And what else?

A: I like to be outside, it is very relaxing.

C: Yes, it must be, given how much time you spend in here, where it's very hot and stuffy. [pause] So, do you have any friends who are having a barbecue?

A: No.

C: You don't know anybody?

A: No.

C: Oh, well, that's a pity . . . I suppose you *won't* be having a barbecue, will you?

A: No. I won't.

C: Oh, what a *shame.*

After Mr. Campbell left, Sam peered round the shelves. Mr. Asham was staring at his palms whilst opening and closing his eyes. He brought his hands to his face. He sighed. He began speaking in a language Sam did not understand. It sounded like a prayer, perhaps a lament, and then Mrs. Maclean came in. When she bought a newspaper, Mr. Asham was his affable self once more. He spoke of the weather; she was polite; barbecues were not mentioned. But there was something forced about his cheerfulness. When Sam brought his ripe avocado to the counter, all Mr. Asham said was, "Sixty-five."

Mr. Campbell can't have been the only person who treated Fahad this way. His reaction suggests a deeper wound caused by many hands. When he sat in that park, thirty-one years later, it had still not healed. In retrospect, it seems amazing that he could have been so unhappy, for so many years, and almost no one knew. I don't think his wife, or any of his children had any more idea than the hundreds of people who came into the shop each day. Fahad was such a private man. For many years, the only person who knew how he felt was a woman named Trudy. Like Fahad, she was an outsider. Trudy was a Filipino woman in her early thirties who worked as a prostitute. Unlike Fahad, she was not supposed to be living in Scotland, because she did not have permission from its government to do so. In this time without borders it is hard for people to imagine how great a problem this was. No one was allowed to enter another country unless they had permission. If they did and were caught, they would be sent back where they had come from. That they might have a very good reason for not wanting to go back was usually ignored. Trudy's reason was a husband who said he adored her and could not live without her, but who expressed these fine feelings by pushing burning cigarettes against her skin.

In 2016 she had been living in Comely Bank for fourteen years. Whilst she did not like sleeping with strange men, it was an occupation she remained stuck in: If she worked in a shop or office the government would find out that she was living in the country and then force her to leave. Trudy was thus trapped in her job, and the country, with no obvious means of escape. But she was neither passive nor a victim. She made the best of things. She had six or seven regular clients, and she knew what they liked. She took holidays twice a year whose common feature was the sea. Whether sailing round the coastline of Scotland, or walking on the crumbling cliffs of southern England, it pleased her to have so much water in sight. Though the waves were the wrong colour, and it was too cold, it reminded her of home. It is probably for the same reason that so many Survivors like to live close to the sea. When you gaze out over so much water, anything seems possible.

Though prostitution was illegal in most cities, Edinburgh was more permissive. Everyone knew the places with blacked-out windows and signs that said MASSAGE and SAUNA offered another kind of relief, but the police usually turned a blind eye. This tolerance had its limits: Trudy could no more tell people what she did than people could say they had been to visit her. In both cases, there would have been strong disapproval, and perhaps the police would have been informed. As a result, there was still a degree of secrecy about visiting her. Regulars did not use the front entrance, but instead walked down an alley that led to the back door. In some respects, her house was like an exclusive club, albeit one where you couldn't meet the other members. This suited most of her customers, who tried to pretend they were her only client. Sam was the only person who was interested in the idea that she saw other men. Even as early as 2014, his curiosity is obvious.

October 13, 2014

It's the middle-aged men who slow as they pass. Most wear suits or smart-casual clothes and have a taken-care-of look. They neither stare nor furtively glance at the door. Instead they turn their heads in a ninety-degree arc, first one way, then back, so that their interest is concealed. They must walk by every day, thinking how easy it would be. They work hard, they deserve it, their wives will never know. All they need is the nerve.

For all his curiosity, it took Sam almost two years to walk the short distance from the gate to Trudy's red door. In his diary entry for August 24, 2016, he offers a long, involved justification that begins with Lucifer, his Friday volunteer, telling him about a "friend" who went to see Trudy, then meanders for six pages through the rights and wrongs of prostitution and the importance of understanding all forms of sexual relationships, and then concludes by saying it is fine if he goes in the name of research. I omit this for a simple reason: It is total rubbish.

August 25, 2016

At three o'clock I went and pressed the bell. I stood and waited, as many must do, but unlike them I felt neither anxious nor fearful. I didn't care who saw the back of my head, what conclusions they'd draw, whom they'd tell. There's no one to divorce or dump me. I won't lose my job. The only reason I was relieved when the intercom spoke was because I wanted to see inside. "Do you have an appointment?" it asked. "No," I said, "Shall I come back later?" After a few seconds of confusion or thought, I heard a bolt being drawn back (the sound of which always makes me think of a gun). The door was opened by a small woman who was Thai or Malaysian, but definitely not Chinese, Japanese, or Korean. She had shoulder-length black hair with red streaks and was wearing a white T-shirt and a pair of pink shorts. When she smiled her teeth looked sharp.

"I'm Trudy" she said, and I put out my hand, forgetting where I was. She laughed and took it, and her hand was warm and limp. I followed her down a dim corridor brightened by photos of "exotic" scenes: a white sand beach ringed by palm trees, two red pagodas surrounded by bamboo, a swath of rainforest with blue and yellow parrots in flight. "I'm glad you came," she said. "I was getting so bored."

She led me into the back room, which in most houses on that block is the lounge, but in hers was a bedroom. Apart from the bed, whose sheets were grey, there was just a small chest of drawers and a chair, both of which were that pale Labrador colour that marks something as coming from IKEA. I wondered if she had a second bedroom that was just for her.

"Don't be nervous," she said, mistaking my distracted state for a case of the sexual jitters. "I'm not," I said, and then felt disappointed. For all my efforts to follow in other men's footsteps, their shoes did not quite fit. They rubbed and pinched too much for me to forget they were only borrowed. I did not feel lustful, angry, or nervous. I felt I'd been miscast.

"Sit down," she said, and I obeyed. The bed gave a ludicrous creak. She took a step towards me and put her hands on my shoulders, and her breasts, up close, seemed bigger. I could smell coconut, and my tongue felt large in my mouth, but my dick was nonexistent. I wondered if this was how some of her customers felt. Did the scene live in their minds for weeks, or months, a well-scripted fantasy of which they were the star, only to find, after all the rehearsals, that it was not as they'd imagined? The legs in their fantasies had been smooth and long; hers were short, thick, and fleshy, with large patches of scar tissue on her hips. Perhaps this sight was enough to make some of these men pause.

But the result of contemplating all their non-desire was a minor twitch of arousal. Enough to make me push up her T-shirt and dislodge her bra. Her nipples were brown, large, wonderful in my mouth. "Yes," she said, and put her hand on my groin, and I pushed against it, and then Trudy was no longer there. She was neither Caitlin nor Sinead but a hybrid: Caitlin's eyes, Sinead's black lips, the former's bum, the latter's breasts, the legs of maybe a third. And the fact that this transformation was unoriginal, wholly derivative, made me harder still. That's why we close our eyes when we kiss: so we can think of another. Of course, Trudy and I were not kissing: It is the one thing (besides anal) you aren't allowed to do. She undid my belt, then my zipper, and then she was holding my dick in one hand, my balls in the other, and when it has been a long time—almost three years—you struggle with disbelief.

Her hand moved with slow purpose. For the next few minutes, she didn't speak, except to compliment my dick. And it felt good, amazing at times, but my mind was soon up to tricks. The stupid part was that this was a situation without risk. There'd be no anatomical sleight of hand, no swapping of hand for vagina. I knew it was impossible for her to get pregnant, but in the end it was useless. I imagined the swelling, the birth. I saw the years of sacrifice, the wish to escape, and although her hand kept pulling, I was totally soft. I prepared myself for one of the usual reactions. I didn't think she'd be hurt or angry, and she would not accuse me of being gay. The more likely alternatives were that she would feign sympathy, or worse, that she would regard it as a kind of challenge. An awkward struggle would ensue, with her utilising every method of arousal—lips, tongue, teeth, her hair's caress—until her efforts seemed desperate.

"Don't worry," she said, and her hand stopped moving. "Most are like this first time." Although there is probably some truth to this, it was still irritating. Fucking condescending, I thought, which is why I said, "Yeah, really?" Unsurprisingly, this show of anger didn't bother her: It is hard to intimidate someone who has your flaccid penis resting on their palm. Instead she shrugged and said, "It's true. Yesterday a man could not. He even cried about it. I know that he wanted something but did not want to ask." I asked her what he wanted. "I don't know," she said. "But he will come back. He had something in his pocket. Maybe a rope. Is that what you like?" she asked, for an obvious reason: I had gotten hard. Whilst this probably did not surprise her, I was fascinated. I'm sure I have no interest

*in tying up girls, or being tied up, and definitely none in pain. At the time
I thought it might just be her voice, so I told her to tell me more about
those other men. She hesitated, and as she did her fingers stroked up and
down. I heard about an old man who likes baby talk, an ugly man who
tells her she's hideous, several preferences for lingerie of a particular colour.
Up and down her fingers smoothed as she spoke of their fetishes. I'm sure
some of it was made up, but there were others I recognised even from her
vague description. I'm not surprised about Mr. Campbell, but I'd never
have guessed about Mr. Asham. After a few minutes it seemed as if she
wasn't even talking to me. I'm not saying she'd forgotten I was there—my
penis was in her hand—more that whether I was listening was irrelevant.
When I came she seemed almost surprised.*

Like Sinead, Sam was desperate to avoid sex, albeit for different
reasons. She wanted to avoid an unwanted pregnancy; for him there
was no other kind. It was this that kept him from sleeping with Sinead
or anyone else. Obviously, this was an irrational fear: Though there
was no foolproof method of contraception available at the time, if two
people were careful, if they used condoms, spermicide, and contra-
ceptive pills, it was very unlikely the woman would become pregnant. But even this was too great a risk for Sam. For the previous
three years he had not only abstained from sex, but also from going
on dates, or anything that might be a date, even if the girl had a boyfriend, girlfriend, or husband and seemed completely uninterested
in him in any romantic or sexual way. He did not go to parties. He
did not go to bars.

He did not return to Trudy for several weeks. It was not because
he was too busy in the shop or lacked money; it was because he felt
the blush of shame that often follows pleasure.

Sam wanted to know more about the other men who visited
Trudy, but he was afraid she would get angry if he asked her directly. That she told him as much as she did may seem surprising,

given her need for secrecy. But she had many customers who were stimulated by stranger things than hearing about other men's desires. And after nearly ten years working as a prostitute, Trudy was understandably tired of men and their appetites. She had no close friends, and she had lost her faith in God, so she could not make the weekly confessions that Mrs. Maclean offered up to Father Robert. Sam was not exactly a priestly figure, and certainly could not provide absolution, but perhaps there was a kind of release in being able to tell someone. It might have also made a difference that he did not try to have penetrative sex with her. After that first time, she rarely touched him during their hour together. Instead she talked and he listened while his hand did its work.

October 4, 2016

The first time I see them is strange, knowing they've been with her, knowing what they've done. But after that it's just another piece of information, no different from knowing they like fishing or speak Czech. For example, yesterday, I had to listen to Randall drone on about flour beetles for ages, how they can regulate their population size or something and only once did I think of him doing that really clichéd Mummy-I've-been-naughty routine. Honestly, I don't know how she keeps a straight face. Is it just the kind of men who visit prostitutes, or are they (we?) all like that? If it's everyone, does that make it normal? Of all the things I've heard from Trudy—the humiliations, the choking, her having to hold a gilt picture frame around her head—nothing seems beyond them. Even the weirdest thing ends up seeming banal, like that thing with the shop coat and the mask.

The face on the mask was that of an elderly woman with grey hair and white skin. The teeth were somewhat exaggerated; on her head she had a crown. The woman was head of the British Royal family, and though she had a name—Elizabeth Windsor—she was usually known as The Queen. She was soon to acquire the dubious honour of being the only monarch to lose her kingdom completely.

Why did Fahad make Trudy wear this mask? Given that we have none of his letters or diaries, we can only speculate. But it is surely significant that he had such a powerful person act in a submissive fashion towards him.

But perhaps the mask, for all its strangeness, was only a symptom of a greater frustration. When Fahad was young he thought that the shop would be only temporary, that he'd do it for five, ten years, then leave the street, perhaps the city, maybe even the country. But no one could run the shop as well as he, and why pay someone to do an inferior job? So for three decades he had stood at the counter and suffered people's condescension—hating it, but not quite hating them, at least not fully, because it would only take one invitation, one evening at their house or a restaurant for them to see he was more than a shopkeeper. Word would spread, and he would be welcomed. They'd throw a party; there'd be grilled meat, laughter, dancing, fireworks, his name burnt into the sky.

Part II

The death of oneself is neither impossible nor extraordinary; it is effected without our knowledge, even against our will.

—Marcel Proust, *The Fugitive*

9. Autumn Begins in Us

HER COLLAR ALMOST COVERS HER cheeks; a green scarf
fills the gaps. She has let her hair grow long. She is walking briskly, a
little too fast, because her heels are starting to hurt. She slows,
thinks, *Wish I were Muslim. Then I'd have an excuse.*

The leaves are perfectly yellow and red; very soon they will drop.
They will fall on the path and the river and everything will change,
sort of. Any change you can predict does not seem interesting. It
can only confirm.

The path is not as quiet as it should be. At nine o'clock on a Sunday morning people should be at home. They can have someone to

fuck, a person to hold, a loved one, an intimate friend, and in exchange (though not a fair one) she should be granted these moments when no one is looking at her.

Caitlin brings a hand to her cheek but does not touch it, as if an itch had flared then gone. She looks around, first at the couple approaching, hand in hand; then at the old man with the black Labrador; then at two little girls in pink, one of them hopping, the other skipping, both with great excitement. As if the world is about to be treated to their latest performance.

A blur of brown, then mallards land. She watches them swimming till the couple, the old man and his dog, and the little girls have passed. Did they look at her? Did they stare?

Walk, just walk.

The river runs straight, and so does the path. The ducks quickly recede. There is no one ahead. For the time being, she is safe. Safe and free to think about that moment in the future.

They are at a restaurant on the shores of the Mediterranean. The restaurant is busy, and they have not booked, and so the waiter asks them to share a table with another foreign couple. The other woman is intelligent, beautiful, with a name like Danielle or Sophie. The man is unimportant. The couple do not want to share, yet cannot say so. After they've introduced themselves, said where they're from, the conversation stalls. Then Sam makes a clever joke about the waiter and they all laugh. By the time the entrées arrive it will seem as if they have known each other for years.

When Sam goes to the toilet, the other man will disappear. How, she is not quite sure: either his phone will ring, and he'll go outside, or she'll make him not exist. Then it will be just her and Danielle, who will smile and say, "How did you meet your husband?"

Her tone will not be suspicious or baffled. She will ask in a tone of approval, admiration, maybe even jealousy. This last possibility will make Caitlin pause. She will consider the woman's cheeks, the pout of her lips, the way her hair holds its shape despite the sea breeze. What is her intention? Is she a threat? Does she guess there was a time when it seemed as if she and Sam would never be together? Is she trying to conjure that hateful time into their blissful now? Perhaps she thinks this is a wedge that she can hammer in. That Caitlin will hang her head, acknowledge she once was undeserving. This, like murder or rape, is a crime with no statute of limitations. No matter that her cheeks are whole; that she and Sam have children; that he has held her every night for fifteen years: The fingers of the dead can point just as well as those of the living.

And she loves the colour of the river. It is like whisky, like ale. It is the kind of river people are warned about in fairy tales. Don't drink the water in the forest or you will fall asleep for ten years. But this doesn't seem so bad. Her tomorrow will be like her today. But in a year, or five, or seven, she will be better, not a princess, but not a monster either. When she believes this, she is impatient. The future, her future, is within sight, and she does not want to wait. She wants to be happy.

"We used to work near each other," is how she will answer Danielle. Who will smile as if to say *Go on*. But Caitlin will leave it at that. She will act as if this is a story not worth telling, as if there were no obstacles. They met and fell in love; how and when are details.

Walking and the sound of the river. She likes to hold her breath in the bath, the pressure in her lungs and skull building, the sound of the water no longer outside but something swirling within. This is how she feels about Sam. A stream, at times a river, is flowing from her. To call it love would be an understatement. It is not a single feeling. There is no love without joy, hope, desire, despair, hatred, and jealousy. With adoration comes the wish to hold a pillow over his face.

She is walking more slowly. Starting to relax.

Danielle will have many other questions. How long have they

been married? Have they got children? Have they been to Greece before?

Perhaps she is not so bad. She doesn't want to come between Caitlin and Sam. She just likes them as a couple, albeit in a fawning manner. But this is more touching than irksome. It is what happens to couples greater than the sum of their parts.

The path begins its long bend round the Colonies. These stone houses are where labourers lived when all the area was part of an estate. On a wall, high up, is a carving she has never noticed before. There is a hammer, a chisel, some L-shaped measuring device, what looks like a bushel of wheat.

"Where do you live?" Danielle asks, then blushes, not so much at the question, but the eager way she asked. Caitlin tells her she and Sam live in a converted barn in the Scottish Borders.

"It has a really large pond Sam dug for me because he knows I love ducks."

"How lovely!" says Danielle, as delighted as if the pond had been dug for her. "Do you have any other pets?"

"Two dogs, both from a rescue home."

"What are their names?"

"Bobby and Trick."

"Or Trick and Tricky," says Sam as he sits down. Which makes Danielle laugh, though she doesn't, couldn't, get the joke, not knowing Bobby, what he gets up to, or frankly, anything about her life with Sam. It makes her seem pathetic.

But when Sam puts his arm around Caitlin, when his hand caresses her shoulder, she sees Danielle flinch. And who could fail to pity her. Beautiful, intelligent, but with a husband who is not Sam.

The ducks return. Unless they're different ducks. Although Caitlin cannot tell them apart, these do seem happier. Their quacks are like a laugh. She smiles, rubs her cold ears. This has been a good walk: She has spent time in the future. She will go as far as the bridge and then turn back.

A jogger overtakes her, and for the next half a minute she must watch the smooth action of the woman's arms and legs, the confident bob of her ponytail. She runs with the resolve of someone trying to punish herself.

The woman goes under the bridge, then disappears, for that is where the path loops back on itself. The river takes a strange route. Though it flows down straight from the hills, seemingly intent on reaching the sea, during its last few miles it meanders and switches direction, as if the prospect of losing its freshness to salt suddenly makes it shy. Caitlin doesn't know the reason; it is probably something to do with rocks, or soil, or maybe people changed its path. It is definitely a good thing—if the river were straighter, more canal-like, there'd be no surprises.

Under the bridge it is dark and cold and the stone presses down. As a child, this frightened Caitlin. Any tunnel, underpass, or bridge made her shut her eyes and take quick breaths, and sometimes she passed out. Her mother thought she was claustrophobic, but that wasn't the problem. She could hide in wardrobes and cupboards for hours without fear. What terrified her was the idea that it only took a second for the tunnel or bridge to collapse. Whatever rules or forces kept the tunnel intact, however many centuries the bridge had stood, no one could guarantee these forces would not fail.

But Caitlin is not a child. She is an adult who believes that although the world may not be kind or fair, it is at least consistent. The sun rises in the east. The seas shall never boil. She can stand beneath this bridge for years, and it will never fall.

A pause to listen to the river. To look at leaves, at smoke, at the limbs of trees. Then she is heading home. Past the Colonies, round the first of the bends.

When you know someone well, you spot them at a distance. Their overall shape and height is a pattern you recognise. So when Caitlin sees Sam, he is still half a minute away.

Disbelief; a moment of wonder; then she slowly exhales. She has been holding her breath since she last saw him, on Thursday, when they hardly spoke because so many people were bringing in donations. She does not recognise the green trousers or black jacket, but it is him, she is sure. She wants to raise her hand and wave. She wants to call his name.

She puts her hands in her pockets.

Bites her lip.

Lifts and moves her left foot forward.

Ditto the right.

And though it must look like she's blushing, that is not it: Her blood is just impatient. It wants to be nearer to him. She wants this, as it wants this, but she also wants the opposite. She wants to walk past him. To disappear. She has no idea what to say.

He might not have seen her. Perhaps she can turn, walk round the bend, throw herself in the bushes. She wants to do this, and without warning a laugh leaves her. She is so stupid. She is obsessed, would die for him, but she is not a teenager, not a virgin. This is the man she wants, and she will walk towards him. She will be normal, interesting; she will not say, *I love you*.

She is seen. Recognised. He raises his hand. There on the riverbank, in the terrible present, he is speaking to her.

"Hey," he says. "How's it going?"

As if there were nothing remarkable about their meeting; as if they were always bumping into each other.

"Good," she says, which although not sparkling, is certainly better than *fine*.

"What have you been doing? Did you work yesterday?"

"No, did you?"

"Half a day. I yawned, and then it was over."

She laughs briefly, through her nose. And how would he react if she pulled off her jumper and T-shirt in one fluid motion? Just to show him there is nothing wrong with the skin on the rest of her body.

"What are you doing today?" he says. Which might be an invitation. If she says she's doing something, he'll think she's saying she's busy. But if she says she's doing something he thinks is fun, maybe he'll want to join in. It's an opportunity and a risk. If she says she's doing nothing, he might think she's boring (which he probably already does). Or he might say, "All right then, let's do something." It doesn't matter that Sam has never, in the fifteen months of their acquaintance, asked her to have even a cup of coffee. There's always a chance.

"I don't know," she replies. Then shrugs.

To which he says, "OK." He shifts his weight to the other foot. Looks past her as he says, "Yeah, me neither. Hang on a sec—"

He puts his hand in his pocket, brings out his phone. He touches a button and looks at the screen.

"Anything?" she says.

"No," he says, and sounds disgusted. In ten seconds he will leave. Then there will be months of standing in his shop or her shop, talking about fucking books. And if she is this pathetic now, how will she be in six months? She will be like that scary goth girl who pretends to be looking in the bookshop window. There are days when Caitlin times her. So far the record is thirty-seven minutes.

He looks at his phone and says, "So, are you going home?"

"That's right," she says. "I'm going home. I think my face is bleeding."

He looks up.

"It probably looks like meat."

And other people would say "What?" or pretend not to hear. They would look at the river, the trees, the sky and its very few clouds.

Certainly from embarrassment, but also from kindness: The afflicted cannot be expected to control themselves.

"No," he says. "It doesn't. It's not as bad as that."

And when he raises his hand there is no swell of music. Time does not slow. This is still the present. He pulls aside her scarf, and in doing so, a fingertip brushes her face. This is how, at twenty-seven, she learns that memory is useless. She will remember him doing this, but only as an event. The sensation of his finger, its slight caress, will elude recall.

Caitlin closes her eyes. She refuses to see his expression.

"I'm not a doctor," he says. "But no one has these conditions forever. It can just take time to find the right treatment. Maybe it's an allergy, or maybe you shouldn't use soap."

When she opens her eyes, he is looking at her with his usual expression: calm, interested, but without more emotion.

And when you have tried to show someone you love them, and got nothing back in return, the only way to save yourself is to try to hate them.

"You know what? I've tried everything. I gave up milk, coffee, and cheese. I rub steroids into my face. I don't have an allergy to wheat, dairy, gluten, or yeast. I don't use fucking soap. I wash in tepid water. I stay out of the sun. I don't use washing powder, and my clothes are never properly clean. My thyroid is fine. The only thing left to do is graft skin from my tits, or maybe the tits of a mouse, or just grow me a new fucking head."

Sam's expression does not change. So fucking what if he stops talking to her. Better to live without hope or joy than be an idiot.

Better for him to hate her.

Better to read one novel, then another, then another, and whatever she thinks about each—whether she liked the minor characters, or found the book confusing, its plot predictable—to speak to no one about it. Better to treat each book as a dream that happens only for her.

Better to feel nothing.

Better to be dead.

"Come on," he says. "I'm getting cold."

"Come where?"

"This way," he says, and turns towards the direction he has come from. For an instant Caitlin is confused. He does not appear annoyed or angry. If anything, he seems pleased. He is whistling, or rather half-whistling—the notes are often just blown air—as he looks upstream.

When she steps forwards, he smiles. "All right," he says. "Shall we?"

For the next minute Caitlin's mind is occupied with several difficult tasks. She must move a body that no longer feels like hers. She must accept that this is real. She must focus on the fact that she is walking along the river with Sam. She must pay attention to everything so she can remember it. She must recall the brown and foaming water, the green-headed ducks in a hurry, the plastic bags shredded by branches. She gathers these details; she hoards them. But they are only twigs from which to make a nest. The shiny, precious things inside will all come from him. The pout of his lips, his cautious stubble, the lean line of his jaw.

As they walk, she swipes these glances, but they are not enough. If she looks longer, it will be staring, which is what she wants to do, but cannot. She needs to be patient. As soon as he starts to speak, she can look all she wants.

They pass under the small stone bridge, where Alasdair is squatting, possibly defecating. He glares at both of them.

"What do you know about him?" Sam asks.

It is like the first bite when hungry.

"Not much, except that he's a bastard. Can I say that? I know he's homeless, and I know he probably has mental health problems, but does that make it OK for him to be horrible?"

Sam looks at her, which means she can stare. His lips are so red they look sore.

"I mean, have you heard how he speaks to people? He makes them feel awful. It's very aggressive. He dresses it up in this new-age diet crap, as if he cares about their health, but he's just a bully. He knows they wouldn't take it if he weren't homeless."

And maybe she shouldn't talk. Every word is a risk. He is already looking at her in a way that makes her head feel like it's made of glass.

"So what did he say to you?"

"All kinds of stuff. Mostly about my face."

"Like what?"

"I don't know. One time he said I needed to eat raw onions with every meal. He also said I should avoid direct sunlight at all times."

She laughs. Looks. There are grey hairs above his ear.

"That doesn't sound mean. He just tells me to eat more fruit. Especially apples."

She snorts. Not an attractive sound, but she is too indignant. "He also said my face wouldn't get better unless I stopped hating myself." This so clearly vindicates her opinion that Sam needn't say anything more. But it would still be nice if he did.

They keep walking. The river widens, seems slower. They pass a play area where every child seems possessed. Shrieking, screaming, they run in tight circles, spinning, colliding, falling over, hurting and being hurt.

"What's wrong with their parents?" he says. "Why don't they take care of them?"

"They're just playing. They're fine."

He shakes his head.

"What is it?"

"Nothing."

He begins to walk faster. As they round the curve of the river, he neither looks at her nor speaks. He has either forgotten her or (more likely) is trying to pretend she is not there.

The path stops at steps. Something is burning. She cannot see the smoke. The sky is blue, incredibly pale, as if the atmosphere has grown thin.

This is so autumn, she thinks, then says, just to hear the words out loud.

"Everything must end in autumn," he says.

He is smiling, not looking at her, as if this is a joke. And she has thought him many things—wonderful, brilliant, kind, cruel, cold, and indifferent—but this is the first time he has seemed weird. For the last twenty minutes he has been someone else. In some ways she likes this, because it makes her feel they are closer, that he has shared something with her. Except this is not quite the man she loves.

The river is ten feet below; black railings block off the drop. To their left the land rises in steeply terraced lawns, each with a waist-high chain-link fence separating it from the path. Though there are no signs saying *private*, it seems wrong to imagine opening one of these gates and trying to climb the slope. The grand houses above seem to forbid it.

It is ten thirty, perhaps eleven. There are now prams and tricycles, scooters, children running, children refusing to walk. There are also couples hand in hand, arm in arm, hands in each other's pockets. A lot of people, too many eyes. A cold voice in her head says, *Quit while you're ahead.*

As they near a domed stone building they are forced to stop. Two families are blocking the path. A boy is turning slow circles on a tiny bike while two little black-haired girls have a skipping rope stretched taut between them. From their pinched expressions it is clear they mean this as an ambush.

None of the adults is paying attention. The three men have their backs to the children; the two women are caught in a state of delicious outrage. "Totally ruined," says one with a French accent. She is wearing earrings that are miniature wind chimes.

"So what did you do?"

"I had her put down," she says, then chops the air with her hand. Her earrings chime their approval. As for her friend, she shows her appreciation by laughing and taking a step forwards to put her hand on her friend's arm. With this there is a gap in their ranks. The children freeze as Sam and Caitlin approach.

"Come here, darling," says the Frenchwoman, then places her hand on the nearest girl's head. The girl, who is seven, maybe eight, drops her end of the rope, then clings to her mother.

As they step over the rope Caitlin smiles and says, "Don't shoot." The Frenchwoman stops talking to her friend. *Fuck off,* she says with her face, while her lips say, "Alan." With that, the three men turn. This no longer feels like a public path; it is their living room into which two strangers have walked.

Something is wrong with these people. She has smiled, made eye contact, tried to sound friendly, and although Sam has done none of those things, he hasn't been rude. She wonders if something terrible happened to one of these families. Perhaps there was once a young man and woman who walked up to one of their girls and hit her in the face. Or worse. Did they have a boy or girl who disappeared? A child who was found dead? A child that was molested?

It doesn't matter. They will soon be gone. They will not form part of a story told to a couple in a restaurant on the shore of the Mediterranean.

"Zombie," says the girl who is still holding the rope. "Mummy, she's a zombie."

"That's right," the boy says. "There's blood."

"Blood!" the girls squeal, then point. The adults stare. Caitlin stops walking. She looks at the Frenchwoman, who stares back at her, and only after a long moment, during which she meets Caitlin's gaze without flinching, does the woman turn her head and make her earrings chime. "Ni-co-las," she says to the boy, then smiles at him. "He's at that age," she says, without turning back to Caitlin. "He watches too much TV. He likes soldiers and monsters and guns."

And time travel is real, it must be. Because the Caitlin of 2016 would pull her collar up, wind her scarf round her face, and flee with her head down. It can only be some her from the future who points at the girl and says, "Is it yours?"

"Her name's Estelle. She's not an *it*."

"Well, a *person* wouldn't say that."

"She's just a little girl."

"She's a little girl who doesn't understand that people have feelings. You haven't taught her that. Maybe you don't understand that either. Maybe you're not a person."

"That's enough," says the husband.

"No, it's not. Your children have said something horrible, and you don't give a shit. Is that how you're raising them? That they can treat people badly and there are never any consequences?"

"Listen, we're sorry," says the other woman, who sounds Scottish. "But they're just kids. Can't we just forget it?"

"You probably will. That's why you're all so smug and pleased and think that you're good people."

And as the faces shift, as anger replaces disapproval, Caitlin realises she has lost. So long as she focussed on their kids, she had a chance to shame them. But who can accept that their entire way of life might be deluded and wrong? Who will let themselves be casually destroyed?

"What's your problem?" says Alan, and steps past his wife. "We're not doing any harm. So what if they said something? What do you want us to do?"

Something definitely happened. Or is still happening. A school bully or a chronic condition. Something to make them scared.

Alan jabs his finger at her. "Leave us alone." He pauses, and when he next speaks blurts, "Just fuck off."

He swallows and looks somewhat pained, as if this has taken great effort. He keeps glancing at Sam, but Sam is looking away. He is pale and biting his lip.

"Go on," says Alan, with more conviction. "Fuck off, both of you."

She might as well. This is pointless. He will not back down.

"Why don't you?" she says. "You're in the way. You're the selfish cunts."

She is almost as surprised as Alan. She thanks people for donating clothes that smell of sweat and piss. She stares at the ground when schoolgirls laugh. If there were truth to the notion of biting one's tongue, hers would be a stump.

But what does it profit a person not to speak their heart? The meek inherit nothing. If they are going to be crushed, put in their graves, they might as well cry out.

Alan's face is red; spittle flecks his lips. "Cunt," he says, then pushes her. Then pushes her again. The corners of his mouth twitch up, as if he is trying to smile. As if he is delighted by his honesty.

And so what if he hits her. As Caitlin is pushed, takes another step back, she thinks this would be impressive. Swearing and pushing, though unpleasant, are still acceptable. But although there is no question that women deserve equal pay and can do virtually any job as well as a man, few say it is no worse to punch a woman than a man. Even if the woman hits first, the man is not supposed to retaliate. No matter that women are the same as men in one crucial aspect: Some of them deserve it.

"How fucking dare you," he says, and this time, after he has pushed her, his hand contracts into a fist. And no one is telling him to stop or trying to grab his arms. The others are standing and watching as if this were merely an interesting spectacle they have chanced upon. Even the children are rapt.

A hand takes her wrist, then pulls; the rest of her body follows. She steps closer to Alan, who quickly steps back, and she is pleased to glimpse fear.

Again, she has travelled through time. She must have, because she is walking hand in hand with Sam. To be precise, wrist in hand, because he is gripping hers. Only when they have turned the corner does he let go. He steps away a short distance, then puts his hand on his heart, as if he is about to propose. "Sorry," he says, and turns. Then he bends and vomits.

"What's wrong?"

He wipes his mouth. "Nothing. It's fine."

"Are you ill?"

"No, I just have an allergy."

"To what?"

"Certain kinds of people."

"Really? No."

"OK, well, maybe not an allergy. But they make me feel ill."

"No shit."

He raises his eyebrows. Takes several deep breaths. Then he says, "Hygieia."

"What?"

"Who." He points at a statue of a woman on top of the domed building. She wears a loose fitting dress that acquires folds as it descends her body. In her right hand she holds the base of a cup; her left rests on a pillar being embraced by a snake.

"OK, who?"

"She's the Greek goddess of health. Daughter of Asclepius. It's where the word 'hygiene' comes from. And I think it's actually open." He goes towards a gap in the railings. "Yeah, it is. Amazing."

She follows him and sees a metal door in the side of the round building. A sign above the lintel says *St. Bernard's Well*.

"I'd forgotten. Today is the day of open doors. How lucky is that?"

"Very," she says, but with no idea what he's talking about. Her heart is beating fast, and she also feels sick. She is back in the awful present where she and Sam are not together. This walk will be no foundation. If they had not run into those people, if she had not said those things, they might have gone on. They would have reached that place where the river is broad and slow. There are benches there dedicated to people who sat beneath oaks and alders watching the river pass, the sway of the trees, and irrespective of the year, the age, whatever their troubles were—the factory had closed, their husband was in prison, their son had said he was gay—the sights and sounds made them feel better.

She follows Sam down the steps. An old man in a green blazer sits on a metal chair in the doorway. "Hello," he says, and Sam says, "Hello," and then there are more steps. As they descend, the air is cold, and they should not be here. They should be on a bench with a plaque that bears the name of a man who sat and stared at the river. They should be sitting as close to each other as they will be in that restaurant by the Mediterranean. Instead they are going down into a tomb. How appropriate, she thinks, and remembers what Sam said about autumn. Was this his bizarre way of telling her she should give up? If so, she cannot disagree. There is really no chance.

It is not this thought that stops her halfway down the stairs. It is, after all, not new. She thinks it almost as often as she imagines their future. What cuts her from the inside—the knife is dull and slowly twists—is that she now accepts it.

"Where are you?" he says.

"Here."

The knife moves through her gut. It is awful, depressing, and to her surprise, a relief. There is something tiring about hope.

"Come here. It's amazing," he says.

"Coming," she says, then descends. She ducks through a low doorway and is surrounded by cornflower blue sky. It is, however, a strange sky, because it is supported by pillars. And yet it is, without doubt, the sky—it contains the sun.

Sam stands beneath, gazing upwards, his head to one side. She hangs back and does not speak. The moment seems private.

"We're so lucky," he says. "This is closed every other day of the year. There are probably people who've lived in the area all their lives and still never seen it. You know Mrs. Maclean, who volunteers on Thursday?"

She nods, although he cannot see. Mrs. Maclean is one of those old women who seems terrifyingly nice. They bake, they knit, they do volunteer work; they poison thirty-seven people at a summer fête.

"She was telling me about this a few weeks ago. She said she saw it in 1955, and I said, 'What was it like?' and she said, 'Wonderful.'

But when I asked if she'd seen it since, she shook her head. Which seems pretty strange. If she liked it so much, why hasn't she seen it since?"

"I don't know," Caitlin says. She stands next to him, under the sun, the sky all around. It is then that she understands she will have to leave. Not just her job, but also the street, probably the country. There needs to be an ocean between them. She'll go to Australia, maybe India. It's the only way.

Sam is still looking up. They are standing so close. Anyone else would lower their head and tell her, "Don't stare."

It is the start of the agonising process of taking her Last Looks. This will go on for weeks, months, but now that she has decided to leave, never to come back, she is entitled to be thorough. The skin on his neck and throat is stretched. It is like she can see every follicle, hair, and line. He is all detail, and she wants to focus on each one completely, but all at the same time. Why is that kind of looking impossible?

Yet even as she studies his cheek, his chin, she cannot properly focus. There is too much stone over their heads, underneath them, surrounding them on all sides. They are as enclosed as if they were in a mouth. And the decoration does not help. What gives the illusion of openness, space, is actually worse than blank stone. It is a blue weight that presses down. It reminds her of a documentary she saw about a coffin artist. He painted only on the insides of coffin lids, usually landscapes. His audiences had to get in and close the lid and then a light came on. He claimed that under such conditions, people paid attention.

The air is poor, lower in oxygen: She needs more of it. She sucks it in, takes quick, shallow breaths, and at first this helps. She feels happy, almost giddy, but then the ceiling drops an inch. As if the stone briefly forgot whatever is keeping it up.

She should just run. Take his hand and drag him out.

Like she hasn't been crazy enough.

She will stand her ground, outstare the sun, say fuck you to the sky.

They will be crushed together.

He lowers his head, turns his face to hers.

"I really enjoyed today. We should hang out more often."

And suddenly she can breathe.

The sky is not going to fall.

10. Found

ON DECEMBER 15, MR. CAMPBELL was stabbed seven times in the chest. He died on the way to hospital. He was sixty-five.

The first Sam knew of it was when he saw the trail of blood. It ran past his shop, finishing on the corner. It was early, he was still sleepy, and the blood was hard to believe. He stood in the doorway, drinking coffee, wondering who it had come from. When it began to rain, softly at first, then heavier, he thought it would quickly wash the blood away, but it took a long time.

Over the next few days, many people said how dreadful, shocking, awful, and terrible it was. Though they shook their heads and looked grave, none said, *He was a fine man* or *He was a good man* or that they would miss him. There was speculation about the will. Some said Mr. Campbell had relatives in France; others that his money would go towards a sanctuary for old horses. What everyone agreed on was that Stephanie would get nothing. Her divorce from Mr. Campbell had been protracted and bitter; it had taken the court three months to rule that there was clear evidence of mental cruelty on his part, more than enough to offset her single act of infidelity with Charming Robert. The settlement was generously in her favour, so much so that Mr. Campbell took out a full-page advert in the local paper that consisted of a jeremiad about the biases of the judicial system, in particular "its susceptibility to the pathetic lies of weak, attention-seeking people."

The police had no suspects. They did not know that the last person who had seen him that night was Trudy (who told this only to Sam). She said Mr. Campbell seemed no different. As usual, he lay on the bed and closed his eyes tightly and made her slowly undress him. This was by far the most difficult part, because he made no effort to help her, did not even raise his arms. It took twice as long as the sex itself, which was over quickly. "Thank you, Stephanie," he said, then put on his clothes and left. Within ten minutes he was dead.

When the will was read, only Trudy and Sam were not surprised. Barring a few small bequests, he left everything—the house, the antique shop, the contents of his bank accounts—to the ex-wife he had bullied and belittled for seventeen years. Almost equally surprising was how modest his estate turned out to be. Though he had aped the manners of the upper classes and often referred to his antique shop as "a hobby," he was no wealthier than most of the storekeepers of Comely Bank. He was certainly not as successful as Mr. Asham.

In addition to the main bequest, the will stipulated that all his clothes should go to Caitlin's charity shop, and all his books to Sam's. Neither could remember him ever entering their shops. He also specified that his gas-powered barbecue should be given to Mr. Asham. The general tenor of the will was thus one of making amends. The question was why an otherwise healthy man should have put his affairs in so final an order. Of some relevance might have been the fact that he was not killed for his money. His moderately expensive watch stayed on his wrist. His wallet was untouched.

The only possible motive was found by Sam in Mr. Campbell's desk. The executor of the will had asked Sam to help box up the deceased's extensive library. After three hours, and thirty-two boxes, he had finished except for a set of Gibbon's *The History of the Decline and Fall of the Roman Empire.* The books were heavy, covered in dust, mostly on high shelves that could be reached only by ascending a metal stepladder broken in a number of places; not only was the ladder unstable, it also had sharp pieces of protruding metal. During the entire exhausting, dirty process, the executor made no attempt to help. He hovered on the edges of the room, speaking on his phone in a voice so horribly nasal his mouth seemed uninvolved. Only when Sam had run out of boxes did the executor interrupt himself to say he had more in his car.

As soon as he heard the front door close, Sam went to the mahogany desk. He didn't know what he expected to find. He just had to look.

The top drawer was empty.

So was the middle.

The bottom one was locked.

He grabbed a letter opener from the desk then pushed it into the lock. He had no idea what he was doing; he was in a frenzy.

The lock must have been old, fragile, or poorly set in the wood, because Sam was able to push it in. Inside the drawer was a large tin box. Inside it was another box. Inside it was a third that contained a black ski mask and three photographs. One was of Stephanie sleeping in a patch of sunlight. On the back it read: *St. Albans. 1998.* In the second Trudy had her arms tied behind her back. The third picture was of a boy who was crying. He was eight or nine and wearing makeup, far too much. Behind him was a full-length mirror in which the photographer was reflected. It was not Mr. Campbell or any man that Sam recognised.

Sam put the mask in his pocket and the photos inside a book. A moment later the executor returned empty-handed. "I'm afraid you'll need to come back tomorrow," he said.

It took most of the next morning to transport the boxes to the shop. Sam spent the rest of that day, and most of that night, going through the books. He turned the pages slowly and with great care, anxious not to miss any ephemera. Most of the books were bound in leather and had had many previous owners. Their names were written in ink over a century old. He learnt that first Nathaniel Murray, then Elizabeth Griffin had owned a booklet entitled *Mastering Shyness Through Auto Suggestion.* He found anti-Semitic remarks throughout the Old Testament of a family Bible belonging to the Mac-Allisters of Dundee. There were tram tickets and pressed flowers, banknotes from countries that had long since vanished. It was an embarrassment of riches, but Sam was disappointed. He had never seen so few traces of someone in their books.

In part, this was unsurprising. These were rare, valuable books that Mr. Campbell had probably never read. Even if he had, he would not have turned over the corners of their pages, or written notes in their margins.

By the time Sam got to the last box he had given up hope. At first glance, the books inside seemed no more promising than the rest. They were bound editions of an Edinburgh newspaper from the nineteenth century, not the sort of book to inspire a reaction from Mr. Campbell. On all but one the year of publication was stamped on the spine in gold letters, but there was a single volume whose binding was darker and whose year had rubbed off. It was only to ascertain whether it was from 1870 or 1879—the other volumes covered the years in between—that he opened it. The binding felt odd, much rougher than leather—if anything, more like scales. If the book was smaller and lighter than the other volumes, this was because it was not one of them. Instead of columns of newsprint and illustrations, there were brown boards on which photos were mounted. They were mostly family pictures from the 1920s and '30s. There were photos of weddings.

There were photos of holidays:

And of people dancing in their gardens.

There were almost sixty photographs in the album. They were from a time that no one could remember, not even Mrs. Maclean. Which is not to say these scenes seemed strange to Sam (as they must do to us). When he looked at these people and places he saw many things that had changed, but also some that had not. Maybe it was not the same world as his, but they were related.

It was three o'clock in the morning when Sam finished looking at the album. He felt a pleasing throb of sadness. These people were long gone, but they had been happy, felt love for each other. The children seemed content; the parents looked dependable. His only regret was that their family name was McRae, not Campbell.

That night he slept in the shop. In the morning he washed his face and hands in the sink, then began to price the books. When he came to the album, he hesitated. Perhaps it was too soon to sell it. He had been so tired; he might have missed something.

He was still hesitating when he opened the shop. His first volunteer was bulimic Dee, who sat at the till and gripped her elbows while he priced the rest of the books. Boring Lesley came in at eleven, shortly after which they sold one of Mr. Campbell's volumes for £500. In some respects, not a lot of money. But enough to pay a social worker for an extra day's work—so they might visit a child a week earlier, so they might see bruises before they healed.

That afternoon Sam put the album in the shop window and felt a tremendous relief. Sometimes he felt he was wasting his time on questions he did not need to answer. Perhaps he didn't need to understand why apparently good people could make terrible parents, and vice versa, in order to take the risk that everyone took without thinking. It wasn't as if he'd have to justify having children: It was the "normal" choice. It was not wanting to have any that required explanation. And if he did have sex, and it led to a baby, and if he and the mother raised this child, perhaps it didn't matter that there was no way to guarantee that they wouldn't fuck it up. If, for example, they were emotionally distant, and their child subsequently grew up with trust issues that made it hard for him/her to form meaningful relationships, they would be breaking no law. They would not be publicly condemned. Even if the child grew up to be a murderer or tyrant, they would still get away with it. It was not like hitting a child: That left marks others could see. If they were cruel, no one would ever know, except themselves and the child—and sometimes, if they were lucky, the child might not know either. But they would, and always.

Sam sold two more of Mr. Campbell's books. Magda came in at four. She was an elegant lady with bright silver hair who had buried three husbands. She was carrying a small cage wrapped in a blanket that contained her rat. "She doesn't like the cold, do you?" she said into the cage.

Sam went into the back office, shut the door, and put his head on the desk. Magda could look after the shop. He needed to sleep.

He closed his eyes and soon was dreaming of climbing a steep hill to watch an organised flood. Sinead was admiral of the fleet; Toby was dressed as a whale. There was a mock battle with pirates and cannons. Metal balls roared through the air, blasting through timbers and rigging. The air was full of smoke and shouting, the screams of people injured. As he felt the table under his head, and knew where he was, there was a shout about thieves.

"Stop shouting," Magda shouted.

Sam stood and opened the door and saw Alasdair at the counter. He was holding his bicycle with one hand while jabbing a finger at Magda.

"It's mine, and you took it."

"Stop shouting," she said more quietly. "You're upsetting her. She doesn't like it."

This confused Alasdair long enough for Sam to interrupt.

"What's wrong?" he said.

"He says we stole that photo album."

"It's mine," said Alasdair. "Those photos are mine." He stopped talking and put a hand on his chest, as if the words were causing him pain.

"We didn't take them," said Sam. "They were donated."

"By a thief. They are—" He hesitated. "My family. Give it to me."

"I'm sorry, but I can't, not unless you can prove it's yours."

"They took it. They beat me, and they took it."

"Who took it?"

Alasdair shook his head impatiently. "I don't know. They had masks, they had black faces. I want it back," he shouted, and then Magda hit him hard in the throat. Alasdair made a choking sound, then staggered from the shop.

"I warned him," said Magda.

"Did you?" said Sam, but she wasn't listening. He watched as she kissed Daphne. The rat's tail twitched with pleasure. Could she feel that way about a child? Somehow he doubted it.

For the next hour he dozed and thought about Mr. Campbell's black mask. If he was willing to beat up the homeless, what else might he and the others have done? Perhaps one of them was the man in the picture with the boy. Why did Mr. Campbell have this picture? It was definitely not a picture you wanted someone else to have. They could blackmail you. You would have to give them money, do exactly as they said. You would become desperate. You would do anything to make them stop.

But although this is plausible, it remains speculation. All we have is what Sam knew. There cannot be more.

When he woke up, the rat was looking at him. She was sitting on Magda's shoulder. She had such pink eyes.

"She likes you," said Magda. The shop was quiet. He could not hear music or voices.

"What time is it?"

"Half past five. But I thought we should close. We're both tired. Today was very stressful."

"True," he said, and she kissed him. Her mouth did not feel old. At first he was too surprised to pull back, and then he was not sure he wanted to. That was when she stepped back and steadied Daphne, who had almost fallen.

"Don't worry," she said, and smiled. "That was just because of today."

"OK," was all he could say.

"I'll see you next week," she said.

After she had gone he replayed the kiss. Soon he was thinking of Sinead. It did not matter that she was unstable, obsessive, obviously bad news. Even now, she might be outside. He could go to the window and beckon, and in less than a minute they'd be having sex on the desk. Her teeth biting his lips, his cheek, her nails digging into his back as he pushed into her, harder, faster, till she had come several times, at which point he might start to slow, but she would dig her nails in, tell him not to stop, and this would go on until they were exhausted, perhaps in pain, and only then would he come. It would feel incredible, overwhelming, like a little death. He would lie on her, still inside her, as they softly kissed. Desire would be transmuted from something physical, a basic hunger, into the start of an emotional connection, or better still, the recognition of a bond that had been present, albeit neutered, during all those times he had feigned disinterest. Only with reluctance would he lift himself from her. As he slid off the condom, he'd see it was torn.

Sam did not go to the window to see if Sinead was there. Instead he put the money from the till into the safe. He vacuumed the floor. He turned off the lights. He locked the shop, then walked down the street to where Trudy lived. It was not his usual time, but she was glad to see him.

Sam was there for two hours, but he did not masturbate. He did not remove his trousers or lie on the bed. He spent the time looking at the bruises on her neck, trying to get her to say who had done it, asking her not to see Mr. Asham again. When he offered to compensate her for the loss of earnings, she said she'd think about it. He was on the verge of telling her she needed to leave Comely Bank. Until she was living and working somewhere legally, she would always be vulnerable.

He was about to say this when his phone rang. It was the police. The officer was calling from the shop. "You need to come here," he said.

Someone had thrown one of the heavy batteries that vehicles used in those days through the window. The floor was covered in broken glass, and the wind had pushed over the displays. Books were strewn over the floor, their pages flapping in panic.

"Was anything taken?" asked the policeman, who looked very cold.

"I don't think so."

"Are you sure?"

Sam scanned the books in the window. All of Mr Campbell's books were present. Except the photo album.

"Nothing's gone."

"It was probably just kids," said the policeman.

Sam had to wait for someone to come and nail a board to the window. He picked up the books and shook them to make sure there was no glass in their pages. As he did, some photos fell from one of Mr Campbell's volumes.

Both had *Mum, 1956* written on the back. Assuming this was Mr. Campbell's mother (notwithstanding the fact that there was a girl in the picture and Mr. Campbell had been an only child), it seemed unlikely that *she* could be blamed for any of his failings. These scenes were not from an exceptional day. Such warmth could come only from quotidian kindness. For the child in this picture (and perhaps Mr. Campbell), love was not a treat dispensed on weekends—when there was time, perhaps the will—but a constant star in her sky. She could rely on it. It would not shoot, or fall.

Why shouldn't a man as horrible as Mr. Campbell have had good parents? The kind of adult you became was not due just to your upbringing. Where you lived, the school you attended, whether you could think or run quickly: All these things could shape you. Every parent made mistakes, was sometimes impatient or cruel, confused their interests with their child's. But the day could still be saved (and, of course, ruined).

Sam remade the displays, then swept up the glass. The emergency glazier came and boarded up the window.

"Bad luck, eh?" he said, and hammered.

"More like bad karma."

"Haven't we all. Can I get a coffee?"

When the glazier left, Sam sat in the dark for a while. He did not want to go home, but the shop was cold from the wind that came past the boards. It was a freezing night, not one to be out in, certainly not for long. It was definitely not a good night to spend by a river under a bridge.

Sam locked the door, buttoned his coat, and went to see a thief.

11. No Place Like Home

THERE WAS NO MOON, AND some of the streetlights were off. The wind was a cold hand trying to push Sam over.

When he reached the bridge he called Alasdair's name. Although there was a chance Alasdair would run away, Sam didn't want to sneak up on a man who had just committed a crime (not to mention been punched in the throat).

He went down the icy steps with care, but on the last he slipped and badly grazed his hand. He couldn't tell how deep the wound was, just that it was bleeding. It hurt a lot, so he put it in the river, till there was no feeling.

It was even darker by the water. He had to wait for his eyes to adjust before he saw the narrow path that ran along the bank. When he reached the bridge he called out again. He told Alasdair he did not care about the window. He offered him a place to stay. Sam said this with conviction, but the echoes emptied his voice.

He went under the bridge and the sound of the river was magnified into a roar. Sam repeated his offer, then felt very stupid. He was standing under a bridge at night, talking to himself. Even if Alasdair could hear him, he would not trust Sam.

"Do you have a bath?" said a voice behind him. Sam was so startled he stepped off the path and into the river. The water came up to his knees; it was so cold that he swore.

"Good for the blood," said Alasdair. "And very good for the brain." He did not seem frightened.

"Did you know the human heart is twice as strong as that of an elephant? That isn't in books, but it's true. So do you have a bath?"

"Yes," said Sam, and got out of the river.

"You'll need to sit in warm water, then cold, or you'll get sick."

"I'll be having a hot one."

He heard Alasdair tut. "That would shock the blood, and you might get very depressed."

"OK," said Sam. "I'm going home. Are you coming?"

"I said I was. But if you try and take the album I'll call the police. They'll put you in prison with the other thieves."

"I won't take it away."

"Fine. But you've been warned."

Sam stayed close to the wall on his way out. From behind came sounds of breaking glass, laughter, bronchial coughing, spitting, more breakage, further coughing, then the sound of something heavy being dragged. Like a body, perhaps a human's, maybe a sheep's. Which was ludicrous, but then so was going under a bridge at night to invite a deranged homeless man to come and stay in your house.

So was not having sex with beautiful women because they might end up having kids that he would fuck up.

They came out into the lighter dark where things at least had shapes. Alasdair was dragging a long, white sack. He was wearing stained yellow trousers, black tennis shoes, and at least four coats.

"Stabbing me in the back," he said. He stopped, rummaged, pulled two golf clubs out of the sack, then threw them into the river. The sack was so heavy he needed Sam's help to get it up the steps. That was when Alasdair noticed the wound on Sam's hand, which was bleeding again. Most people would have recoiled at the sight of so much blood; Alasdair reached into a pocket and pulled out a plastic bag. Without asking, he put it over Sam's hand, then wrapped it several times around. He tied it with a complex knot that made Sam think of ropes on boats.

"Is that a sheepshank?"

Alasdair stared blankly at him. "What's that?"

"A kind of knot. Where did you learn it?"

"It's how I tie them. But you need to have strong fingers. Most people's are too weak."

"Yes, but did someone teach you?"

"I taught myself."

When they reached the top of the stairs the wind tried to push them back down. It was a mark of how hostile the weather was that no one else was on the street. Traditionally during that time of year— just before Christmas—it was socially acceptable for people to drink until they passed out or told each other the truth. It was a time of staggering, shouting, kissing in doorways, weeping, begging for forgiveness or punches in the face.

They took turns dragging the sack. All the windows were dark.

Sam lived on his own in a two-bedroom flat on the ground floor of a tenement building. He did not think of it as home; most nights he slept on an inflatable bed in the back room of the shop. Although it wasn't comfortable, he slept better there. He did not lie awake listening for the sound of a key in the lock.

They went in, and there was the relief of warmth. In the living room were only two chairs, simple wooden ones that were similar but not quite the same. The only other furniture was an old tin trunk that served as a table, on which there was a lamp. There was no carpet or curtains or pictures on the walls. The floorboards were not smooth and polished, as in Caitlin's flat, but rough and paint splattered. They sat on the chairs.

Alasdair asked Sam if this was his new house. "It's not mine," he said, and Alasdair nodded in approval. He went to explore. The kitchen had a stove, a sink, two saucepans, a frying pan, a fridge, some knives, and a chopping board. There were no gadgets, not even a toaster; the cupboards contained only food.

The bedrooms were similarly plain. A bed, a wardrobe, a small table with a lamp; once again, no curtains or pictures, and a floor of bare boards. Even Trudy's room for clients was better furnished. It was as if the flat had been looted by burglars so thorough they verged on the vindictive. They had taken everything that was personal.

"Very good," said Alasdair when he came back in. "I will stay."

"All right," said Sam, who had not realised that this was in doubt. "Do you want a cup of tea?"

"Yes, I have my own."

"What kind is it?"

Alasdair cocked his head. "It's very rare. Very rare, and secret. It is Chinese medicine. If you drink it every day you cannot get cancer. No one who drinks it ever has unless they smoke cigarettes or come from a hot place."

"I thought China was pretty hot."

Alasdair tutted at him. "Only some of it." He took a box from an inside pocket of his jacket and handed it to Sam. On the box was a drawing of an old Chinese monk with a long white beard. It was a tea that Mr. Asham sold.

While Sam waited for the kettle to boil he removed the plastic bag from his hand. It was stuck to the blood, so he peeled it off slowly. The cut was not that deep. There was always far more blood than seemed appropriate.

Alasdair was asleep on the floor when Sam came back. He was using the photo album wrapped in a coat as a pillow. He looked exhausted. Sam sat and drank the tea and watched him twitch and groan. In sleep, Alasdair's features seemed better arranged. Sam could imagine a time, perhaps ten, fifteen years ago, when the face had been softer, clean shaven, something presented in boardrooms, classrooms, operating theatres. Or perhaps this was wishful thinking. He could have come from a home where his parents kept him locked in a cellar. There was no way to know unless Alasdair remembered. Until then, Sam could believe whatever suited him.

SAM WOKE TO the sound of breaking glass. Which is to say he woke, gasped in a breath, and *thought* he had heard glass breaking; then, when all was quiet, he wondered whether that sound was only something he had dreamed. He decided it was the latter. He lay back and tried to remember his dream. He could recall several fragments— a rabbit in a cage; the circus; running upside down—but they did not add up.

He closed his eyes.

He drifted.

Something smashed.

Sam got out of bed and went into the living room. Alasdair was standing on one of the chairs. He wasn't wearing trousers. He wasn't wearing underwear either. The floor was covered in shards of china and glass. Alasdair pointed at what remained of the lamp. "It's broken," he said.

"What happened?"

"It fell off the table. And I had to break some bottles."

"Why?"

"Because I'm not going to sell them."

"You didn't have to break them inside."

"I couldn't wait. Will you pass me my shoes? There's a lot of glass on the floor."

Sam put Alasdair's shoes by the chair. He looked away, out the window, as his guest pulled on his trousers. It had snowed heavily. Cars were crunching past.

When he turned, Alasdair was lacing up his tennis shoes. He seemed in a hurry to leave.

"Where are you going?"

"To market."

Alasdair hefted the white sack onto his shoulder. There was then a pause in which each expected the other to speak. Sam was waiting to be thanked. Alasdair was waiting for Sam to offer to help him. When neither did, Alasdair left; both felt aggrieved.

In the shop it took two hours for the glazier to put in a new window, during which the wind blew through the hole and knocked over books. The customers said accusingly, "It's very *cold* in here." All his volunteers cancelled, citing ill health or the weather, except for Spooky (aka Derrick), who was so inept he was worse than no volunteer. Spooky was thirty-five, had a terrible stammer, and loved volunteering in the shop. He spent the rest of his time looking after Lonnie, his vicious father who bullied him to the point where he imitated his stammer in front of other people.

Sam spent the morning apologising for the cold or correcting Spooky's numerous mistakes on the till. Naturally, he blamed Alasdair, and with justification, but it was not entirely his fault. Yes, he had smashed the window, but perhaps Mr. Campbell was also to blame, as was whoever or whatever had caused the calamity that disturbed Alasdair's mind. But even after the glass was replaced and the shop warmed up, Sam remained angry. Just because the man was a homeless amnesiac, that did not give him right to smash the window of a shop whose profits helped save children from cruelty.

And so Sam called the police. For this, we should not judge him too harshly. Blame can be very efficient. So many ills can shelter under one umbrella.

Sam was ready to tell the officer what Alasdair had done, and where they could find him. Fortunately, this was when Spooky spilt his tea on a baby. "You burnt him," the mother shouted, but the tea was only lukewarm. She nonetheless threatened legal action and physical harm, then told Spooky he was a fucking idiot who should never have kids. It was unlikely that Spooky would ever have children, but that this was something he nonetheless wanted was clear from his reaction. He hunched, put his hands on his face, nodded his agreement.

"I want you to leave," said Sam. Spooky stood up, but Sam wasn't talking to him. He said it again to the mother.

"What?" she said.

"I want you to leave now."

"Not after what he did."

"What did he do? It was an accident. Your baby's fine."

"That's not the point. He could have been burnt."

"True. He also could have been kidnapped. He could have been taken by wolves. He could have, but he wasn't. Derrick's said he's sorry. Maybe you should—"

He did not get a chance to finish. The woman swung her hand at his face, but only after bringing it so far back he had time to get out of the way.

"You're banned," he said. "Don't come in here again."

He had never said this to a customer before, and he wasn't sure he was allowed to.

"I won't," she said, and stormed out, and then it was very quiet except for a vibration in the air. The customers were shaking with the pleasurable knowledge that they had a good story to tell. Sam went into the toilet and threw up. Then he made another cup of tea for Spooky. When Spooky took it he looked at Sam with such reverence that the mug was not a mug but a chalice brimming with holy liquid.

That evening Sam was actually glad to go home. He wanted to sit in a hot bath and drink a cold beer and maybe think of Sinead. He would submerge his head so his ears were covered. The only noise he'd hear would be the swish of water. If the floorboards shifted, he would not mistake this for a footstep. If the boiler squeaked, he would not mistake it for an old key twisting in the front door. If voices came from upstairs, or outside, he would not think they were discussing him, passing judgement, saying they had made the right choice.

He went home and ran a bath. It started snowing again. He wondered where Alasdair was, whether he was under the bridge or in someone else's house, naked and breaking their lamps.

He got in and the water was perfect. The bath was big enough for two, especially if the people were lying on their sides, at first not moving, then gently pressing their bodies together. Things would quickly become more intense, but although he and Sinead would want to have sex, they'd stop themselves, because it wouldn't be safe, and she would be fine with that. Instead they'd grind against each other, kiss in wonderful agony. Their heels and elbows would knock against the side of the bath, and the water would slosh out onto the floor, and some neighbours in the imaginary flat below would hammer on the ceiling with brooms because of the water coming through. When that failed, they'd use sledgehammers that made a booming sound when they struck. The hammers would be heavy, hard to swing, and so would strike the ceiling—his floor—at long, solemn intervals like the peals of a bell being rung to warn villagers that smoke had been seen on the horizon. Lives that seemed permanent, fixed, would be shattered by these chimes, and Sam was almost asleep. His eyes were closed; his nose was just above water. He was no longer having his fantasy of Sinead, the sub-fantasy of the village, but still the banging persisted. If anything, it had gotten louder, to the point where it could not be caused by a sledgehammer, but had to be some kind of projectile repeatedly fired at close range.

Unsurprisingly, the ceiling could not take such a sustained assault. It gave way, or sounded as if it had, and this was one of those dreams that did not seem like a dream because every detail—the sound of splintering wood and then a loud bang, as of a heavy door hitting a wall at speed—was vivid.

He raised his head from the water.

Heard a voice shout his name.

They were back.

They were back.

IT HAD BEEN almost two years since Sam had lost his temper. The last time was during the spring of 2015, when he saw two teenage girls shooting an air rifle at a swan from a window overlooking the river. The great bird hissed and flapped its wings, confused, frightened, and full of rage at the pain from above. Sam could have shouted at the girls to stop, rung on their door to see if their parents were home, or even taken several deep breaths and accepted that the swan would soon be out of range. Instead he bent and picked up stones and threw them at the window. Most were small, just pebbles, and if a few hit the girls—who were sixteen, or seventeen, barely children—they caused no more pain than the pellets caused the poor bird.

There were, however, larger stones, what you could call rocks, and it was one of these that broke the window.

The girls with the air rifle screamed. So what if they were little sadists: He was hurting them.

It was the same with his honest, genuine response to finding Alasdair in the hallway, clutching his shoulder, glaring at the broken doorframe. When he shoved Alasdair against the wall, it felt very satisfying, even better than phoning the police. This was an unambiguous way to show Alasdair that he could not do something just because he wanted to (a precept Sam was breaking only to prove a point, and besides, it was different for him, he was not at all crazy). What seemed like a violent attack was actually a lesson.

But Alasdair did not seem improved as he collapsed on the floor. He was shaking and moaning, having some kind of fit, and this made Sam tremble too. Partly because he was naked and the door was open on a winter night. But the fact that he had lost control was what upset him more. He had been on his own for ten years, surely long enough to accept there would not be a knock on the door, a key in the lock, his parent's voices saying they were home. He should have stopped being afraid. He should have given up hope.

He shut the door as best he could and got a blanket for Alasdair. He soon stopped shaking, but stayed curled in a ball. Sam got dressed, then made some of the Chinese tea. It was still too hot when Alasdair drank it, but he was obviously too cold to care. When he finished, he lay down, closed his eyes, and seemed to fall asleep. Sam was tiptoeing away when Alasdair said, "Why did you lock the door?"

"I didn't think you were coming back," said Sam without turning round.

"Where else can I go? It's too cold for bears. And why did you do it?"

"Do what?" said Sam, but he knew.

"Why did you hurt me? Because of *your door*?"

"And the window. And the lamp."

Alasdair made a hissing sound. "You can get new ones. They don't matter."

Sam turned around. "Not to you. But they matter to me."

"But this is not your house. So it is not your door. Not your lamp."

"Yes, but it belongs to someone."

"Who?"

"My parents."

"Are they alive?"

"I think so."

"Where are they?"

"I don't know. Maybe Africa."

"When are they coming back?"

"I don't know."

"When did they go?"

"When I was sixteen."

"Why did you stay?"

"They didn't want me to go. And they didn't ask. They made it look like they were going on holiday. A week after they left, my grandmother got a letter saying they weren't coming back."

"Why?"

"I don't know. They said everything was wrong."

Sam waited for Alasdair to say something about his parents not eating enough. Instead he pulled the blanket tight. He stared at the wall.

"There's a bed if you want it," said Sam. "You'd be more comfortable. It's my parents' room. I mean, it was."

He wanted Alasdair to say something, no matter how insensitive. Even this would be a kind of acknowledgement. Once the secret was outside his head, it wasn't such a weight.

It is the same with most Survivors. We do not expect consolation. We just need others to know.

Unfortunately, Sam found it hard to tell people. He had not told Caitlin or Mrs. Maclean; only Trudy knew. Even with her it was little discussed. She found it painful to talk about abandonment. While she doubted that her husband missed her (and certainly did not care if he did), many others had relied on her. Trudy's mother needed her help on their farm, she looked after her nieces and nephews, her father only enjoyed food that she prepared.

Sam would not get over being abandoned by his parents while he lived in their house. It didn't matter that he had emptied the place of almost all their possessions. So long as he remained, he could not forget.

12. Less

THE WINTER MONTHS IN COMELY Bank were always difficult. It was dark when people woke up, when they ate their breakfasts, when they left their homes. Daylight was something that happened while they sat in a shop or office or school. They might catch ten minutes of frail sun at lunchtime, but it was too cold to linger outside. By four o'clock the moon was large in the sky and frighteningly low, as if part of the earth were seeking to return.

That final winter was no exception. People stayed home as much as possible. They went out only for food. If they met on the street, in Mr. Asham's, conversation was brief.

But it would be inaccurate to say nothing happened during that time. The slackening pace gave everyone the chance to reflect. They thought about what they'd done during the year that had passed, what they'd do in the future.

Caitlin decided to leave Comely Bank.

Mrs. Maclean vowed to help more people.

Toby decided to eat less.

Mr. Asham decided to start seeing Trudy three times a week.

Sinead decided to drug Sam.

Sam started trying to get Trudy a passport.

After a period of deep reflection, Alasdair began drinking his urine.

But there were obstacles. Sinead didn't know which drug to use; Sam had no idea how to get a fake passport; Mr. Asham had to stop seeing Trudy after his wife found short black hairs on his shop coat. As for Caitlin, she read travel guides and looked at brochures but did not book a flight. Only Alasdair was able to start his plan immediately.

Toby's plan had its origins in his visit to Sam's shop. After Sinead saw how the cookbook calmed him, she bought him others. During that autumn she read the recipes to Toby, showed him the photos, talked about how the dishes might taste. But whatever had happened in the bookshop that day was not repeated. His hunger was unchanged. Perhaps this was why Sinead stopped reading to him.

The more likely explanation is that she was too obsessed with Sam. In addition to following him and waiting outside his shop, she took pictures of him on her phone at every opportunity. Most were partial, blurry images, but this did not matter: Each photo was a piece of him. Instead of reading to Toby, she looked at these pictures on her phone till she was squirming in her seat, crossing her legs, smoothing her hands down her thighs. Only when her desire reached wonderful, torturous levels did she return her attention to Toby. Even with Sam's face before her, Toby put her off sex.

When Toby returned to the cookbooks in February 2017, it surprised Evelyn and Sinead. Toby could not read and rarely enjoyed looking at pictures. Yet now he spent hours gazing at the cookbooks. This had no effect on the way he ate—he still cleared his plate in a ravenous manner—but he stopped asking for food at other times. He no longer tested the locks on the cupboards or went through the rubbish. He did not cry or beg.

Toby's self-discipline had dramatic results. By the end of February, he had lost twenty kilograms. By the middle of March, he had lost a further five kilograms, bringing him down to 139 kilograms. Though still obese, he was no longer elephantine.

Sinead couldn't understand why the cookbooks were working. The crucial difference, I suspect, was that Toby now *wanted* to eat less, but this only begs the further question of *why*. Sinead wondered if he was jealous of her feelings for Sam; perhaps he was trying to lose weight so she'd find him attractive.

That she could even consider this notion speaks volumes about Sinead's inflated idea of her attractiveness. Toby had no sexual inclinations, not even towards himself. When he got an erection he guffawed and pointed at his crotch.

It is interesting to compare the different urges of Toby and Sinead. Both were primal needs that seemed irresistible. Yet throughout history there have been people who abstained from sex or eating, even (in the latter case) to the point of death. In virtually all these cases some political or spiritual motive was able to override these desires. But although Sinead admitted that she had a problem, nothing she could think or do made any lasting difference. In some respects her situation was that of the world writ small. At the start of this century our societies were in constant crisis. The ice caps were melting; the stock markets kept crashing; the gap between rich and poor was widening every second. We were running out of trees, fossil fuels, fish, and clean water. There was perpetual war.

Everyone knew about these problems; they were topics of daily conversation. Yet few people were prepared to change the way they lived. It was essential that they were able to speak to their friends at any time. If they couldn't eat bananas, or fly on jet planes, they would rather die. Their problem was the same as Sinead's: They simply lacked the will.

If it seems ludicrous to equate the plight of a young nymphomaniac with that of the entire world, that is entirely fitting. An absurd comparison for an absurd situation.

If she could not change, if *they* could not change, how did poor mentally challenged Toby manage to overcome his craving?

These are the wrong questions. They assume that the decision to want and eat less was made by a conscious mind with plans and intentions, i.e., by Toby. Given his somewhat limited mental capacities, it makes more sense to give the credit to his body. Perhaps it suddenly realised it could not expect to function much longer at its present size. Never mind that his body did not actually "realise" this fact, or "decide" to make him eat less, at least not in the way these terms are used when speaking of sentient beings. We need not speak of intention or purpose. The body has ways of restoring balance, which though they may appear goal-directed, with a clear end in mind, are in fact just emergent properties of the system as a whole. For example, when a pregnancy is spontaneously aborted, it is often due to a conflict over resources between the mother and foetus. When the stability of the mother's body is threatened—for instance, by the foetus utilising too much of the available blood sugar—the mother's pancreas will automatically secrete more insulin, thus reducing the amount of glucose available to the foetus, which can lead to its death. This is done without ill will: It is regulation.

There are such patterns and mechanisms within all systems. Though we need not speak of "design" or "purpose" when discussing their properties, sometimes they perform a function that an impartial observer—who desired only the greatest good—might think desirable. This could range from reducing a chronically obese person's interest in food, to increasing the height of the tree line, or even something like the Cretaceous–Paleogene extinction event that destroyed the dinosaurs which had arrogantly ruled the land for really far too long.

In Toby's case, he was saved by whatever property of his digestive or nervous system led to the metabolic and behavioural changes that reduced his appetite. Though we might wonder at the timing—why, after so many years, did this internal switch get flicked?—the mechanism that caused it was as blind as those superheated rocks that struck the earth. No matter that he began losing weight at a crucial time: In the weeks before Toby's dramatic change, Sinead caught his mother wrapping a tea towel tightly round his neck on several occasions. Although she did not know her predecessor's suspicions (Sinead and Mortimer never met; she thought Trudy worked in the Thai restaurant), the furtive look on the old woman's face was enough to make Sinead suspect Evelyn was losing what little patience she had left. However, let me repeat, we should not be swayed by how fortuitously timed, and probably life saving, Toby's diet was. Likewise, we should not take the apparent precision with which the meteors struck what was then North America, Europe, and Australia, and nowhere else (excepting the small fragment that struck poor Socotra, "The Island of Bliss," whose people had never attacked or enslaved anyone, and which had such beautiful trees)

as anything other than one of a set of equally probable patterns of impact. And to those who still insist this was a balancing of the karmic books, let me point out that there were plenty of spared nations with an equally inglorious history. I would like to think, if I may dare—postulating the eradication of several billion people is a thorny proposition—that if the meteors had struck elsewhere, the eventual outcome would have been the same. Decades of shock and rebuilding; a fairer, better world.

However, just because that tragic, awful loss of life was ultimately a good thing does not mean it was willed or caused by any entity, force, or power. Though it was, in many ways, a perfect solution to the problems of early twenty-first-century Earth (though one that no government or supranational body could advocate, let alone accomplish), if there was some entity or force capable of such a thing, why had he/she/it/they waited so long before intervening in humanity's affairs? Why had they let things deteriorate to the point where only the deaths of billions of people could effect meaningful change?

Most Believers' explanations are versions of the idea that only a catastrophic loss of life could teach us the lessons we needed to learn. The deaths of millions had proved insufficient. There was no war we could not forget, no famine we could not ignore.

This is probably true. But there is still no need to posit an invisible hand hurling those meteors. It could have been, as I already said, a lucky accident. I also wonder what kind of warped mind feels it necessary to destroy two billion people in order to unite the remaining five billion, when presumably it could have just as easily restored the ozone layer, cleaned up the seas, and crashed the financial markets so badly they would never recover. Admittedly, this entity would have had to do far more if those two billion people were still alive—such as remove our ability to digest meat, stop air travel for several decades, eradicate corporations, form a nonhierarchical world government, and mix the populations of different countries so thoroughly that there were almost no places with dominant ethnic groups and ultimately, no countries, at least not in the classic we-are-one-nation-and-everyone-else-must-die sense of the word. But for a quasi-omnipotent being, this probably wouldn't have been more than a few hours' work.

But if this hypothetical, all-powerful entity were responsible for our collective salvation, then it is only a small logical step to conclude that it was responsible for everything that happened during those final days. That it chose to kill the good people and beautiful trees of Socotra. That it put Mr. Asham on a plane to safety but not his wife and child. The motivations for this are unfathomable. Why, for instance, was Toby freed from his great hunger when the end was so near? What was the point of saving him from his mother if this reprieve was to be temporary?

The only answer I can accept is that it made the people who cared for Toby happy. His mother was delighted; only the most twisted, unfit parents take no pleasure in their child's achievements. Her relief must have been twofold. Toby had done the impossible, and she would not need to commit an unforgivable act.

Sinead was almost as pleased. She had spent most of her year with Toby trying to achieve this. Sitting with him during his TV programmes, stopping him from going through the rubbish, trying to keep him distracted. Spending hundreds of hours reading to him about the worm that ate and ate because it wanted to fly. Telling him, over and over, that the worm in his tummy had to be starved so it would leave, so it could eat, so it could be a butterfly.

Given how much time and effort she had spent, it was entirely understandable that Sinead took most of the credit (even if it was not down to her, but Toby's body, or perhaps that invisible hand). At the end of March, when Toby's weight was down to 130 kilograms his mother threw her arms around Sinead and sobbed. Never had she seemed less like an old witch.

That month Sinead's pay packet contained an additional two hundred pounds. She used it to buy new clothes and the different drugs she was thinking of using on Sam. She wanted to know how *he'd* be feeling when under their influence. Did Toby's transformation make her happy? Was it like a shiny ring on her finger she could not take her eyes off?

When I think of Caitlin's many troubles—her skin problems, her infatuation with Sam—there is at least the consolatory knowledge that she still found pleasure, or at least escape, in books or walks by the canal. Her unhappiness was an understandable reaction to having a physical disfigurement in an incredibly superficial culture; without it, I am certain she would have been no more unhappy than anyone else.

Sinead didn't have this kind of release. She did not read, and her musical taste was limited to what she had listened to at school. Like many people, she watched a lot of television, but in a more indiscriminate fashion than most. She had no female friends, and her relationships with the men she knew were primarily physical. She must, of course, have had those small moments of euphoric joy that everyone has privately, when she glimpsed the sea between buildings, or got in a bath so perfectly hot it made her bones give thanks.

Even Mrs. Maclean and the sour Mr. Campbell must have had such interludes, though it would be naïve (and perhaps insulting) to claim these brief moments made their lives less miserable.

So there is all the more reason for hoping Toby's transformation made Sinead happy. I can imagine her doing some mundane task like tidying Toby's room, or vacuuming the lounge, feeling tired and somewhat bored, worrying that Sam was talking to some unconventionally beautiful girl from Denmark or Croatia with charmingly inflected English, a compelling neurosis, and very firm, high breasts. In her diary she imagined them fucking, sitting in cafés, holding hands and kissing as they walked past her.

But there must have been times when she looked over and saw Toby reading quietly, and this derailed her train of thought. Perhaps the knowledge that she had helped him was a small, bright thing.

What Toby thought about losing so much weight is difficult to say. Hunger had ruled his life for so long; what was it like to lose that obsession? To have so many seconds not coloured by want? The people of Comely Bank would probably ask us the same thing.

Although Toby would have struggled with such questions, there was no doubt how losing so much weight made him feel. Everyone could see the change. He'd had a bounding enthusiasm; his laughter had been panting, delighted, prone to induce hiccups. In place of this joyful, swollen child was an overweight man in his thirties. He was like one of those patients who has drastic, life-saving surgery that is deemed a great success, delighting relatives, friends, and doctors—everyone except the patient. They feel so drained, so hacked at, they're unsure it was worthwhile. There was an air of loss around Toby, and with good reason. Our body is the world we know best; its changes are supposed to be gradual. In three months he had lost a third of his. He must have felt like a different person.

13. The Trial of Samuel Clark

APRIL WAS NOT CRUEL THAT year. The weather was unusually mild. There was little wind to bully the trees, so the blossoms stayed on their branches. The flowers had a subtle fragrance that entered people's homes and made them long to be outside. Bedding and carpets, rugs and mats, curtains, cushions, pillows, and blinds: all were beaten, cleaned, made fresh. Dusty objects that had been kept for years were casually thrown out. Lawns were cut, trees pruned, many seeds got planted. It was a time of great energy and purpose, of starting afresh, and it was all quite pointless. In four months their bright, clean homes would cease to exist.

This was also the time of year when most people, either on their own, as a couple, or as a family, decided where and when they would go on holiday. Of all the choices they made that spring, this was the only one that mattered.

The notion of "having a holiday" was of great importance to these people. They wanted to relax and feel nothing except the hot sun on their face, a cold beer fizzing in their throat. They wanted to spend two weeks without responsibilities.

And yet this was somehow not enough. They also wanted to eat new food, see incredible landscapes, feel the push and spark of being in a strange crowd.

Unsurprisingly, most people's holidays did not satisfy these contradictory goals. They got bored or started to crave the familiar. Even those who had a happy time felt that they had failed to escape.

I think this is where we differ from people back then. We do not place such a burden of expectation on our trips. Last year I spent an enjoyable week amongst the limestone pillars near Vang Vieng, walking or sitting to sketch and rest my old legs. At the end of each day, I returned to my guesthouse and ate a simple meal, then sat and talked with the other diners till my eyes grew heavy. At no point did I forget that I was far from home. The green curry was thinner; the insects were larger; people's Mandarin sometimes had a French inflection. But it did not feel bizarre, exotic, or as people used to say, *foreign*. I doubt there are any places that feel like that now, with the exception of a few Arctic towns. These days we are all so mixed together: The only thing more foolish than speaking of nations is to speak of race.

In 2017 the people of Comely Bank (and Scotland, and for that matter, the United Kingdom of Great Britain and Northern Ireland, to give it its full, bloated title) chose the same kinds of destinations as they had in previous years. I am sure they had good reasons. The exchange rate between the British pound and the currency of their destination was good; they had been before, and liked it; many of the local people could speak English. Unfortunately ninety percent of these individuals, couples, and families made the wrong decision. In July they went to Barcelona, Paris, Rome, or Athens. They went to New York or Los Angeles.

It should come as no surprise that few of Comely Bank's eccentrics had holiday plans. The last time Mrs. Maclean had left Edinburgh was to go to her sister's funeral forty years before. Sinead was not going to risk going away, not when she was so close to her goal. Trudy was as trapped as ever. Sean and Rita seemed rooted to their bench. As for Alasdair, he was too busy enjoying four-hour baths in tepid water laced with urine and sage.

Only two people in Comely Bank had plans to go away. One was Toby, though strictly speaking, it was his mother who made the decision. She had a brother in Hong Kong she had not seen since he had visited Comely Bank fifteen years before. That visit was cut short after three days, following an unfortunate incident in which Toby bit his uncle so hard he needed stitches. The wound was on a hand that was holding a sausage. He had been teasing the boy.

Evelyn had never expected to be able to get on a plane with Toby: How could he behave himself in a confined space in which so many people were eating? After booking the flight for July 26, Evelyn opened all the windows of the house, then played a scratchy vinyl record of a woman singing in a voice so joyous and loud that it was almost a scream. She turned the volume up so high it could be heard at the other end of the street. As she stood at the window, looking out over the river, she must have breathed in the scent of blossoms and thought she was finally free.

A few days later Caitlin also booked a flight. Hers was a one-way ticket. Its destination had not been part of the long list of places she had first considered. Although there were many places that sounded

good—Istanbul, Kyoto, and Vienna were her top three—in each case
her enthusiasm quickly waned. When she pictured herself walking
down their streets it seemed absurd. She would be as out of place,
as much a freak, as she was in Comely Bank. The only improvement
would be not understanding their shouts of scorn and disgust.

In the end she decided to go to the travel agent, tell them how
much she wanted to spend, and let them decide. It didn't matter
where she ended up. So long as she left Comely Bank, she would be
leaving Sam. In a new place, in her new home, she would face many
of the same problems (and probably some new ones). But by virtue
of living in a different flat, having a different job, shopping in different places, making new sounds with her mouth, she could not be
entirely the same person, which meant she had a chance of being
happy. She would wear different clothes (smarter, not secondhand),
exercise more (she would get a bicycle), and alter her appearance (either dye her hair or cut it very short). She would also change her
name. "Caitlin" had lived in Comely Bank; "Stella" (or perhaps
"Yasmin") would live in Trinidad or wherever.

Such changes of identity are not uncommon amongst Survivors.
No one knows how many changed their names; my guess is thirty
percent. When asked why, most Survivors say they wanted to begin
again. When they talk of wanting a new life, it is barely a metaphor.
I hope it does not sound melodramatic to suggest that losing everyone and everything you have known is a kind of death. But it is still
a metaphor. However much they grieved and wished they were dead,
the fact is that they lived. But therein lay the problem. It made no
sense for Julie from Paris, or Alan from London, to be lying on a
bed in a room on a different continent while their houses and the
streets they were on, and the districts those streets were in, and the
cities that contained the districts, were only a crater. Alan and Julie
were out of place, and always would be, because their places no longer existed.

Some have said that these identity changes were an attempt to avoid the truth, a way for Survivors to pretend their loss had not occurred. To which I can only reply that this was something beyond even human denial.

When Caitlin told the travel agent what she wanted he showed no surprise. He looked at the computer screen, clicked twice with the mouse, then said, "What about Egypt?"

She had not considered there or anywhere else in the region. Like most people, even supposedly well-educated people, she regarded it as a dangerous place where people were perpetually angry in the name of God. She thought of women covered head to toe in black cloth, their eyes looking out a rectangular strip like the viewing window in a prison door.

"That sounds great," she said.

Ten minutes later she was walking down a street that now felt unfamiliar. Though the shops, cars, and faces looked outwardly the same, they seemed provisional, less solid, a draft of themselves. It was as if she were struggling to remember them from far ahead in the future.

Most of Comely Bank's residents had these dreams of escape. They said, "When I have a little more money," or "When the children are grown." They said, "After Mother dies." They said these things and meant them, and they were good excuses. But the only way to leave was hurting those they loved. It would be like telling them they were dispensable.

The only person Caitlin thought she'd hurt by leaving was Sam, and this was far from certain. Even if he was hurt, it wouldn't be her fault, because he was the reason she had to go. Of course, she didn't *want* to hurt him. He hadn't done anything wrong; he just hadn't done what she wanted. The important thing was that she tell him about her departure. That way, if he needed to say something to her—such as his honest reaction to the news that she was leaving forever—he would have a chance to do so. Sometimes it was only at the very last moment that people knew what they really felt.

He was tidying the shelves when she entered. The only customer was a woman in a tweed skirt at the back of the shop. Sam turned, saw Caitlin, and smiled. "Hey," he said, and it was amazing how the sight of him, his voice, could still make her feel as if some wave of energy were burning through her.

"I have good news," she said, then wished she hadn't said *good*. *Big news* would have been all right. *Good* was insensitive.

"What is it?"

"I'm going to Egypt."

"Oh. When?"

"July 27th."

"Wow. For how long?"

This was the awkward part. She couldn't say *forever;* it would sound like bragging. As if she were presenting this as a fait accompli (which of course it was). The polite thing, the *friendly* thing, was to pretend that the decision was not set in stone (although it was) and that she therefore wanted his opinion.

"I'm not sure," she said. "Definitely for a while." Which struck just the right note. It showed him her conviction without being final.

"Any idea what you'll do?"

"I don't know," she said. His question irritated her. There was something patronising about *any idea*. It implied that there was no possibility of her having some amazing job already organised.

"You could always teach English."

"I don't want to teach. It's boring."

"Oh, you used to, didn't you?"

"Yes."

"Well, it might be less boring doing that in Cairo than Edinburgh. I mean, how—"

"It's all the same."

She didn't want to hear any more. Sam was speaking as if leaving were not an achievement. He clearly did not regard it as a big event, and it was obvious why. He had been in Comely Bank, in his shop, for so much longer than she had, and yet she was the one who was leaving. It was fine for him to be jealous, that she understood. But there was something pathetic about him trying so hard to sound casual. So what if he was good-looking, clever, incredibly well read: He had done nothing with his life. He hadn't been to university. He hadn't even travelled. If she came back in twenty years he would still be there. He'd have grey hair and inch-thick glasses and be horribly stooped. He'd be one of those broken old men who inhabits second-hand bookshops the way a bear, when it is dying, will quietly wait in its cave.

"What's the matter?" he asked, and she could not answer. She was getting too angry.

"Nothing. I have to go."

"Wait," he said, but she did not. Stupidly, she was crying.

CAITLIN WAS RIGHT: Sam *had* achieved almost nothing. At twenty-nine he was still a sixteen-year-old boy who thought that reasons mattered. Despite having read many novels that featured men and women in various stages of love—not to mention all the "real" feelings in the letters and diaries—he remained emotionally naïve. He let things with Sinead and Caitlin get to the point where they were both crazy. Although he hadn't led them on, he had also never told them he wasn't interested. Perhaps this would have made no difference; it could not have hurt to try.

Sam's naïveté had mixed results when it came to Trudy. Whilst it would be an exaggeration to say he was in love with her, if he hadn't felt some form of affection he wouldn't have tried to get her a passport. It was also his way of proving that he was different from her other clients. In his defence, it must be said that he was no less susceptible to the confusing effects of an orgasm.

The kindest assessment of Sam and Trudy's "relationship" would be that he was her best client (or the one she disliked least). All she had to do was talk. He didn't touch her or ask her to touch him. Sometimes he didn't even masturbate. This allowed him to think there was something special about their time together. The money was just for the sake of appearances; if one day he forgot to pay, he thought she would probably say nothing. It might, however, be awkward for her, and that was why he kept paying.

But Sam's real mistake was his insistence that Trudy stop seeing Mr. Asham as a client. When she said she'd think about it, he actually believed her. The only explanation is his belief in their "special relationship." Which is not to say he was entirely convinced. He would not have worked so hard to get her a passport if he thought she'd make a quick decision. He phoned government departments, and spent hours searching online. He started conversations about immigration with many people, including his volunteers, during which he asked, in throwaway fashion, if they knew anyone who could get a passport for a friend of his.

All this is to his credit; there is no doubt that Trudy wanted to leave. He was also right to say what she already knew: that Fahad Asham was a dangerous man who enjoyed hurting women. Sam's error was to assume that her subsequent silence on that matter—throughout the winter of 2016 and the following spring—was due to her having made the right decision. He thought she'd followed his advice because they were close.

This situation was complicated by the fact that Mr. Asham *had* stopped visiting Trudy. But after four months he thought it safe to resume his visits. He paid double the usual rate and never hurt her face.

———

CAN ANYTHING BE said in Sam's defence?

If one considers the short life of Samuel Clark, in particular the period from his eighteenth birthday to his twenty-ninth, there are certainly positives. There is no question about his commitment to raising money for the charity. In its first year the shop made sixty thousand pounds; in its second, seventy thousand pounds; for its final year, the projected takings were just below one hundred thousand pounds. It is reasonable to assume this money helped protect a number of children who would otherwise have been harmed. The other group that benefited were the volunteers. For most, it was somewhere they could come and feel valued. For people like Spooky, it was a safe place where they could start to reconstruct themselves. They could sit behind the till and take money and put books in bags. They could clean and tidy shelves, alphabetize the fiction, cull books from too-full sections, build towards the realisation that they were OK.

Sam's other good deed was letting Alasdair live with him. This required considerable patience and self-control. During Alasdair's first few months in the flat he acted as if Sam weren't there. He had conversations with himself that began as a series of muttered phrases then quickly turned into shouting. Most of these ended with him yelling, "WHAT?" or "I DON'T KNOW." He also left blood in the sink after cleaning his teeth. Whenever Sam asked him not to do this, Alasdair smirked and said, "You don't like blood, do you?"

He had no respect for the few objects Sam possessed. Within the first few weeks Alasdair ripped two cushions and broke three plates, all the glasses and mugs, the bathroom mirror, two light bulbs, and one of the windows in the lounge. He often smashed things with a hammer then left the debris on the floor. The flat was his storeroom and personal junkyard. Sam had to wear shoes in the house; he took them off only to get into bed or the shower. As Sam lost his possessions, he gained many new ones. He'd come home to find a lawnmower in the kitchen, a child's bicycle in the hall.

Alasdair also threw out one of the few objects that had any sentimental value for Sam, a small jade crocodile he had been given by his grandfather. The crocodile was on Sam's bedside table in a big glass ashtray, along with a few stones he'd taken from the river because he liked the veins of quartz in them. One morning, when Sam was at work, Alasdair went into his room in search of a glass to urinate into. In some respects, he had good reason to do so, as there was only one left in the flat (and it wasn't really a glass, but an old jar), and Sam had taken to hiding it. When Alasdair couldn't find it—Sam had taken it to work with him—he considered the ashtray, but only briefly, because its capacity was too small. Alasdair did not know why Sam had the thing at all. Neither of them smoked. He took the ashtray and put it in the box of broken plates and glasses that Sam had been asking him to get rid of for weeks. After that, he carefully filled a bottle with his piss.

When Sam came home and found the ashtray and its crocodile gone, he calmly went into the kitchen. He was used to Alasdair moving objects around—not just small ones, but all the furniture. Alasdair thought the flat had irritable feng shui.

"Where did you put the ashtray?"

Alasdair was putting handfuls of what looked like grass into boiling water. "Which one?" he asked without turning.

"The one by my bed."

"You don't smoke," said Alasdair, sounding pleased.

"That's right. But where is it?"

"I put it in the box with the plates."

"Where's that?"

"Outside."

Sam went and looked. There was no box. It was the day rubbish was collected.

He went back into the kitchen. Alasdair was pouring a yellow liquid from a plastic bottle into the saucepan. He was whistling. Sam was not angry, but nonetheless wanted to say something. Surely Alasdair needed to know that he had upset Sam. He had thrown away something precious. Now all he had left of his grandfather was the tin chest in the lounge.

But all he said was, "What are you making?"

"Soup."

Later, after they had eaten, Sam wondered why he wasn't bothered. All he felt was calm. He would experience this feeling many times in the weeks that followed. Though Alasdair continued to dispose of objects in the house—he threw out Sam's parents' bed because it was too soft; the kettle because they could boil water in saucepans—it didn't seem to matter. It pleased him to watch the slow destruction of his parents' home. He was no longer afraid they might return; now he wanted them to come back and see the state of the place. Their possessions gone, the rooms littered with junk, the sweet ammonia smell of Alasdair's urine.

Having a place to live definitely helped Alasdair. One evening after dinner they were sitting quietly in the lounge. Alasdair was looking at the photo album; Sam was reading a crime novel in which the members of an aristocratic family were being fed to circus animals.

"This woman," said Alasdair, "is not my mother." He tapped her face with his nail. Then he turned the page.

Sam waited for Alasdair to continue, but he seemed engrossed in the album. He returned to his novel and read two chapters, the second of which ended with someone hearing the roar of a lion. He yawned, closed his eyes, reopened them, and saw the photo album coming toward him. This was the photo he saw.

Alasdair's long fingernail tapped the boy on the left's face, moved right to his father, then tapped along the line.

"This is not my family," he said. He sounded sad, but only for a moment. Then he closed the book and handed it to Sam.

"Take it back. Sell it tomorrow. If you don't, I will."

"Thanks," said Sam, and Alasdair nodded. Sam felt he should say more, but he didn't know what. He returned to his novel and read about an aunt being chloroformed.

"You are not an object," said Alasdair.

"I hope not," said Sam, and laughed. Alasdair did not.

"Just because they threw you away doesn't mean you're a thing. You weren't something they owned."

"I know," he said without thinking. He felt uncomfortable.

"They were wrong, but they don't know that. No," he said, then shook his head. "They won't be coming back."

"They might," said Sam, his heart beating faster.

"Why? So they can own you?" Alasdair made a noise in his throat. "You should hope they are dead."

"No," said Sam, who had fantasised about it. Prayed it was not true.

"Why?"

"Because that's wrong. I don't wish them well, and I don't want them to be happy, and I hope they're living a shitty life in some air-conditioned condo with ex-pats who moan about the beer. But just because I can't forgive them doesn't mean they deserve to die."

"Why not?"

"I just told you."

"No, you didn't. You said that isn't what you want. Not why they don't deserve to die."

"Because no one does. Or only people like Hitler or Stalin."

"Why them and not your parents?"

Sam shook his head. "You're fucking crazy. It's obvious."

This accusation did not bother Alasdair. He knew it wasn't true. He tilted his head. "Not to me."

Sam sighed. "Because they killed *mill*ions of people. Because even putting them in a cage for the rest of their lives doesn't seem like enough."

"What about your parents? Would that be enough?"

"No! They didn't kill millions of people. They didn't kill *any*one. They didn't kick me or hit me or put cigarettes out on my legs. They just left me without saying *goodbye* or *we're sorry* or even that shit parents tell their kids when they're getting divorced about how it isn't their fault and Mummy and Daddy still love them very much. It was a horrible thing, and I guess it's fucked me up, and I don't think I'll ever understand why they did it. But it's not the same thing as killing millions, or even one person. Lots of people are total fuckers who only hurt and destroy other people, but that doesn't mean they should be killed. What my parents did was horrible, and just because they could have done worse, doesn't make it less so. They just—"

He stopped, because Alasdair didn't seem to be listening. He was concentrating on an old piece of rope he was twisting around his fingers. Sam felt stupid, then angry that Alasdair had brought up the subject then gotten bored. He stood up and went into his room and closed the door very hard. At that moment, if you had said to him that he was right about his parents, he would have told you to fuck off. But what was true of them was perhaps also true for him. Just because someone makes a stupid, naïve, catastrophic mistake, one that they cannot forget, not even after sixty years, this does not mean we must condemn them completely. I have heard too much talk about people getting what they deserved. About karma and so forth. To my mind, this is the kind of thinking we should now be done with. We can admit the faults of the dead without saying they deserved to die.

14. June

DURING THAT PENULTIMATE MONTH CAITLIN stopped coming into the bookshop. It had taken her a long time, and it had been painful, but she had finally given up. Any interaction was a risk; the last thing she wanted was hope.

She would have been surprised (and maybe pleased) to know how much her behaviour upset Sam. After all, he was not in love with her, and—though it may seem cruel to say so—they were not really friends. What upset him was the fact that she was leaving. He felt the same when his volunteers left. Though this was usually cause for celebration—it meant they had found permanent employment, true love, a level of self-esteem that made them realise their time was too precious to be spent sitting behind a cash register—it always bothered him. It suggested that his world was not as stable as he thought. This, perhaps, is another reason he stayed in Comely Bank. It was like one of those little lakes a river sometimes leaves behind. A place to meet the same fish all the time.

Sam was especially sensitive because four of his volunteers had left that month. Clive and Penny were the first to go. They announced that with the help of Jesus they had beaten their addictions and in gratitude were going to work with street kids in Bolivia. Next was Mehmet, who clasped Sam's hand and said he was going to open an ice cream shop in Ürümqi. As for Boring Lesley, she had found a job at the airport. But although Sam would miss them, they were easily replaced. There was no shortage of people in Comely Bank whose lives had hit bottom. Only a week later there were three new volunteers: Abena (who had just converted from Buddhism, her ninth religion, to Islam), Paige (who was on probation), and Douglas (who had had surgery then chemotherapy for his cancer and whose prognosis was good).

But Caitlin meant more to Sam than his volunteers did. One does not have to reciprocate love in order to enjoy it. No wonder he found the loss of Caitlin's attention distressing. If someone stops loving you, or seeming to love you, it casts a shadow backwards. Treasured Memories lose colour, light, and become Things That Happened. Perhaps she had not enjoyed talking about books or the oddities of their volunteers. Perhaps he had bored her.

Sam started having dreams in which he was continually late. Usually these involved him running to catch a bus because he had gotten the time of departure wrong. When he woke his heart was racing and his chest felt tight; sometimes he had to drink whisky to calm down. The worst part was that he couldn't disagree with what Caitlin was doing. Anything except ignoring him was basically self-harm.

Sam dealt with the loss of Caitlin's attention in a way Mrs. Maclean would have understood. He lent Lonnie fifty pounds. He allowed Lucifer to separate Crime from Fiction. On Sunday afternoons he started going to Mrs. Maclean's house, even though this involved two hours of halting conversation with the three elderly ladies she invited from church. Some days he went to the toilet three times during his visit, just to get away from the talk of bunions and floral arrangements. It was during one of these escapes that he happened to look in a room whose door was usually closed. Inside he could see a writing bureau and a long shelf full of boxes. On that day he went no further; the next week he took as many letters as he could hide in his pockets.

He also tried to be a better housemate to Alasdair. It took three hours to find soybean paste, ginger-marinated tofu, organic spinach, organic flat parsley, wild garlic, freshwater mussels, buckwheat noodles, rice wine, single cream, and saffron. He marinated the mussels for six hours. The sauce took another two. When Alasdair came in he sniffed the air suspiciously, then looked in the pot.

"What's in that?"

Sam told him, then could not help adding, "It tastes pretty amazing."

Alasdair picked up a wooden spoon. He dragged it through the thick sauce, then brought it to his mouth. He sniffed.

"No."

"What?"

"It's no good."

"Why?"

"You can't put these together."

"Come on. Just taste it."

Alasdair put his finger in the sauce, then licked it.

"So?"

"It's very good."

"I told you."

"Yes, but that's not the point. The point is—" he said, and paused, as if he was only then picking a reason. "The point is they don't work together. The wheat upsets the mussels. The spinach blocks the cream. Just because it tastes great doesn't mean it's good for you. You'll get more nutrition from rice crackers."

Which is what he ate for dinner.

That same week Sam brought the laptop and image scanner from the bookshop and set them up by the old chest. When Alasdair came in, Sam made no attempt to explain the piles of photos, notebooks, and paper scraps on the floor. Even if Alasdair wasn't interested, it was a job long overdue. A small fire, a minor flood, and they would all be lost.

It wasn't an unpleasant task. He got to remember (or try to remember) when and how he'd found each item. For the first two years he hadn't bothered to record this information, which meant that some items were even more of a mystery than when he'd first seen them. I doubt anyone will ever know why the boy on the left looks so scared.

Sam didn't dwell on any picture. He preferred to lose himself in the repetition of the task. Nowadays we only need to hold something up to our screens for a second; back then it could take thirty seconds to scan an item. It was boring, but soothing.

Sam was about to scan a photo he'd found in a book called *The Price of Glory*, in May 2011, when he realised Alasdair was standing over him.

"I don't know them," he said.

"I didn't say you did." Sam turned over the photo. "The women's names are Val and Cynthia; it doesn't say what his is. It's from 1961."

Sam put it down and picked up another. "You probably don't know them either."

"That's right," said Alasdair. "They're not my family." He squatted and turned over several more photos, then stood and went to the chest.

"You should give these back."

"I didn't take them."

Alasdair thought for a moment. "Maybe you are not a thief. But they belong to someone who didn't mean to give them away."

"I thought you didn't believe in people owning things."

"These are not things." He sat down and started looking through the piles. Sam scanned a few more pictures, then yawned. He stood and stretched.

"I'm going to bed. Do you want to take over?"

"All right. Just pass me that cup."

It was half-full of yellow liquid. At least it wasn't warm.

That night Sam woke several times and heard the whirr of the scanner. How many people were in that trunk? At least several thousand. More than the number of living people he knew in Comely

Bank. Even that small amount, perhaps three hundred, was overwhelming when he considered all the things they'd said and done, what people thought about them. It was a lot of information, most of which would vanish when they died—except that which persisted through their children and friends, and then, after they were gone, through letters, photos, or videos posted on the Internet. For a moment, as Sam lay in the dark, he saw himself in a playground holding the hand of a child with curly yellow hair and a nose like his. He protested, and the child vanished.

The idea of "living on" in others' memories, and through offspring, was for many a great comfort. Every society has its delusions, some of them necessary. Just because the people of Comely Bank had peculiar notions of how to be happy doesn't mean we should judge them. Hindsight is too sharp. If someone is writing about us in sixty years' time, he or she will certainly find fuel with which to burn us. They might, for example, remark on the contradiction between the way we think of the present and the future. As someone who remembers how it was Before, I can attest to the fact that most people now are more focussed on what is happening in the present. We are not always rushing to the next experience, hoping it will be better.

The usual explanation for this shift is that we accept what Sam could not: how quickly things can change, how swiftly they end. Though this is probably true to some extent, it is my belief that most people believe the opposite. Few think that a cataclysm will happen again.

But in ten years, or sixty years, the same thing could happen again, and it might be worse. The world's population is now smaller and by no means as dispersed. Any thoughts of stopping another cataclysm are only science fiction.

TOBY BECAME A problem for Sinead in June. She had decided to take him to the park, because the exercise was good for him, and they could stop by the bookshop. He was reluctant to go; in the absence of his hunger, the street had lost its allure.

They did not need their coats. The sky was an encouraging blue.

They walked down the street, past a restaurant, then a café. Toby didn't even pause. When they passed the delicatessen he glanced in the window, but for only a few seconds. She didn't even have to stop him reaching for the mangoes and melons arranged outside Mr. Asham's.

When they reached the bookshop, Sam was on his knees. He was putting new books in the window, the last from Mr. Campbell's collection, including the photo album. Sinead usually watched Sam from near the kerb, perhaps to preserve the fiction that she was not staring into the window as if it were a television that needed only one channel. On that day, she went to her usual place. Sam had his back to the street, so he did not see her and Toby. This had the advantage of letting her look as much as she wanted, but stopped her from seeing his face. She didn't bother to take a photo; she had plenty already. For an enjoyable, though average five minutes, she stared at his back and bottom, knowing she would soon be seeing them without clothes. She had tried all the drugs she had bought except gamma hydroxybutyric acid (GHB), a central nervous system depressant said to induce euphoria. A low dose would not put him to sleep, as so many of the other drugs had done to her. Best of all, it was said to remove a person's inhibitions.

When she saw Sam lean over to put books in the corner of the window, she closed the distance fast. Her hand went into her pocket; she brought out her phone. By the time his shirt had moved up, and his trousers slipped down, her phone was ready to capture the band of flesh revealed. She took a photo, then another, and a third to be sure. Though she had, of course, seen the top of his buttocks before, she had been too dazed, too slow to take a decent picture.

She zoomed in until it seemed there was no glass between them. While Sam was arranging the books he saw a spray of white light on their covers: The flash in her phone had gone off. When Sam turned, she was already moving away.

Sinead and Toby walked quickly down the lane that led to the park. It was as if she were holding a box that contained a present she had been wanting for ages, and so what if she had bought the present herself: The pleasure was no less.

Sean and Rita were on the bench but didn't see her and Toby. Sean was busy feeding cubes of mango into Rita's open mouth. Sinead decided that she'd get Sam to do the same for her. She thought of his sticky fingers needing to be sucked.

She steered Toby to a bench under a tree that offered enough shade for her to see the phone screen properly. When she looked at him, he was staring at the ducks and swans. He started to cry.

"What is it? What's the matter?"

He covered his face with his hands. She didn't know what else to do but stroke his head. Eventually, his sobs grew quieter. He rested his head on her shoulder.

She kept stroking his hair with one hand, but with the other held her phone. She opened the first picture, which was from farthest away. She stared at the several inches of his skin and it made her feel good, but also bad, because it made her want the real thing more. She moved to the next, which was fractionally nearer, and this gave the illusion of getting closer to him.

Next to her, Toby drowsed and made a whimpering sound. He was such a comfort. Without him she'd be in jail or a mental hospital. She stroked the top of his head and then resumed looking at the pictures that got closer and closer to the skin she would soon be touching. They'd be in bed, and she'd be on top, but only at first, because they'd do everything.

The thought made her close her eyes, and yet she still saw the pictures. If she'd been alone, she might have gotten lost in this fantasy, but Toby was still upset. To quiet him, she smoothed her hand down his hair until it reached his neck. There it lingered, rubbing, kneading, moving blood around.

After a minute of her doing this he went quiet, allowing her to return to the thought of Sam pushing into her. They'd do it until she was sore, or until he passed out, whichever came first. And when she woke, he'd be holding her. Neither would speak; there'd be no need. After a long look they'd kiss. It would be a slow, tender kiss; she'd touch his face, and then her hand would slip down from the neck to his nipples, then down his chest.

When Toby started whimpering, it seemed natural to do the same for him. She didn't usually do this, but he was so upset there seemed no other choice. The strange thing was that his stomach was so diminished. It was not the stomach of the Toby she had known for the past year, as he was not quite the person she had known for that time. Again, this was unsurprising. She had been wrong to think that Toby might not become someone else. His body had changed, and so had he. As Sinead's hand moved in circles, she wondered whose stomach she was rubbing. If he was not Toby, then who was he?

This was a troubling thought, one that made her mind and hand seek comfort. She put her hand under Toby's shirt. His skin was warm, and hairier than she remembered. And it was nice to trace circles on Toby's stomach, but they seemed abridged. Their natural orbit was wider, several inches more, with the navel at the centre. What stopped her hand, what spoiled the motion, was the top of his trousers. But this problem was like Sam's reluctance: It was easily overcome. A little powder in his drink, the opening of one button. Beneath Toby's shirt her hand turned perfect circles. When she was with Sam, on their first morning together, her hand would not stop there. It would travel down between his legs, then be joined by her other hand. His balls would be in one hand, his penis in the other. It would be large, though not at all hard, but that wouldn't be a problem. There was a special pleasure in coaxing it from that state.

She was beginning to squeeze when Toby groaned into her ear. It was a bovine sound that brought her back to his penis in her fist. She snatched her hand away and stood. He yawned and stretched, and as he did his penis poked out.

"Put it away," she said, and took a step back. She had passed up hundreds of chances. She wasn't going to fuck *Toby*.

But they could be in his bed in five minutes.

"Come on," she said, and pushed Toby's penis back into his trousers. She took his hand and dragged him out of the park. When they passed the bench, Sean laughed and whistled the wedding march.

As they turned the corner her heart was beating fast. If Toby didn't know what to do, she would go on top.

Past the Chinese restaurant, then the dry cleaner. She needed condoms, but the chemist was on the way.

She was in such a hurry she did not see the dog coming out of the bookshop. He had thick black, tufted fur; his name was Mr. Perfect. The fact that he didn't see her either was not the dog's fault. He was old and almost blind, and she was going too fast. Sinead's foot caught his front paw. Mr. Perfect yowled.

"The fuck?" said Lonnie, Spooky's father, who loved the dog far more than he loved his son. "What the fuck did ya do that for? What did he do to you?"

"Nothing, I'm sorry," she said, and she was, but she did not want to stop.

"Wait," he said, and grabbed her wrist. "You need to say sorry to *him*."

She looked down at Mr. Perfect. "I'm sorry," she said, "It was an accident. I just didn't see him."

"That's fine," said Lonnie, but he did not let go. "Do you want to meet my son?"

She hesitated, not only because the question was unexpected, but also because he had moved his hand up her arm. Only then did she remember how she had almost kissed him.

"Come on," he said. "He's just inside." His hand slid up to her elbow.

"I have to go," she said, and looked at Toby.

"It'll just take a minute."

"No, really, I have to."

"Why?"

"We need to have lunch."

"Does he?" Lonnie pointed at Toby's stomach. His hand crept up further.

I am not particularly sorry that Lonnie did not Survive. If he hadn't interfered, Sinead would have had sex with Toby. This would have been indefensible. But better than what happened. So what if she fucked him every day for the next six weeks? Yes, it would have been abuse. But Toby would have Survived.

This, then, is why I blame Lonnie: He prevented a lesser evil. Though of course the blame must be shared, and not just with Sinead. On that day, Sam's mistake was being friendly to her. When he saw her with Lonnie, it was too unlikely a pairing for him to ignore.

"Hey," he said, and raised his hand. "Do you know each other?"

"Yes," she said, and smiled. Lonnie looked confused.

"Have you been to the park?"

"Yeah, it was great."

"Cool," he said, then Lonnie took his hand off Sinead's arm. "See you," he muttered to Sam, then yanked the dog's leash.

Sinead did not care. She looked at Toby, then back at Sam, and the usual dynamic was reversed. Sam stopped her wanting Toby.

"So what have you been up to?"

She shrugged. "Mostly looking after him. But that's much easier now. He's really made progress."

"I can't believe how much weight he's lost. What happened?"

"I don't know. He just lost his appetite."

"Amazing," he said, and she blushed. As if he meant it as praise.

"I guess it's partly to do with all those cookbooks we buy. I think they've really helped. He spends ages looking at them."

Sam turned away from her. "How do you feel, Toby?"

"OK," he said.

"Really?"

"Yes." Toby was not a good liar.

"So are you sticking around this summer?" Sinead asked.

Sam laughed. "Where else would I go?"

"What about on *holi*day?"

He shrugged. "I don't even *know* what that is. I don't know where I'd go. Anyway, I have a guest at the moment, so I can't really leave."

"Who's that?" she said quickly.

"Alasdair. You must know him. He used to live under the bridge."

"Cool," she said.

"So what about you? Are you around this summer?"

"I guess so. Toby and his mum are going away, so I could do that too. But it might be nice to stay here."

"You should," he said. "It will be a great summer."

"Maybe I will," she said, and turned away. "We have to go now. Toby needs his lunch."

"All right, see you later," he said, and seemed sorry she was going. When Sinead got home she wrote in her diary:

June 4, 2017

Today was really horrible and really fucking amazing. I got so turned on in the park I nearly fucked Joby. If there had been any bushes, or it had been dark, I would have done him there. I don't know what happened. Maybe it was because of the photos. I don't even know if he could fuck me, but he definitely can get hard. Anyway, I don't want to think about it. The main, most awesome thing was that when I saw Sam he didn't do that whole you're-just-another-person thing. He seemed really pleased to see me! We talked for ages, and I was totally cool, because this disgusting old guy had been perving on me so much that I was too pissed off to throw myself at him. We had this really normal conversation, like we were actually friends. After a while he wasn't just talking to me, he was actually flirting. It almost makes me think that I don't need the drugs.

She may have been right. Sam *was* attracted to her. In his own, stumbling fashion, he was making progress. Given a little more time, he might have stopped being stupid. Perhaps, if there had been an August. If there had been a September.

But she couldn't wait.

June 6, 2017

Another almost-fuck today. I wasn't even thinking about Sam. When I got to Joby's he was lying on his back on the lounge floor, reading a book about cakes. He had his legs open, but I couldn't see anything because he was wearing baggy tracksuit bottoms and there was no bulge. I thought it was fine, so I sat down next to him and for a while it was OK. We looked at cream cakes and black forest gateau, and even though I was sitting really close I didn't want him. I was leaning all my weight on one hand, and so when Joby twitched and knocked my arm I fell on him and it was kind of funny. He laughed, and I did too. It was nice to see him happy, and it was nice to be lying on his *chest, and so I stayed there. When he started reading again, he rested his hand on my shoulder, and I liked that too so I moved his hand down onto my breast, and after that I lost it. If his mother hadn't come back, I definitely would have.*

After this, Sinead took precautions. She masturbated before going to Toby's house. She kept him out of reach. Despite these measures, she had two more near misses during the following week. She feigned illness for several days. She considered quitting her job. On June 13 she wrote:

I'm sore, and every time I look at him I think about his cock. But I can't afford to quit. I need to pay my rent and all the bills and buy more GHB. But if I don't I'll probably end up having his baby. I could take out a loan and stay home as much as possible. But I could also start taking the pill and get a new diaphragm. It's better I fuck him than someone else.

Though Sinead was far from rational, she wasn't entirely wrong. Both options had advantages. If she quit she'd have more chances to spend time with Sam. They could get to know each other, and then she could drug him.

How bad would it have been if she and Toby had had sex? Though it was morally and ethically wrong, I doubt it would have damaged him much. It might have been upsetting, even traumatising. But he would have Survived.

As for how it would have affected Sinead, that is hard to say. She might have loved it so much she forgot about Sam. It could also have unhinged her further. My guess is that it would have troubled her at first, but after two or three times she would have found ways to justify it. Reasons can always be found.

Sinead's solution arrived when she was at the dinner table with

Toby and his mother. She was trying not to look at him, probably staring at her plate. Despite her best efforts, she glanced at him eventually. She saw his jaw, the saliva on his chin, the mulch of food inside. A disgusting but by no means unfamiliar sight. It was just how Toby ate. Toby, who had been so grotesquely large that she could never want him.

I wonder how long it took her to realise that she'd stopped wanting him. In my experience, this kind of shift happens so quietly it can go unremarked. At the start of my daily walk along the shore I feel so awful I don't see what's before me. No fishermen on the wharf, no couples on the beach. There is only a migraine of names and faces that block out the present. Only when I sit down to rest do I notice the palm trees, the green parrots amidst their fronds; only then do I realise I'm feeling better.

Sinead didn't quit her job. She didn't fuck Toby. On June 17 she wrote:

> This is going to cost me a fortune. I never thought he'd be so picky. At the start he'll only eat stuff from that delicatessen. I guess it's what he's always wanted but never been allowed. Even so, I have to hold the food under his nose and sometimes push it through his lips. But once he's started eating, there's no problem. If I switch to cheap stuff he doesn't seem to notice.

There were, however, difficulties.

> Even though I've started doing my shopping on the way to his house, I still can't bring enough food, not without Evelyn getting suspicious. I have to space out the food, which makes it even more expensive, as I need to use the posh stuff to get him going. He loves those little macarons. Pushing my hand away and shaking his head is just for show.

Though Toby (or Toby's body) had managed to reduce his cravings for food, there were clearly limits to his/its self-discipline, such as being teased with exquisite French sweets. He could not resist such temptation. After two weeks, Toby was ten kilograms heavier. His mother was baffled. She asked Sinead if he'd found money or been hanging round the dustbins.

Losing weight was Toby's great achievement. He had shown more willpower than Sinead. He had sacrificed a third of his body, his world, in order to save the rest. But this change did not suit her, and so she stopped it, seemingly without remorse. At the end of June she wrote, "It's great to see Toby getting back to his old self."

15. Five, Four

SPOOKY WAS LATE. HE HAD been due at ten, and it was half past, and Sam should not have cared. But a small voice had been whispering to him since Caitlin started snubbing him. *They are all leaving,* it said.

When Spooky finally arrived at eleven, he didn't even apologise.

"I was t-t-talking to a f-f-friend," said Spooky. "I think he can h-help."

"Great," said Sam, who had no idea what he was talking about.

"I just n-n-need some pictures of your f-f-friend."

"Which one?"

"Who needs the p-p-pass p-p-port."

Sam tried not to laugh: It was hard to believe Spooky had contacts in the criminal underworld. Was he preparing to hand over envelopes of cash to shadowy figures in alleys? Did he have some dark secret he had been concealing all along?

He did not. He was just a bullied son. But his father had been in prison. His father hung around with men who had scars and tattoos and dogs that liked to bite. Men who might do a favour for their old friend's pathetic son.

"When do you need them?" he asked.

"N-now?"

Sam left the shop in such a hurry he knocked into Rita. She swayed from side to side, her eyes unfocussed, the scent of wine leaking from her mouth. She staggered, grabbed hold of him, and giggled. Only then did she realise who had bumped into her.

"You clumsy cunt," she said. "You *nosy* clumsy cunt."

"Sorry," he said, and ran down the street till he got to Trudy's. He went to the back of the house and rang the bell twice. There was no reply, but he thought she was home because she rarely went out in the day. If she didn't answer, it was because she was with a client.

Sam sat on the doorstep and looked at the windows. Crows shrieked in the trees. He could see the outline of a slim figure on the top floor of the nearest house. She was so tall she must have been standing on something, perhaps a chair or stool she meant to kick away so she could jerk and twist.

The woman adjusted the curtains. Stepped off the chair.

He didn't like waiting there; it wasn't a good place to be seen. He also didn't want to ask Trudy for the photos. If he actually succeeded and she got a passport, it meant he'd lose her as well. But he also thought that the more he did for her, the greater the chance she would love him.

Obviously Sam was not thinking clearly. He certainly shouldn't have sat there. Given that he had already considered the possibility she was inside with a client, how could he have thought that remaining there was a good idea? During the eleven months he had been visiting Trudy he had never seen another client—she was careful to allow plenty of time between appointments.

However, even if Sam had expected to meet one of her clients, it wouldn't have been the figure that emerged. Because Mr. Asham was no longer seeing Trudy. She had told Sam this—perhaps not in words, but certainly with her silence. He felt betrayed, then foolish, but there was no time to think. Mr. Asham was coming towards him. Something had to be said.

"Hello," said Sam.

"Good day," said Fahad with such bonhomie it conjured his other, blue-coated self. He showed neither guilt nor embarrassment. Sam wanted to grab or hit him. Instead he watched him leave.

Afterwards he stood there stunned for a minute. Then he muttered, "Fuck." He knocked on the door and there was no reply, so he knocked again harder, and this felt good because it seemed purposeful. His third knock was a punch.

The door opened. "What are you doing?" asked Trudy. She was wearing a red bathrobe and had wet hair.

"I saw him."

"Who?"

"Mr. Asham. You said you wouldn't see him."

"No, I didn't. You just asked me not to. Now I need to get dressed." She went inside and into the bathroom and shut the door hard. Sam went in and sat in the lounge. He thought she seemed angry, but he wasn't sure why. Probably because she had been caught in a lie.

He heard the sound of water running. He looked around the room. Though Trudy had bought the sofa, the tacky gold cushions, the cabinet of cheap black wood, and the framed photographs of Paris and London, the room was still impersonal. Perhaps she could only be herself, not "Trudy," when she was in that other bedroom he had never seen.

On the table in front of him was a book in Filipino. When he opened it an envelope fell out. It was addressed to:

Malea Ocampo
106 Comely Bank
Edinburgh
EH4 1HH

Sam had never dared ask her real name, but that didn't mean he didn't want to know it. It was a nice name, and as he said it quietly, slowly, Sam felt his lips push out in almost a kiss. He liked the hum of his vocal cords, the feel of his tongue pushing against his teeth.

She came out the bathroom and sat on a chair on the other side of the room. Her hair was still in a towel, but she was now dressed in jeans and a sweater. "Do you want a tea?" she said.

"No."

"I want one," she said, and left the room. He heard the rise of the kettle. The sound of cupboards closing. He sat in the room and waited. The kettle clicked off.

Malea came in holding a mug and a packet of biscuits. She sat down, sipped her tea, then said calmly, "It is not your business. It is *my* business. He is a client, and he pays a lot, and I need the money. I cannot always do this. Maybe for five years, but no more."

She sat and smoothed her hand through her hair, first on the right side, then on the left. "You are nice," she said. "But you are not my boyfriend. I do not want this. I do not need this. If you don't like that I see this man, perhaps you should not come anymore."

Sam stared at the steam that rose from her tea. He did not know what to say. He had been looking forward to telling her the good news. He had expected her to be grateful. Instead she was virtually threatening to break up with him. Perhaps it was inevitable. He was too fucked up even to sustain an arrangement with a woman he paid. And if it was really over between them, he might as well help her leave.

"So, I came here to ask you something."

"Yes?" She looked at him warily.

"Do you have some photos of yourself? Small ones? Two will be enough."

Which would make anyone curious. "Enough for what?" she'd have to say.

Malea put her mug on the table and stood. She stood and went to the cabinet and opened a small drawer from which she took a strip of photos. She handed them to him.

In the first two she was smiling; in the third she looked serious; in the last her expression was hard to identify.

"Why do you have these?"

She shrugged. "They are useful. And sometimes my clients want them."

She must have thought that he too wanted to look at the photos while his hand moved back and forth. The worst thing about this idea was that it was true. Although he had never looked at a picture of her whilst masturbating, he had thought of her many times. Until that moment, this had never seemed shameful. But it was just another way in which he was like them.

ON JULY 12, Sam hit his head and blacked out, then was slapped awake. There was no time to think, but this didn't matter, because thinking was no help against being kicked in the chest.

There had been no warning. It was lunchtime, and he had been looking up whilst walking towards the park. He couldn't stop staring at the sky. It was so blue and clear that any change seemed impossible. He wasn't walking in an entirely straight line, which didn't matter as there was no one around but Sean and Rita, and they were asleep on their bench. As Sam walked past the bench he barely glanced at the sleeping couple. He had given up hope of finding out what bound them so tightly.

He gazed into the sheet of blue and thought of falling up. Then he was pushed so hard from behind he staggered and slammed into a parked car. He hit his head and lost consciousness; when he came to all he saw was the sky that was still implacably blue. *This isn't my bedroom,* he thought, and then Sean slapped him, initially without much force, but then Rita yelled and he gained conviction.

"Wait," Sam said, and tried to stand, but Sean kicked him in the ribs. Then there was no chance to stand; taking a breath was all he could do. But as soon as he had, he was kicked again, and all the good work was lost.

He managed to roll over, so all Sean could kick was his back, but the change of target didn't matter.

A kick to the small of his back.

A kick between his shoulders.

His spine was like a lightning rod conducting the shock. The next one was sure to be to the back of his head. As it went forwards his neck would snap.

Instead there was a cry of pain, a sound of breaking glass. Sam rolled over and saw Sean kneeling on the ground. His forehead was bleeding and there was glass in his hair, and Sinead had the neck of a bottle against Rita's throat.

"Can you get up?" she asked, and he nodded, though he wasn't sure. Slowly, carefully, he sat up, then immediately had to lie back down. When he coughed, it felt like being stabbed in the lungs. He tried again, and it hurt, but he managed somehow to stand. He leaned against the car and wondered if any ribs were broken.

"Come on," said Sinead, and he obeyed. He went warily past

Sean, who was crying while attempting to get the glass out of his hair. For a moment Sam forgot that this man had been hurting him only a minute before.

"Call an ambulance," Sam said to a man taking photos with his mobile phone.

"Why?" asked Sinead, then punched Rita in the face. Rita screamed, but Sinead slapped her hard, and the shock of this silenced her.

"I should cut your throat," said Sinead, then took Sam's arm. Next he was moving, which meant he was walking, but he did not know how. His brain was doing nothing except broadcasting pain. As the sound of Rita's screams faded, he wondered whether the brain was overrated. The body knew how to take care of itself. Feet and legs could be trusted. All the same, it was strange to feel that he was not moving, but being moved.

Did it then grow dark? Did he walk with his eyes closed and Sinead's hand trapping his arm? Afterwards, he could not remember. She might have said where they were going, but he might not have asked. The only thing he could recall with any certainty was when they had to wait to cross the road. A van transporting a large mirror came to a stop in front of them. The driver leaned out the window, his arm dangling loosely down, a cigarette between his lips. A song with a slow, heavy beat was blasting from the stereo, and it was either this, the van's engine, or a combination of both that made the mirror vibrate. Sam's reflection seemed to ripple, though only slightly, not so much that it affected the clarity of the image. It was as if some different reflection were struggling to be seen.

"I think you're in shock," said Sinead. She put her arm round his back. They walked down the street, towards the bridge, and although Sam said they should go back, because Sean was hurt, he was talking to himself.

Sinead's flat was on the fourth floor; on the way up he had to rest.

He looked at the blue weight pressing down on the skylight and wondered why all that glass didn't fall. It was a judgement suspended; in a week, or ten years, the sky would drop through.

"Nearly there," Sinead said, and her hand slipped down to his hip. This was comforting, because he felt light-headed; he was breathing deeply, but the air wasn't entering his lungs. He started taking quicker breaths, and this seemed to help. With each gasp his head inflated until it felt gigantic, and this was definitely a good thing, because it meant more space for thoughts. His body seemed to weigh nothing, and he felt like laughing because in an almost infinite space was the freedom to hatch thoughts that were dinosaurs compared to the chickens and cattle that usually roamed his brain. One was the notion that it was good his parents had left him. What he had mistaken for loss and desertion was nothing of the sort. They had removed the bars of his cage.

The more Sam considered this, the better it sounded, and as they climbed the final stairs he began to laugh. Admittedly, it didn't sound like laughter. It was a panicked sucking of air that more closely resembled choking. He couldn't blame Sinead for asking once again if he was OK, if he needed to rest, because it certainly was a horrible sound, not one of his best laughs. But it still deserved that name, because the idea was so monstrously true it had to be something else as well—truth was just one category, in no way sufficient to contain the saurian nature of the proposition. And so the idea was not just true, but hilarious as well, and if something was funny you had to laugh. Since laughing proved that it was funny, you had to laugh far more, much more than breath could satisfy, but still you had to try. He gasped like he was drowning. Saw colours, shapes, nothing.

When Sam opened his eyes, his head was being cradled. He tried to speak, but his throat stayed closed. "Shh," Sinead said, and pressed his head against her chest. He remembered his mother doing the same whenever he got hurt. Before the plasters and antiseptic cream, there was the softness of her sweater, the support of her breast, her saying, as Sinead was saying, *It's going to be all right.*

This was what you had to believe. What he had believed until the day he woke late after a night of drinking cider in the park. He'd smoked a lot, and so his throat was raw, and though he could have drunk from the bathroom tap he wanted the ease of a glass. The house was quiet, but he didn't trust that; they might still be in. He opened his bedroom door, listened a moment, heard the heavy hand of a clock. He went into the kitchen and filled a pint glass.

"Water," he said, and regretted it, because then his head was no longer being held. He couldn't see where Sinead went. All he saw from his place on the floor was coats hanging over him. The toes of three pairs of shoes were aimed at his face, and it bothered him. No feet were in those trainers, so they couldn't kick him; they were just too close. He rolled over, which hurt but was worth it. Now all he saw was a wall painted yellowish white. It was so uniform that he could believe he was not seeing it, that it was not outside of him. It was like the sun on closed eyelids. It was the shade of that piece of notepaper on the kitchen table thirteen years ago.

That day, he had found a stack of twenty-pound notes wrapped in the folded paper that could only be believed by holding them. He had to look into each queen's eyes for confirmation.

Yes, this is real, Her Majestys said. But even the word of so many monarchs was not proof enough. He turned over the notes and counted the faces of Michael Faraday, midwife of electricity, who once amused himself "by watching the meteors vaulting through the sky."

Only after counting two hundred faces did Sam accept the money was real. Four thousand pounds. Until that moment the amount had seemed as hypothetical as a million pounds or ever having sex. Obviously, the money wasn't his, but while he held it, met Michael's eyes, he could believe otherwise. There was almost nothing he couldn't do with it. He'd buy a car, have a massive party, fly to Sydney, hire a bunch of strippers.

"Here you are," said Sinead, and helped Sam sit up. She put a mug in his hands, and he drank. The water tasted salty, but that was from the blood in his mouth. There must have been a lot, because even after several gulps the water tasted the same.

"More?" she asked, and he nodded. He stared at the wall that was still a surface free of marks, the way the sheet of notepaper had seemed when he took out the money. But when he had eventually turned it over—with reluctance, because it meant he'd find the actual reason his parents had left this ludicrous amount of money—he did not see instructions about bank deposits or solicitors. Just a few lines written with a careful hand.

Your Grandma will call.
Good luck.

Which was confusing, because they weren't supposed to be going on holiday until the following day. He went into the hall and entered their bedroom, saw their suitcases were gone. The idiots must have got the dates wrong. This didn't explain the money, but he guessed this was what his grandmother would call about.

"How do you feel?" asked Sinead, and put a hand on his chest. It was odd what a difference being beaten made. The day before he would have pushed her away. She was still the same crazed, obsessive woman who had been stalking him for months, but it was hard to distrust someone who'd fought two people to save him.

She put a cold cloth to his forehead then wiped the blood from his face.

"I think it's just your nose," she said. "Do you think you can stand? You'll be more comfortable on the sofa."

He stood up slowly, with one hand on the wall. He was in awful pain, and he wanted to throw up, but he could walk okay. At least nothing seemed broken. Sean had been drunk and wearing trainers, and not a very good kicker.

He lay down on the sofa, and Sinead took off his shoes. She gave him two extra cushions, then said she'd be back in a minute.

"No problem," he said, and looked around. The room reminded him of Malea's lounge except in better taste. There were magazines on the table, a shelf of DVDs and another of books, two paintings of Edinburgh's skyline, a TV, a yucca plant. These things went together, and they had been carefully selected, but not by Sinead. She didn't own the furniture; she hadn't chosen the carpet or the colour of the walls. In five minutes you could have removed all trace of her.

When Sinead came back, Sam thought she was wearing different trousers. They were black and tight and ended midway down her calves.

"Those are nice," he said.

She put down two glasses of water. He reached for one and took a sip. Again he tasted blood.

"What's wrong?" she asked, and quickly laughed. "I think that one is mine."

"Is it? It tastes salty."

"I was drinking margaritas last night."

"I thought it was just me."

"Maybe it was," she said, and laughed again. Although it wasn't funny, he laughed as well. He couldn't remember the last time he'd felt as relaxed with someone. When he was with Mrs. Maclean, it always felt formal; with Malea, the clock was ticking; with Alasdair, there was a constant apprehension that he might break something. Sam felt comfortable and very warm, and although he suddenly wondered who was going to close the bookshop, he immediately had an intimation that things were going to be fine.

"Things are going to be fine," he said, because it wasn't enough to think this, feel this; it had to be heard. It was more than a mental conviction; it was a pulse that travelled the length of his body, the kind of thing you saw in films when magic spells were cast to heal the wounded hero. His fingertips felt as if sparks might emerge; rushes of electricity travelled down his muscles. These rushes felt like ants, but much faster than ants. They did not march in slow columns; these ants rode on trains.

Sam rolled up his sleeve, took her hand, and placed it on his lower arm. Her hand clenched his wrist, but that wasn't right, so he put his palm on her hand until her fingers opened. He gently put her fingers back on his arm, and then only the smallest motion, an inch's journey, was enough to show her what he wanted. She smoothed her fingers along his arm as another wave passed through him. That was the only word for it, *wave;* it captured the way the sensation broke on him in an intense collision. *Wave,* because the feeling was not going to stop, just as the sea and its waves do not.

Sinead's fingers were moving in such total accord with those waves of certainty—they were coming in faster—that she had to know what he was feeling.

"Come closer," he said, because although she was touching him, she still seemed far away. She shifted nearer, but there was still distance between them, and so he said, "Closer," and she came closer, and then he said it again. With Sam lying down, and Sinead leaning against the sofa, there was almost no space between them. Her face hung like a moon above. Her lips were far too red. Their intensity hurt his eyes and made him think of that old film where nuns living on a mountaintop go demented with lust. Her lips looked as if a child had coloured them in quickly.

He was so thirsty. He was about to ask Sinead for water when she asked, "Do you have any gum?"

"Gum?" he said, and liked the sound of the word. "No, I don't. Do you?"

"No," she said, and looked quite sad, but for only a moment. "I have sweets," she said, and stood up quickly. She went out the room, and he heard something break, and then she came back in. "Open wide," she said, and he obeyed, and then she put something in his mouth. He was so curious about it, so impatient to taste it, that he closed his lips on her fingers. It was a mint, and her fingers were soft, and when she took them out she took the mint as well. She put it into her own mouth. "That's better," she said, and only then did he realise that the pulses had stopped. For a moment he felt dizzy, and he was still thirsty. She passed him a glass.

"How did you know?"

"Because I'm thirsty too."

They drank and looked at each other. Her lips were no longer as red. He wondered about his.

"How do they look?"

"What?"

"My lips," he said, and pointlessly pointed. She brought her thumb to them. She smoothed it along his lower lip, which felt like it was swollen. *The lips are big in the brain,* he thought. *And so are the hands.*

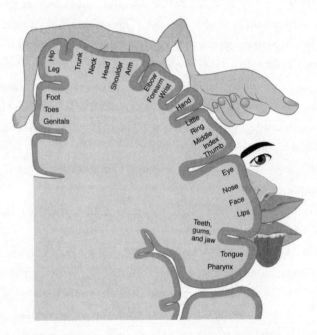

He pictured a man with his face, but distorted. With the hands and lips of a giant. As for his brain, Sam's brain, it looked like a city seen at night from a plane—in some places dark, in others light—and although he could not quite map this image onto that of the man with giant hands, he knew they were connected.

"Great," he said, then could not say more, because her mouth stopped him. Her kiss was passionate, almost rough; he expected to taste blood. But it was not long before her tongue slowed and the biting stopped, and there was a tender meeting of mouths. Then he was touching her face, the back of her neck, his hand pushing into her hair. It had been years since he had kissed anyone properly, because Malea wouldn't, and that one kiss from Magda had happened so quickly. There was nothing wrong with kissing Sinead; if she thought it would lead to sex, that was not his problem. The only thing which troubled him was that the waves had stopped. Her hand was still stroking his arm—that had not changed—but the euphoria had gone. Perhaps their kissing was confusing things. He took his mouth from hers.

She looked surprised, then worried.

"I'm so fucking thirsty," she said, and drained her glass. "Be back in a minute."

She was gone a long time.

He thought he heard rain.

Out the window the sky was still blue.

His legs felt hot, so he took off his trousers, albeit slowly and with a certain fear, because there was no telling what kind of wound he might see. He was almost disappointed to find how little damage there was; it devalued the beating.

When Sinead came back in he asked, "Where were you?"

"In the kitchen. Why, did you miss me?" she said, and laughed. This laugh didn't stop, and she seemed to be having so much fun that he joined in. They laughed as she knelt then kissed him again, and somehow they kept laughing as their kissing continued. It was just as funny when her hand travelled down his chest. But he stopped laughing when she touched his penis through his shorts. The wave broke over him again, but now it was a constant feeling of pleasure. Perhaps it could no longer be called a wave, but he didn't know what else to call it. He didn't care either, after she pulled his penis through the slit in his shorts. "I love you," she said, and put it in her mouth.

Nothing in his life had ever felt as good. Many things had made him happier, or more pleased, but all those emotions were corrupted by words, thoughts, the fear of being seen to enjoy something too conspicuously. But this sensation did not need interpretation. When Sam thought of his brain, that city at night, most of it could have been dark, or absent, and he would still have felt the same pleasure. Only the oldest parts were required, those places lit by flaming torches instead of electric light.

But when he gasped out loud, it was not because of Sinead's oral skills. It was the realisation of how incredibly stupid he'd been. He could have felt this good every day for the last year. Admittedly, he would have had to reciprocate by having some form of penetrative sex, but he could have worn two condoms dipped in spermicide and made sure she was on the pill. They might not have needed to go out with each other: Plenty of his volunteers had regular sex with friends, or just acquaintances, with few complications.

Sinead took his penis out her mouth and slapped it on her protruding tongue. "Do you like that?" she asked. She did it again, then put him back in her mouth. She pinched the base of his penis, squeezed his balls, and pushed his penis deeper in her mouth till it touched the back of her throat. As she moved her head back and forth she gagged but never broke eye contact. The whole thing seemed both completely real and utterly made up. It was not, in Sam's experience, how sex usually worked. She was acting as if this were a porno film. He had no idea if this was something she enjoyed or whether she was just trying to please him. Although it certainly did, now there were lights in other parts of the city, not as bright as in the old quarters but enough to distract. From then on, every moment of pleasure was analyzed. Sam was no longer wholly within the moment; he was outside it as well. When Sinead leaned back and took off her T-shirt, then started to remove her bra, she did so with exaggerated slowness. First one strap, then the other, after which she arched her back as she reached to undo it.

Though this was exciting, there was something performative about her actions that made him uncomfortable whilst really turning him on. The sight of her breasts was equally thrilling and discombobulating. They were medium-size, on the small side of large, with such a remarkable heft that they were without doubt the best breasts he'd ever looked at that weren't on a screen. The old parts of the city could not wait to touch and taste them; the newer districts noted the way she rubbed her nipples while biting her lower lip. She wasn't doing this for him, she couldn't be: She didn't know anything about *him*. Not his childhood, or his parents leaving, or what books he liked to read. As she undid her trousers, Sam considered the possibility that he wasn't special. Maybe all she wanted was an audience.

By the time her trousers were off, he was certain he was wrong. If all she wanted was an audience, she could have found a different one each night.

Sinead stepped out of her trousers and bent over him, so her bottom was in his face. This received mixed reviews. The residents of newer districts rolled their eyes and groaned; in the old town, the midbrain, lights pulsed in applause. The reactions between these districts differed so greatly that perhaps they were no longer one place. They were more like separate cities linked by history, not all of it good. Sam wasn't one brain, one person, but two: the first fully in the moment, the other somewhat removed. Who enjoyed Sinead taking down her pants while looking over her shoulder? Whoever it was, whether "Sam" or not, this person was clearly in charge. When Sinead got on top of him there were no objections.

She took his penis in her hand.

She lowered herself.

He did not say, "You need a condom."

She gasped then began.

16. Three, Two

WHEN SAM WOKE HIS HEAD hurt and his mouth was dry. Most of all, there was panic. He was in Sinead's bed, and he didn't know why.

He sat up, and the pain was so bad he lay down again. He looked at the clock on the bedside table. It was only nine a.m. Next to the clock was a framed picture of his face. It had been taken in the shop; he was looking right at the camera but not seeing it. He had probably been talking to a customer, but it looked as if he were making meaningful eye contact with the photographer. He didn't know when the picture had been taken, but it was at least three or four months ago, because his hair was very short. Sinead had been looking at his face each morning for at least that long.

If he'd found a similar picture in Caitlin's or Malea's houses, he would have been pleased. Seeing it in Sinead's bedroom was upsetting. It was only a photo, and far from private, but it bothered him. He imagined Sinead putting it in different rooms, having conversations with it, touching herself while gazing into his eyes. It was invasive and a violation, and it made him furious. At no point did Sam consider the thousands of photos he owned, all without the knowledge or permission of either the people in them or those they had belonged to. If this had been pointed out to him, he would have shaken his head and said, with special vehemence, that it was not the same thing.

As he lay on top of her black sheets he remembered them fucking. Her on top. Then from behind. None of it made sense. After years of self-control, why had he given in? He smashed the photo of his face; it made him feel better.

But there was nothing more twentieth century than thinking you could destroy a piece of information. There would be copies on her phone, camera, and computer; it could be her profile picture; she might have a blog entitled *Will I Ever Get to Fuck That Guy in the Bookshop?* that featured candid snaps of him from every angle. It had probably already been updated with new and adult content, its title changed to an affirmative.

Sam got out of bed, put on his trousers, and started searching Sinead's flat. He wanted to know something about the woman he had just slept with. It didn't matter if she caught him; the worst had already happened.

He began in the bedroom. In the chest of drawers he found sweaters, scarves, T-shirts, underwear, nothing interesting except a small pink box that contained a pair of handcuffs. They were engraved with the message *For S from P. You will not want a key.*

The wardrobe was more rewarding. He found two shoeboxes full of photos of Sinead on beaches with boys in shorts who looked like they exercised a lot. The earliest photos were from 2006, the last from 2010. None showed her wearing dark colours or with the heavy makeup he was used to seeing. Without the latter, she looked younger, more at ease. There were also birthday and Christmas cards from her parents—though the most recent, from 2013, was signed only by her mother.

The predictable vibrator was in her bedside drawer. Under it were six laminated photos. He saw himself in profile in different places on the street—in Mr. Asham's, in the post office, in the French delicatessen—with no particular expression. All but one of the pictures were taken from at least ten feet away; the exception showed him at the bus stop, close up, and must have been taken through a bus or car window. There was nothing provocative or suggestive about any of the poses. Whatever she found erotic she supplied herself. Perhaps their banality was the point. These everyday moments were starting points for any fantasy. A chance meeting could lead to conversation, which could segue into a coffee, a beer, his tongue in her mouth.

He looked through the photos again, unsure of whether to take them. Perhaps they did no harm. He was about to put them back in the drawer when he dropped one. He bent to pick it up and saw a notebook with a plain brown cover underneath her bed. Its pages were filled with entries chronicling the last few years. The most recent entry was from the previous week.

July 4, 2017
Still not sure about the dose. Not enough and it won't work. Too much and he'll feel sick. It would be so fucking typical if he threw up and passed out.

It made Sam feel both better and worse to know he'd been drugged. He wasn't to blame; it was basically rape. He sat a moment, letting the thought throb. Then he stood and left the flat, taking the diary with him.

Outside, people were wearing shorts, eating ice cream, and walking very slowly. It was the first day that actually felt like summer. There were expressions of disbelief and sweaters tied around waists. People squinted at the sun as if it were a bright light suddenly switched on. It is probably bad taste to envy those about to die, but in one respect those people in Comely Bank, London, Paris, and New York had something we can never recover. They could look into the sky with absolute trust.

When he got home, Alasdair was hunched over the scanner, holding a photo Sam did not remember. It was a black-and-white picture of a woman wearing a bonnet with ribbons tied under her chin. In her arms she held a small goose, or perhaps a duck, Sam really couldn't tell.

"What does it say on the back?"

Alasdair turned the photo over.

"It's blank," he said, and put it in the trunk. The next item he took from the pile was a notebook bound in black leather.

"Oh, I remember that," said Sam. "It's really smoky. There must have been a fire."

Alasdair brought it to his nose, breathed in, and nodded.

"It's pretty strange, but also boring. Just this list of things the person bought, it's really quite path— What are you doing?"

Alasdair's tongue travelled down the notebook's spine. When he finished, he said, "This is good."

"Why the fuck did you lick it? It's filthy."

"Because it's a chemical sense. I wanted to see if it tasted different from how it smelt."

"And did it?"

"No."

Alasdair grinned as if he knew a tremendous secret. He opened the book but only glanced at the page before looking back at Sam. His smile was still there, and Sam waited to hear that smoke was good for the body because it contained carbon, or that it was good to lick things because the tongue needed exercise. Instead Alasdair said, "A man came here last night."

"Who was it? What did he want?" Sam pictured Sean, or Mr. Asham. He thought of Sean holding him down while Mr. Asham hit him.

"He didn't say who he was. But he looked sick. I think he eats the wrong fruit."

"What did he want?"

"To give you something."

Alasdair put his hand under his topmost sweater, then seemed to be feeling his nipple. He brought his hand out, looked at it, flexed his fingers several times, then slid it under a different layer of clothing. He produced a brown envelope.

"Here," he said, and Sam took it. The envelope was damp.

"Tell him to eat peaches. The best ones are in cans."

Inside was a small red book with thirty-two pages, most of which were blank. It was Malea's passport.

The next day, he booked her a plane ticket for the Philippines. The flight was for August 1. He put the passport and ticket through her door that evening. Though Sam would have liked to see Malea's confusion, then joy, he decided it was best not to give it to her in person. If he was present, it would put too much pressure on her response. There was even a chance she would refuse the ticket, not because she didn't want it, but to avoid being in his debt. It might even upset her; maybe she'd be angry he'd found out her real name.

But it could also be a chance for them to start again. In another place, where she was not "Trudy," he could be someone other than Sam who used to pay for sex. Obviously, they'd have to take things slowly, get used to their new roles. It was far from guaranteed. Yet not impossible.

And so he booked himself a ticket on her flight. He did not think there was any need to mention this to her.

THE LAST TWO weeks in Comely Bank were almost without incident. A black cat called Lucky was rescued from a tree three times, a driver lost control of his vehicle and drove into what had been Mr. Campbell's antique shop, and a fire broke out in a house near the bridge. Even in the glare of hindsight, none of these events seems auspicious. Only the betrayal, murder, and vicious beating that befell several of the human relics seems to have anticipated the impending cataclysm. Finally, in those closing days, those people were of the present.

It would be a stretch to say that Sam was responsible for all of these mishaps. Yet even the most indulgent view of his actions, from someone who was privy to his every feeling and thought, would find it hard to deny a degree of blame. All that can be said in his defence is that he was badly shaken by his violation. If he hadn't seen Sinead for the next few weeks, perhaps he might have calmed down. But when he looked out of the bookshop window on July 19, she was on the other side of the street. He stared at her, thinking she would quickly, guiltily leave, but she didn't seem bothered. In fact she was smiling.

Sam went into the back room and worked his way through twelve bags of novels featuring violent, unhappy men who loved their country so much that they were willing to kill other violent, unhappy men who wanted to harm that country. Though every donation told him something about the people who gave the books, in that particular case all he learnt was that their owners a) enjoyed the idea of global catastrophes being narrowly averted and b) had no respect for books. The spines were broken, the covers loose, the pages water' damaged. By bringing them in, the donors had wasted his time and their own. The books would raise no money; no child would be saved. But at least when he went back into the shop, Sinead had gone away.

When she came back that afternoon, it wasn't a surprise. Having read her diary, he guessed that in her mind this was just another phase of their courtship.

Sam decided he wasn't going to be angry. A giddy sense of dislocation was starting to build. Now that he was leaving, nothing really mattered. Perhaps his parents had felt the same way before their departure. He wondered how long they had planned it. Whether it had always been an option.

Sinead was back three times the next day, on each occasion for at least forty minutes.

On July 21, she was outside the shop for the whole morning, then most of that afternoon. She wasn't always looking in his direction. Sometimes she was looking at her phone, most likely at pictures she had taken when he was unconscious. He wanted to take the phone from her hand and smash it on the ground. He wanted to say, "Fuck you, I'm leaving."

But these were fantasies: If he had really wanted to confront her, he wouldn't have stayed in the bookshop for an hour after it closed. Only when he saw her walk away so quickly she was virtually running (even stalkers need the toilet) did he dare to leave.

Alasdair was exactly as Sam had left him that morning, lying on the sofa looking at the leather-bound book. It reminded Sam of the way that Alasdair had coveted the photo album. Perhaps it would be best if he sold it as well. They wouldn't get much for it—it was just a list of things and their prices—but there was a buyer for every book.

Sam took off his shoes. "Why are you still reading that?"

"Because it's very good. The man knows exactly what he has bought, and how much he paid for it."

"How do you know it's a man?"

"By the handwriting. Look." He thrust the page at Sam.

Date	Item	Price
June 24	Bosch dishwasher	£500
June 28	De'Longhi coffeemaker	£300
July 5	Panasonic microwave	£350

"Fine," said Sam, who had a greater objection. "I thought you were against owning lots of things."

Alasdair tutted. "You know, you can be very obtuse. And I don't think you've read this properly. Listen to this: 'A Bosch dishwasher, £500. A De'Longhi coffeemaker, £300. A Panasonic microwave, £350.'" He looked at Sam expectantly, then continued. 'A Bugatti Volo Toaster, £120. A Santos Classic Juicer, £220. A Rangemaster Dual Fuel Range Cooker, £1100. A Bunn coffee grinder'—"

"All right, I get it. This guy loves buying expensive things."

"No," shouted Alasdair, and hit the top of the chest so hard that Sam jumped. "That isn't the point. Why is he listing these things?"

"For insurance purposes?"

"No!" shouted Alasdair. "How can you be so stupid? It's obvious. He's making a confession."

"Of what?"

"That he's bought a lot of things he doesn't really want."

"Perhaps that's true. But that doesn't make it a confession."

Alasdair paused so long that Sam thought he'd conceded the point. When he did answer, it was in the calm, considered way my doctor tells me that eighty-nine is a stupid age to start smoking.

"Do you ever wonder why you're so curious about other people?

Why you *enjoy* finding things out?" He rubbed his cheek with his palm, then tilted his head to one side. "I think it's an interesting question."

"In what way?"

"Because I don't see how you're different from the people who buy those books you don't like."

"Which ones?" asked Sam, then laughed in a truncated way. "Most of the books we sell are rubbish."

Alasdair smiled, but in a way that suggested indulgence of an almost parental kind. "The ones about people abused by their priests or stepfathers. What you call 'misery lit.'"

Sam shrugged. "I don't see the connection. Those books are bullshit masquerading as autobiography. I'm interested in people's actual lives."

"It's mostly letters and gossip. Just because you do the filling in, the inventing, that doesn't make it more true."

"You've no idea," said Sam. "You'd be amazed what I know about some people."

"What you *think* you know."

"What I actually know."

"Fine. You know that someone's cheating on their wife. Or that they're a thief. But that doesn't explain why you want to know these things."

"I don't have to explain myself to you."

"No, you don't. But maybe you have some idea."

"Look, I think people are interesting. There's nothing wrong with that."

"But you find some more interesting than others."

"And?"

"And the people you're most interested in are the unhappy ones."

"That's not true," said Sam with a trace of anger, because Alasdair seemed so sure of himself. It was insulting to be thought so easy to explain.

"Isn't it? What about Caitlin? And Toby? That old woman who always looks disappointed? And that couple poisoning themselves. All of them are miserable. Is it, uh, a *coincidence*"—he paused, as if to savour the word—"that these are the people you're most interested in?"

Sam had a quick answer. "It's not because they're unhappy. It's because they're different."

"Because she wants to be better looking and he eats too much? Because that couple are trying to escape their lives?" Alasdair shook his head. "I'd say they were very normal."

"What do you know about normal? You used to live under a bridge, and you don't even know your full name."

Other than a slight compression of his lips, Alasdair did not respond.

"Your life, if you can call it that, is a mess. And yet you still feel you can tell people how they're supposed to live. This from a man who drinks his own piss and doesn't have any friends."

It felt good to speak freely, and really, Alasdair had it coming. Sam had put up with a lot, more than most people would have. He didn't see it as being cruel, more a moment of total honesty—and how could that ever be bad? It was OK to temporarily discount the many mitigating circumstances, such as the fact that Alasdair was an amnesiac who was mentally damaged and had little control over what he said.

Alasdair's response, when it finally came, was somewhat tangential.

"Actually, you're dying. You have cancer. Right now it's only in your brain"—he tapped the side of his head—"but very soon it will spread."

It was a horrible thing to say, but too crazy to take seriously. Alasdair wasn't finished.

"Instead of trying to get better, you look for people you hope are even sicker. You don't care about them, and you don't want to help them. You want to look at their misery and think you're better off."

"Shut up," said Sam, because this was unfair. Being crazy didn't give Alasdair the right to say anything.

"I have a suggestion," said Alasdair. "Why don't you spend time at the hospital? They have people in terrible pain. I suspect you'd find them even more interesting than—"

"Get out. And don't come back. Go back to your fucking bridge."

Alasdair did not argue. It took him barely a minute to gather his things. Sam expected him to make some absurd remark, maybe break a window, but all he did was take the front door key from his pocket and place it on the tin chest. Then he turned and left the house, closing the front door quietly.

For the next few minutes Sam stayed in the kitchen, feeling both pleased and ashamed. That these emotions contradicted each other didn't matter. Neither seemed about to displace the other.

I feel exactly the same when I look out my bedroom window. My eyes start at the horizon, then move down to the waves, which today are a shade between blue and green. After only a few moments I feel a sadness so familiar it is almost without sting. No doubt this dilution stems from a nagging sense of foolishness: Like Trudy (or Malea), I am gazing in the wrong direction, squinting to see what could not be seen even if it were still there.

When I lower my gaze, bringing it towards shore, I am perhaps of two minds already: the foolish and the sad. But to me these are not incompatible; to be foolishly sad is still to feel a single emotion. Only when my gaze reaches land, and people, does a separate emotion begin. Then I feel my breathing slow and my thoughts calm. I look at the people lying on the sand, in couples and small groups, either having sex or watching others; although I can't see their features from this distance, I'm certain most are happy.

It was much the same for Sam as he stood in his kitchen. He wanted to hear, but also feared, a knock on the door. He felt both relieved and guilty, which made it hard to know what he should do, just as I, when I stand at the window, don't know whether to turn or keep watching. If the two states alternated, it would be easy to choose. Whilst sad, I could start to turn away from the window. Even if this act was interrupted by my mind switching back to the people on the shore, those few seconds of movement might generate enough momentum for me to ignore this mental reversal. Likewise, Sam, if he had taken a few steps toward the front door, to go after Alasdair to say sorry, might have been able to carry on despite his mind returning to the satisfaction of a house without urine. If only we could be of one mind. Even our unhappiness feels half-achieved.

WHEN SAM OPENED the shop the next morning, there was a note from Malea. It was on a postcard that showed Comely Bank as it had been a hundred years before.

Comely Bank Avenue, Stockbridge, Edinburgh.   J. & W. Gim.

All she had written was *Thank you,* which was both disappointing and entirely expected. At least it was an acknowledgement. He inspected the picture in the hope that this ordinary scene might have been chosen to convey a message. It did not seem promising. The street was without people. The only sign of life was the horse in front of the carriage. If there had been words on shops or street signs, they might have had meaning, but there were just the tenements, their mute windows, the mist blurring the roofs.

He was about to put the card down when he noticed the woman. She stood on the corner, by the carriage, as if waiting for someone. She was going on a journey, and she was not going alone.

This is the danger of pictures. Even when they contain so little, they contain too much.

The rest of the morning passed in a blissful haze of imagining. He saw himself walking with Malea hand in hand through emerald rice fields. They ate noodles at a roadside stall, and she laughed at his failure with chopsticks. He met her family, her friends, and they embraced him, because even though they spoke no English and he was a stranger, they knew he'd brought her home.

The prospect of a new life, in a new place, made everything in the present seem trivial. The large donation of German textbooks, the three boxes of theatre programmes, and the bag of maps swollen with damp were all expressions of people's disrespect for books and the charity, but because he would not see these things again, they also possessed a minor pathos, just as a man who has had a rash for months or years may find its scarlet patterns pretty once they start to fade.

Sam's peace of mind was unassailable. When a woman with a bristly chin spoke loudly in Spanish on her mobile phone for ten minutes all he had to do was think of sitting with Malea on a porch at dusk. When a black poodle came into the shop, trotted round the shelves, yawned, then vomited quietly, this did not upset him either. Once again, he thought of himself and Malea sitting outside together, only this time the sunset was a smear of red. He was drinking a beer so cold it made his hand burn; when Malea sighed her breath caressed his neck.

He was able to enjoy this delusion until he saw Toby. His first reaction was fear; Sinead was sure to be with him. He had been stupid to think she would be content with watching him from a distance. This was a woman who saw nothing wrong with drugging someone who had rejected her. *Fine,* he thought, *if she is here, then so be it.* Exactly what he meant by this decisive and dramatic pronouncement he did not really know. But he wanted there to be a confrontation in which he was able to throw rocks at her from the moral high ground.

Toby, however, was not with Sinead. He was with his mother. Evelyn had never been in the shop before and seemed bewildered. "Do you know where they are?" she asked, and Toby nodded. They went towards the cookery section, him in front, and there was a slowness to the way she followed, as if she were moving against a headwind. But it was only when two women had to stand aside so Toby could pass that Sam realised he had put a lot of weight back on.

"What about this one?" asked Evelyn, pulling a book from the shelf. "Have you got it already?"

Toby turned the pages, his eyes wolfing down the pictures. Then he shook his head.

"All right," she said. "You can get one more. And can you please not do that?" she said to a woman who had just unwrapped a chocolate bar.

"What? Why not?" asked the woman, surprised.

"Because it will upset him."

"I don't understand," said the woman, and took a bite. Although Toby wasn't looking at her, he must have heard the crunch, because he dropped the book he was holding and stepped towards her. She jumped back and shouted, "Fuck!" This reaction was so extreme that several customers laughed, as did Sam, until he saw that Evelyn was crying.

"I'm sorry," she said, and put her hand over her eyes.

Sam brought her a chair. She sat and dabbed her eyes with a tissue whilst some of the customers stared. The woman whose chocolate bar had been imperilled put her hand on Evelyn's shoulder and said something Sam did not hear, which made Evelyn nod. As for Toby, he hovered by his mother, shifting his bulk from one foot to the other whilst emitting a whine of distress.

"I'll be all right," said Evelyn, then started crying again. Her shoulders shook as she wept.

Toby was almost as upset. He stroked his mother's hair and began to make a whispering sound that lacked actual words.

"You can't help it," said Evelyn. "I know you tried, you really did. You were a very good boy." She turned her head towards Sam. "He really did try."

"I know," he said, then hesitated, thinking she would wonder how he did. But either she wasn't listening, or she mistook his words for a platitude.

"He was doing so well," she said. "We were going to visit his uncle in Hong Kong. We were supposed to go next week."

"And you're not going?"

"He can't even go on the bus. Yesterday he put his hand in a woman's pocket because he'd seen her putting chocolate in there. No," she said, and wiped her eyes. Sam expected her to continue, but she let the negative stand.

Evelyn stood up and took Toby's hand. "Have you got your books?" she asked. He nodded, and they walked out slowly, pausing only for Evelyn to say to Sam, "You have a very nice shop." He could smell gin on her breath.

They had been gone for five minutes before Sam realised they hadn't paid for the books. It didn't really matter. The charity couldn't stop children from being hurt. Taking parents to court, putting kids into care, was merely damage limitation. It wasn't pointless—it did reduce harm—but however many thousands the charity raised, it could not solve the problem: people.

Sam put the chair back in the corner, then straightened some books. It occurred to him that what Sinead had done to Toby was basically child abuse. Obviously not in a literal sense—although Toby was not fit to look after himself, it was demeaning to his age and experience to label him a child—but more in the sense that he was vulnerable. Like Mortimer, Sinead had abused the trust that had been placed in her. The more Sam thought about what she'd done, how she'd used Toby like an object and by doing so destroyed all he'd achieved and crushed Evelyn's hopes (both for Toby and herself), the harder he pushed the books into the gaps on the shelves. They made a satisfying noise, like a block of wood being hit by a hammer, a block of wood that deserved to be hit.

Imagine a huge rock travelling though the coldness of space. Imagine that this rock is thirty million miles from Earth. Further imagine that this rock is moving towards the Earth at an average speed of twenty miles per second. At that speed, it will reach the Earth in 1,500,000 seconds, which might seem a lot, but this is only twenty-five thousand minutes, a mere 416.66 hours (which is still more than the number of hours Comely Bank had left when Sam decided he had to get out of the fucking shop).

Even though our imaginary rock is large and travelling fast, it is not unstoppable. All kinds of immovable objects can bring it to a halt, not just major planetoids, but also dwarf planets, trojans, centaurs, and plutinos. Though the stopping of our rock is an exciting prospect—the silent collision, the plume of dust, the shockwaves reaching out—this is only the most dramatic way in which the rock's heading might change. Many forces can bend or deflect it away from Earth, just as Sam could easily have been delayed from reaching the street. If our rock passed close to any sizable planetoid, it would be subject to its gravitational field, which, if strong enough, might shift the rock's trajectory towards Saturn, Pluto, or Neptune or through our solar system without any collision at all. If Sam had first met anyone he knew, he would have had to pause for five, perhaps ten seconds; enough to prevent collision.

If she'd been a few steps farther away, he wouldn't have seen her.

If she'd been a few steps back, she'd have had some warning. She could have smiled, said hi, carried on right past.

But she was right in Sam's path. Caitlin, who loved him, whom he did not love, who was leaving in four days. The only reason she stopped was that he'd walked into her. There was a moment of non-recognition. Then she knew him. She took a step back, and in that moment, with the sun behind her, he was pleased to see her but also sad, because she was virtually gone.

"Are you all packed?"

"Yes," she said, and the corners of her mouth twitched. Perhaps she thought of escape. She was looking in his direction, but not directly at him, as if there were someone next to him whom she greatly preferred.

"I'm leaving too," he said.

She did not seem surprised. "To where?"

"The Philippines."

"Cool," she said, but didn't ask why. She just kept staring to the side of him.

"Well, best of luck," he said, and immediately felt ridiculous. This was *not* what you said to someone you were never going to see again (and certainly not someone you had known well). But if Caitlin found this inappropriate, or simply stupid, she hid it admirably.

"You, too," she said, and then she did smile, a broad, unforced curving of her mouth that spoke as plainly as words. She honestly wished him well.

"Thanks," he said, and she took a side step, and that was when he saw Sinead. She was outside Mr. Asham's shop, and she had definitely seen him, because she was holding her phone at arm's length to take a picture. Having done so, she slowly started towards him.

If the probability of two bodies colliding is so minute, how much smaller are the chances of a third body converging on the same place? Whilst it is possible that Sinead had been waiting there a long time, it was not her habitual spot. Her being there as he stepped towards Caitlin and put a hand on her arm was truly a miracle of the most unfortunate kind.

It is difficult to say how many minds Sam was in at that moment. Perhaps we should start with his best and most basic thought, which was that suddenly Caitlin's hair was infused with the sun; every strand had an aura that made it singly worthy of wonder. It was not that he was blinded, or couldn't see her face, just that it was washed in unexpected light. When she had sidestepped, so as to leave, she had moved into a narrow sunbeam, no more than a handbreadth wide, all that could sneak through the luxuriant tree branches (though no match for the trees of Socotra, the "Island of Bliss"). The light was behind her, though not directly, so that the side of her face and the surrounding hair were illuminated—and not just in the sense of being brightened. They possessed a radiance that spoke of deeper enlightenment, a quality present in old religious paintings in which the women were angels or saints. Yet it was a look much older than Christ. When we lived in huts, perhaps even in caves, the sight of sunlight parting a person's hair must have inspired a similar feeling. What Sam felt was as old as our brain's ability to perceive beauty. And so there was definitely one healthy reason he leant towards Caitlin.

His lips were two feet from hers when he realised she wasn't responding. She was as glassy eyed as an animal that perceives danger. It was very confusing. If she wasn't interested, why didn't she protest? If she did want to kiss him, why didn't she lean in?

Over Caitlin's shoulder he saw that Sinead was only ten feet away. For the last week he had been wondering what she was going to do next. He'd been hoping that his violation had brought her some peace—albeit for his sake, not hers. But the look on her face was enough to disprove this idea. Her front teeth were hurting her lower lip, and she was breathing fast. He saw a level of desire that was akin to fury.

When one first considers the odds of our imaginary rock reaching Earth and the many things that might distort its path, the idea of it doing so seems implausible. But as the hours pass, and the rock continues—close calls with comets notwithstanding—it no longer seems unlikely. By the time the bluish dot of Earth appears, the impact seems fated. The rock will strike our planet; Sinead and Sam must collide.

But the wonderful, terrible truth is that hope persists. A wormhole, a nuclear bomb, the hand of a merciful God. Though salvation now seems as impossible as destruction once did, all those 416.66 hours ago, there is always, no matter how bright the lights in the sky, how tall the tidal wave, that pinch of disbelief.

Sinead was eight, seven, six feet away, close enough to see Sam's eyes as he kissed Caitlin. He was staring back at a rock that had seemed unstoppable only a moment before. Kissing Caitlin felt amazing, though not because of her mouth. What made it enjoyable was not the way she smelt—like lavender—or her knuckles pressed into his back. It was the broken look of the rock that made him kiss Caitlin as if it were New Year's Eve and they were drunk and there was fire in the sky. He put his hands on her neck, then smoothed them into her hair; she pressed herself harder against him. She took her mouth from his, but just for a moment, to gasp in air, then they were kissing again. He did not want the moment to end. He wanted to keep kissing Caitlin, and for Sinead to see, for it to hurt in a manner that never became familiar. He wanted it to be a jagged and surprising pain that shifted like the bloody beads of a vicious kaleidoscope. Turning, shifting, opening new cracks in her mind, her heart, wherever pain came from. Sam was glad when Sinead's hand covered her mouth, pleased when she went pale; when her shoulders dropped he felt satisfied. These reactions, her distress, were certainly revenge, and gratifying, and still not enough. He was disappointed when, with leaden feet, and tears in its eyes, the rock began to reverse. He kept kissing Caitlin even after Sinead ran, just in case she looked back.

Joy is a weaker feeling than hate: It was Caitlin who took her mouth away. She looked at Sam, brought her palm to his cheek, and kissed him very softly. Her tongue did not push through his lips; it explored without entering, flicking left, then right, and Sinead was definitely gone. For several heartbeats there was disbelief, a sense of anticlimax. Then Sam's body was subject to an intense thrill that resembled an orgasm, but only the way a breeze can be compared to a hurricane. It was the euphoria that follows a victory so implausible, so unexpected, that there is a twitch of embarrassment to the winners' smiles. Though it would peak, then ebb—which was both regrettable and merciful, because just as one cannot function when in terrible pain, so pleasure can be equally debilitating—the parallel ended there. Though an orgasm can influence how we feel for hours, days, it does not transform us. Only a sense of great deliverance can accomplish that. This has always been so. Those who survived the Black Death, the Holocaust, the Siege of Leningrad might have kept the same names, might have resumed the trades they had practiced before, slept in the same beds with the same people, but they were, each one of them, now cast from different metal.

As for those who say, *But we are always changing*—and in support of this platitude offer a parable in which a man steps into a river and consumes a kilo of grapes, but when he steps out with only a stalk and all that fruit in his gut, is apparently not the same man—to those people, most of them young, I say: Go ask your parents. Ask your grandparents. See how many say they died on August 2, 2017. The day that, in many cases, is now also their birthday. Whilst I find this adoption of a memorial day entirely understandable, it does mean that people tend not to believe me when I say that this is actually *my* birthday, and always has been.

I don't suppose it matters. These days I do little to celebrate; it has been years since I spent an afternoon on the beach, and alcohol gives me heartburn. At my age no one expects some kind of bacchanal, which is doubly a relief. Even if I were capable of such excesses, it seems disrespectful to celebrate on a day when billions died. This was particularly the case during the fifties and sixties when parades and reenactments were still popular, but even now, when the day is marked in more modest fashion, with banners, skywriting, and commemorative films, I feel the same discomfort. This isn't a common reservation. Lots of people whose birthday is on the second (both originally, and adopted) have no qualms about throwing a large party with musicians that goes on till dawn. The only concession is that they avoid fireworks.

I have friends who roll their eyes when I say that I'm not having a birthday party. "Again?" they ask. "Life goes on," they say, sometimes in a jocular fashion, but just as often in exasperation.

"Of course life goes on," I reply. "That's undeniable. It shouldn't be any other way. We have to live as fully as we can. But I think 364 days a year are enough for that."

This answer, or some variant of it, satisfies most of them. Only rarely do I have to go further, like with Shun Li yesterday. She's having a difficult time right now; her husband is having gene therapy, and it's not going well. Some of this anxiety was involved in her attack on me. She said my refusal to celebrate had nothing to do with the anniversary. She accused me of being morbid.

I wasn't having a good day either. My back was very painful. This was why I spoke at length of what I had seen in Manila on my birthday in 2017. After the first meteors hit Europe, everyone was in shock. The streets were lined with cars whose drivers had pulled over when they heard the news. People kept glancing up at the sky. Strangers put their arms round my shoulders, or embraced me fully. I think they saw me as a representative of those former places.

I was in a bar when we heard about the second wave. By then, nobody was paying for drinks; the bottles were on the counter. Many were crying and screaming; the rest stood or sat in small groups, repeating brief phrases I couldn't understand but guessed were "How terrible" or "I can't believe it." We stared at the TV, on which there were satellite images that were just a mess.

When it started raining, I left the bar and walked till I was lost. There was nowhere I wanted to be. I barely registered that I was in a foreign city surrounded by sights and words I did not understand. Only the corporate logos were familiar, though even they seemed strange, not as confident. The rain was hot, and so heavy it stung; when I got tired of walking I lay on the pavement and let it strike my face. Maybe I passed out, but probably not; I don't think I lost time. When I stood up, it was dark and I didn't want to be drunk. The city seemed incredibly bright, as if every light that people owned had been switched on, the way children do at night when they're left alone.

I walked on. At first the streets were broad and lined with apartment buildings with lush, well-tended lawns. Some people passed at a run. Cars were sounding their horns and flashing their lights as if they were returning from a sporting event where their team had won. Soon I heard music, a fast song with heavy bass and a woman singing in Filipino. The music was too loud, distorted. I didn't want to hear it; I only wanted quiet, but the road I was on led me towards its source. I entered a large square surrounded by grand colonial buildings that had a fountain in its centre, around which were clustered a crowd of perhaps five thousand people, almost all of who were dancing. Most were young, but there were also some elderly people tapping their feet on the margins. A lot of the dancers were drunk, or maybe high, but none seemed deranged, hysterical, or in any way out of control. There were many smiles, frequent laughter; it was one of the happiest crowds I have ever seen.

In hindsight, I can think of many reasons why they were enjoying themselves after finding out that more than a billion had died. For some it must have seemed like the end of the world; if they were going to die, they wanted it to happen whilst they were fully alive. I'm sure that for others the dancing and singing were just an expression of their great relief. It could easily have been Asia that did not exist. There might have been such parties in Paris and New York.

But at the time their joy disgusted me. Though I was too distraught (and drunk) to think clearly, one idea kept repeating like someone jabbing me with a sharp stick: They were celebrating the deaths of everyone I knew. The longer I watched, the more insensitive their party seemed. It was so obviously wrong, so disrespectful; its offensiveness had to be deliberate. They were not content with turning happily away from the disaster; they also wanted to laugh.

If someone hadn't put a bottle in my hand, I might have left and passed out in an alley.

If I'd been standing somewhere else, I might not have seen those five young men.

But they did, and I wasn't, so I got even drunker and saw the five young men with their arms around each others' shoulders. They were between eighteen and twenty-one; each was wearing a cloak. They were facing me, so all I could see of their cloaks was the part around their necks: one was yellow and red, another black and yellow, while the others were red, white, and blue. They were slurring the words of the song they were singing; two had their eyes closed as they swayed back and forth. One of the boys kept blowing a whistle I hoped he'd swallow. They seemed like football supporters because of the way they acted in tandem, chanting and clapping with a coordination that suggested a single mind. When they turned around, they did so in such perfect unison that it was like part of a dance number. That they could do so in such a state of intoxication seems impressive now. But on that humid night all I felt was surprise that quickly shifted to rage. The young men's "cloaks" were flags that had been tied around their necks. All of them belonged to countries that no longer existed. There was the yellow and black of what had been Germany:

There was the red and yellow of Spain:

As for the red, white, and blue, these belonged to two different countries: Great Britain and the United States of America.

At the time, I did not stop to wonder how these young men had obtained the flags. Did they already have them, and if so, why? Were they taken from outside a hotel or embassy during the confusion? Or had they, during this period of grief and shock, gone to a shop and bought them? At that moment, I had no such questions. For the first time since leaving Comely Bank, I knew what I should do. As I raised my arm, I was certain that this was the only thing I *could* do.

If the bottle had been empty.

If the boy wearing the flag of my country had kept his eyes open.

But it wasn't.

And he didn't.

The bottle broke on his temple.

Glass went into my hand.

My arm.

My cheek.

Then the boy was on the ground.

Two of the flags were clutching their faces; the other two were in shock. We were the epicentre of an enforced sobriety that pulsed through the crowd, taking the attention of one layer of people, which was quickly noticed by those in the next, nothing being more interesting than someone else's interest. I wish I could say that the sight of so much blood, or the unconscious boy, restored me to my senses. Instead I shouted at the four standing boys, who may not have understood English—though someone within hearing did, because at my trial the prosecution quoted me. *Isn't that funny?* is apparently what I said.

Of course, when I told this story to Shun Li this morning, I stopped before this part. The party in the square was enough to make my point.

"Maybe I'm wrong," I said. "But every year, when my birthday approaches, I remember that music and dancing and feel overwhelmed."

She was not convinced. She said, "But you still make it to the pier, just like you do every day. If you want to do something special, which isn't a celebration, why not go in the tunnel tomorrow?"

"I might."

"Really?" she said, and her laughter seemed unnecessary. It's not as if I've said I'll *never* go in. I could go tomorrow. I haven't decided.

Shun Li and I have different worldviews. She is interested only in what lies ahead. If I told her about Comely Bank and Sam's last days, I can imagine her response. "What does it matter if sixty years ago a man kissed a girl just so he could hurt another girl?" is what she'd say. She wouldn't want to hear about Caitlin's two minds, her fear and evident joy. She'd shrug away the notion that whilst the dead do not live on through us, our feelings for them persist. She might say, in her brusque fashion, that though this is obviously important for the person feeling the happiness, sorrow, or guilt, there is no reason this should matter to anyone else.

For someone like herself, who never knew Sam, Sinead, Alasdair, or Caitlin, they can only be characters in a story; however vivid or interesting they seem, they cannot be real. Their words ("What are you doing?" asked Caitlin) and their actions (she looked at Sam in confusion) will lack resonance for her. If Shun Li did ask, *What happened next?* it would be with no more interest than she would inquire about a film I had seen (and probably less, Shun Li being something of a movie buff). If I answered this somewhat dutiful question by telling her that Caitlin was as shocked as those flag-covered boys, or that her mouth vacillated between a thin, compressed line of pleasure and a small circle whose bottom half was pulled down as if by spiteful, pinching fingers, Shun Li would nod and say *Uh-huh.* If I dared add that Caitlin's next action was to turn her body sharply away from Sam's, as if she were wrenching it free, then to turn and run away, Shun Li would sigh and turn her gaze to the ceiling. Any further information—that Caitlin then cancelled her flight—would certainly provoke an outburst and her favourite question: *Why can't you just forget?*

She has a right to her opinion. I can't say she's wrong. My only defence is that every person has their history. We begin as caves, grow into huts, spurt into villages. As adults we are towns, and in some cases, cities.

But however high our towers reach, there are always traces of the stage before. Apart from our parents, our siblings, our cousins, there are friends from school, crushes, bullies, people we have not seen for decades but still think of when we are thirty-eight, fifty-six, ninety years old. Everyone has their relics. Even Shun Li speaks on rare occasions of Gezim, her first husband. No matter how high her skyscrapers (she is without question the finest living *guqin* player) the spire of their separation remains just as sharp.

Everything is determined by what came before: I am here because of collisions. Because the rock of Sam struck two other rocks, and the impact was pleasing to him. Yet although Sinead's unhappiness was a kind of revenge, it remained unsatisfying. It was a few hours before Sam found the solution. He opened Sinead's diary and found the page where she had first written about feeding Toby. After marking the page, he put the diary in an envelope. When he put it through Evelyn's door the next day, he felt a satisfaction he knew would endure. So what if he was motivated by revenge? It would also help Toby. Sinead would get sacked, then Toby would start losing weight; it wouldn't be long before he and Evelyn could escape.

17. One

THERE ARE NO CLEAN COLLISIONS. One of the objects—the smaller, the weaker—will certainly be damaged, if not by the loss of a fragment, then certainly with a crack. But this can take time before it becomes apparent. This was why no one was murdered or beaten on July 25 or 26.

On July 27, Sam bought a rucksack and started learning Filipino. "*Ako po si* Sam," he repeated to the bare walls of his flat. His name did not sound right in the sentence. It was a jarring shift that suggested the speaker was trying to be two people at once.

He moved onto other phrases. "*Mahal kita,* Malea," he said, then wondered when he would able to say this to her. Definitely not on the plane. It was better to work up to such a declaration: First he would tell her she was *maganda,* which meant "beautiful." After a few hours he could introduce himself, say his age, thank someone, ask where the toilet was. The only word that defeated him was *pinag-sisisihan.* He hoped there was an easier way to say sorry.

On the morning of July 28, Sam packed his rucksack full of summer clothes. He put most of the rest of his clothes into two large rubbish bags but left himself a change of clothes for the week ahead. He went to the delicatessen to buy a piece of Explorateur for lunch. The owner cut him a piece, then said, "Is that all?" His tone implied that such a small purchase was a waste of his time.

"Yes, thank you," said Sam, and paid him. After being given his change, he said, "No, wait. Actually there's something else. You're a pompous shit and everybody hates you."

The result was a rush of blood to the owner's face that purpled to such a degree it suggested haemorrhage. He was holding the long, sharp knife he had used to cut the cheese when he came round the counter. "What?" he said, but Sam was already out the door. It was only when he was on the pavement that he realised the man was right: He should have bought more. He had nothing to eat with the cheese. The perfect thing would be one of the small brown loaves he could see through the window. But to go back in, after what he'd just said, would require courage.

He went into Mr. Asham's. He didn't like buying from there, but sometimes there was no choice.

When he brought the bread to the till, Mr. Asham was reading a newspaper. On its cover was a picture of the queen, who was visiting Japan, and this gave Sam a brilliant idea.

"Are you interested in her?"

"Who?"

"The queen. What do you think of her?"

"She's very good. A wonderful lady."

"Oh, so you like her. Do you want to meet her?"

"Yes, of course."

"And what would you say to her?"

Mr. Asham turned his hands palms up. "I don't know," he said, and smiled. When Sam did not reply, he said, "That's eighty-five," and put out his hand.

"What do you think she'd say to you?"

"I don't know."

"What would you like to hear?"

Mr. Asham shrugged as if trying to remove a heavy coat. If Sam had gone no further, Fahad might still have remembered this peculiar conversation when brushing his teeth or as he entered sleep. But by morning it would have been gone.

Unfortunately, Sam was determined that Fahad get the joke. He took the paper from him, held up the cover, pointed to Her Majesty.

"Imagine she's here now," he said. For a few seconds Fahad smiled politely. But given the lack of any obvious joke, he stopped. For a moment he looked puzzled. Then Sam saw what he was looking for. Nothing as dramatic as realisation, just a narrowing of the eyes, a contraction of the mouth: signs of suspicion.

Sam ate lunch while sitting on his front doorstep. The sun was so powerful it seemed to be entering him.

Afterwards, he took his clothes into Caitlin's shop; given that she'd left the previous day, there was no risk of seeing her. When he saw a young woman with coiffed black hair standing in the doorway of the back office, he thought she was Caitlin's replacement. She was pale and thin and wore green eye shadow. She was talking to someone he could not see.

"And the head can come right off," she said.

Sam stared at the woman till she noticed him. "Hello?" she said, trying to sound friendly, but her voice had a catch in it.

"I have a donation," he said, and held out the bags. She took a step towards him. "Thanks very much," she said, and her face was carefully blank. Then there was movement in the background and he saw Caitlin. The woman turned and blocked his line of sight. Sam was surprised, but only momentarily. Of course Caitlin had chosen to stay: He had given her hope.

He took a step towards the woman. "I'm sorry," he said. "This is going to sound stupid. But I was wondering if you wanted to go for a coffee sometime. My name's Sam. I work in the bookshop."

"I'm Abby," she said, and her pale skin acquired a faint pink hue. "That sounds fine. But I should tell you that I have a girlfriend, so if we do go for coffee, there won't be any hand holding."

From the back room there were no curses or sounds of breakage or noise of any kind. It was very quiet.

"What about tomorrow?"

Abby looked thoughtful. She pouted. "I finish at six. Come by at six thirty. But I don't know where we'll go. Everywhere round here is shit."

"We'll go to the Italian place."

"Really? My friend worked there for three hours then quit. She said they're all perverts."

She laughed and said "perverts" again. The word delighted her. I used to know a girl from Macao who said *pìgu* the same way. Both she and Abby had this way of completely enjoying something small.

"I'll see you tomorrow," said Sam.

"I expect so," she replied, then walked into the back office. She waited for a few seconds, long enough for him to have walked away, before saying, "Did you *hear* that?"

There was a pause. Then Caitlin said, "Yeah."

"I mean, who does that? Who asks out someone they've only seen for ten seconds?"

"Are you sure he was asking you out?"

"Come on. You heard him. He wasn't exactly subtle."

"He might not have been. Some people are just friendly."

"That wasn't platonic friendly. You didn't see how he was looking at me."

"Maybe," said Caitlin, to which Abby responded quickly.

"Definitely! He was *leering*. He'll probably go home and have a wank about—"

"Shut up!"

"What? Why?"

"I don't want to hear that kind of thing. It's disgusting."

Sam thought it best to leave. If Caitlin came out of the back room and saw him, the shitty thing he'd done would be worse for being pointless. He wasn't even sure it would work. Though it seemed likely their kiss had made her stay, there were many other possible reasons. Some member of her family—about whom he knew nothing, and of which she never spoke—might have had an accident. Or she might just have been daunted by the prospect of leaving her life behind.

Yet for all the mistakes Sam made during that last week, this was one thing he got right. When he met Abby in the San Marco Ristorante, she was exhausted, her makeup smudged. She ordered two espressos and a tiramisu then slumped in her chair.

"Fuck me," she said loudly, then shook her head, perhaps at the way the waiters—of whom there were four, all greying—sharply turned their heads.

"Why," she said, reaching for the sugar, "is everyone fucking nuts?"

"I don't know. I used to think it was because of our parents. Now I think it's probably the Internet. Or capitalism. Or both."

"Twitter!" she said, and laughed at the stupidity of the word.

"I'm guessing you didn't just figure this out. What was today's proof?"

"My boss left me a note that said she's quit and gone to Egypt."

"Amazing. Great," he said, and felt a huge relief.

"Yeah!" she said, with almost as much enthusiasm. "I'd think it was terrific if she hadn't dumped this shit on me. I'm going to have to work for the next two weeks without a break."

"Did she say why she was going?"

"No, but I'm not really surprised. I hardly knew her, but I could tell she wasn't happy. She also had a massive crush on me. When you asked me out, she got really jealous!"

When Sam got home, the police were waiting. They were standing in his doorway, talking to one another whilst looking in different directions. He felt that sudden twist in his chest that even the most innocent feel when confronted with authority (a phenomenon, I am told, that persists).

"Are you Sam Clark?"

The police officer's voice was firm though not unfriendly, certainly not accusatory.

"Yes, I am," he said. "What's happened?"

"I'm afraid I may have some bad news for you."

Understandably, this was frightening; but then a woman's voice spoke from the officer's radio, and the suspense of waiting was worse. It was only a short period, barely five seconds, long enough for Sam to hate the messenger. What the fuck did he mean? "I *may* have some bad news for you." Either he did or did not have "news." What he *meant*, but did not fucking *say*, was he had news that Sam might *think* was bad.

"Copy," said the police officer, then turned back to him. "Mr. Clark, I'm sorry to tell you that Sinead Gorman is dead."

"What? How?"

"We are still conducting an investigation. But we believe she may have accidentally consumed a toxic substance."

He had done his best to hurt her; this was the result.

The police officer stretched his arm towards Sam's door.

"Do you mind if we come inside for a moment?"

"Yes," he said, then "No." There was relief in the actions required. He had to establish which pocket his keys were in. He had to push his hand into that pocket. He had to pinch the metal with his fingers. He had to withdraw that hand. He thought he was doing incredibly well until the police officer asked if he needed help.

"No," he said. He wanted to open the door by himself. He got the key in the lock and turned his hand.

Sam went inside, and they followed. When they entered the lounge, he said, "This is the lounge." He did not know what else to say. One of them sat next to him. I'm not sure what he looked like, except that he was young. The other, who had a beard, remained standing. Sam asked, "How did it happen?" Sinead was dead, and he knew why, but something didn't make sense. They had said *accidentally.*

"I'm afraid we can't tell you much at the moment, except that it happened when she was at work. Do you know Evelyn Boyle?"

"Yes."

"She said her son made Sinead a drink. She said he got two bottles mixed up. She went out this morning, and when she came back in the afternoon she found Sinead, but it was too late."

This seemed odd. He couldn't believe that Toby was allowed to make drinks; anything poisonous would have been in locked cupboards. If it was indeed a tragic accident—the collision of negligence and Toby's mistake—then its timing was curious. Evelyn definitely had a reason to kill Sinead; he had made sure of that. Had she found a way to blame someone who could not be blamed?

The older officer took a step towards him. "Mr. Clark, can you describe your relationship to Sinead?"

He thought this a strange question.

"She and Toby used to come into my shop. He likes books about cooking."

"Which shop is that?"

"The charity bookshop at the end of the street."

The police officer noted this down.

"Were you good friends?"

"Not really. I mean, I knew her, but not very well. We didn't hang out."

"All right," said the police officer, and it was hard to gauge his tone. It could have been an *All right* that meant "If you want to lie, that's fine." It could have been an acknowledgement.

"Do you mind if I ask why you came here?"

The younger police officer replied, perhaps too quickly, "It's just routine. We try to inform family or close friends directly in the event of a death. I'm afraid we thought that you and Ms. Gorman were much closer."

"How come?"

"We found a lot of photos of you on her phone. We asked Mrs. Boyle who you were and she said that you were Sinead's boyfriend."

"Really?"

"Yes, she was quite sure."

He doubted that Sinead had told Evelyn about him. Perhaps she was trying to confuse the police.

"I wasn't her boyfriend. She just had a crush on me."

The younger police officer nodded. "That would explain why she had so many pictures of you." The silence that followed seemed accusatory. But if they had suspicions—of what, he had no idea—it was probably not of anything he could be convicted of.

SAM WOKE ON the sofa with a pain in his back. His first thought was that he and Malea were leaving in two days. Then he remembered Sinead. Who was poisoned, dead.

He barely made it to the sink before he vomited. Each heave was like a serrated spoon taking scoops of his stomach. It cleared the fog of sleep, and he realised what had to be done. He and Malea had to leave at once. It would cost a lot to change their tickets, but this was their future, their lives, so what did that fucking matter? If they didn't, they were asking for trouble. Malea might change her mind; the police could arrest him.

But how could he convince her? He couldn't say he was also leaving. Even though he'd done a good thing for her, she had no reason to trust him. If he insisted too strongly, she might cancel the trip.

And so having made himself anxious, almost panicked, Sam ended up rejecting any course of action. For this, we should not blame him: We never know what is at stake.

All he could do was stay busy. He wasn't going to tell the charity he was leaving. He did feel bad about not telling his volunteers, but that would mean answering the same questions twenty times.

That afternoon he practiced his Filipino. He learnt the words for family members, numbers, dates; how to say *Pleased to meet you*. He read the dialogues out loud, imagining himself asking Malea questions and answering hers.

By the time it was dark, his head felt full. He wanted to sleep. After seven or eight hours he would wake and realise that only one day remained.

But it was only nine o'clock. He had to find something to do for the next few hours. He tried reading, but he couldn't concentrate. He repacked his bag. In the end, he decided to clean the house. It didn't matter that there was no need—no one else was going to move in—it was just to kill time. He started with the bathroom, which took longer than he had expected: The bath had a ring of yellow stains that took a lot of scrubbing. From there, he moved onto the lounge and kitchen. When he moved the sofa he found a book of matches, a green sock, and some screwed-up paper. He opened one piece carefully and found the paper was blank. On the next the word *Environment* was underlined three times. The third was covered by a list of his bad qualities and how they might be solved. It was a long list.

Problem	Solution
Boring	More time with people
Selfish	Drink more water
Violent	Drink less caffeine
Tactless	DRINK URINE
Short-sighted (literal)	6 carrots daily
Short-sighted (metaphor)	Don't know
Flatulent	Keep windows open
Greedy	Eat less sugar
Anxious	Walking
Big ego	Urine
Drug addiction	Urine
Masturbation	Spinach (raw)
Suicidal	Laughter
Bad breath	Keep mouth open
Bad reflexes	45 sit-ups/press-ups/jumps
Bad temper	see "violent"
Bad skin	Spinach (cooked)
Body odour	Better baths
Sleep disturbances	Teddy bear
Constipation	Lemongrass
Guilt	Don't know

Sam screwed up the paper. He didn't have bad breath, and there was nothing wrong with his skin. As for the part about "drug addiction," the idiot must have meant coffee.

Sam swept and washed the floor, which meant he had to move the trunk. He had wanted to have it shipped to Manila; it had been there before, in the 1950s, on his grandfather's first tour with the merchant navy. He liked the idea of it returning after more than fifty years. It would be a point of continuity with the life he was leaving behind, but one whose meaning stretched beyond the bounds of his lifetime, enough to make him feel it wasn't really "his."

Yet the chest was still in his lounge. First he had been too busy; then he had been worried that Malea would see him with it and grow suspicious; after that he had decided to wait till nearer their departure. As he stood in the almost empty lounge with his bags packed and nothing else to clean, he realised that he could not take it. Each photo and letter was a synecdoche of life in Comely Bank. The only reason he wanted them was as a shield. Did he really want to leave? Wasn't he just making the same stupid mistake as all those people who thought they'd "find themselves" by going to India or Nepal? The implication was their current, unhappy self was a costume that concealed a happier, more mentally healthy self that could be coaxed from hiding only by tropical sun, the scent of incense, the sight of orange robes. So what if he learnt Filipino? That didn't make him a different person.

But there was still a chance, albeit a small one, that he could lose his habits. By not taking the chest, he was giving up almost all tangible reminders except the clothes he was taking.

Whilst this might seem praiseworthy, a mark of his good intentions, it was self-deception. Every picture and letter in the chest had been scanned onto his laptop. Sam sat on the sofa and opened the chest. He felt he deserved an extended look at what he was giving up. He was immediately rewarded with pictures he had forgotten. There was the dinner party for cats:

There was a photo labelled *Charlie, 1952. He was gagging for it.*

The leather-bound book was still near the surface. Sam opened it and let his eyes descend the neatly ruled columns. On its own, the book would have been strange; that it was the twenty-ninth such volume indicated that the man was going through more than a phase. The last page was a list of roses he had bought for the garden (three of which are now extinct).

Date	Item	Price
August 8	François Juranville (Weeping)	£12.45
August 8	The Fairy	£10.30
August 8	Paul's Lemon Pillar	£14.50
August 8	Paul's Himalayan Musk	£12.50
August 8	Sophie's Perpetual	£11.50
August 8	The Ingenious Mr. Fairchild	£10.70
August 8	Little White Pet	£13.80

After this came blank pages, expectant columns, things unaccounted for.

The idea did not burst like a revelation; it illuminated his mind like the growth of a flame from a wick. First a quavering idea that seemed about to vanish; then an expansion into a notion that could be verbalised. He got off the sofa and went to the bin. He took out a ball of paper, unscrewed it, and held it against the list of roses. He compared the *F* of *Flatulent* with that of *François*, the *S* of *Sophie's* with that of *Suicidal*.

The next morning, that *last* morning, Sam was outside the library when it opened. It had been six years since he had been inside—like most people in Comely Bank, he preferred to own his books—but it was little changed. Grey metal shelves, fluorescent lights, some plants in agony. He saw a sign that said *Internet Station!*

Sam sat down at a computer and opened a newspaper database. The headline for August 1, 2009 was *MONSTER SAVAGES OUR KIDS*. He skipped forward to August 8.

DEATH DROP OF TERROR was the headline for that day. The story was about a woman who had fallen from a nineteen-storey building and survived with only broken arms and legs. It was interesting, because he knew the woman—she lived next to Mrs. Maclean—but it was not what he was looking for. He wanted to read about fires.

None were reported for August 8.

Nor for August 9 or 10.

There was a fire on August 11, but only in a school.

Each day's paper had forty-eight pages. Although he was able to skip the last fifteen pages of each (they were advertisements or about sports) he soon found it hard to concentrate. By the time he got to August 16, he had to bite his lip to focus. In just over twenty-four hours he would be gone (*they* would be gone) from this place forever; there were surely better ways to spend his last day than staring at a screen. But Sam was, as I have said, a most curious man.

The story was on page eleven of the August 19 paper. It was a short article, only a single column, next to an item about Mr. Carson, who used to run the hardware store. It was only because this caught Sam's eye—Mr. Carson had been forced to close his shop after beating a shoplifter with a plunger—that he read about the "blaze that devastated the mansion on Arboretum Avenue." The mansion had been the home of the Macgregor family: a stockbroker, his wife, and their two children, Emily and Michael, age nine and eleven. They and their mother died in the fire, which began in the night. Their father, Alasdair Macgregor, was missing. The police were appealing to friends and relatives to try to contact him. There was a photo of Alasdair on a small boat. He was wearing a white cap and smiling, never imagining, even in nightmares, that his wife and two children might go to sleep and breathe in smoke and meekly suffocate.

"Fuck," said Sam, and looked around for somebody to tell. There was no one, and so he printed the page, then left the library. As he walked he imagined a hard-working father who came from poor beginnings, a man who counted everything he spent, even when he no longer had to. This did not explain why he had to document their purchases so obsessively, but Sam had ideas. It was the stress of his job, some sexual dysfunction, or both. He had started writing things down as a way to reduce his anxiety, and it had worked, but far too well, because it became a compulsion.

As he turned the corner and the bridge came in sight, Sam considered the idea that Alasdair had been writing everything down so he would have a record for insurance purposes, and this led him to wonder if Alasdair had been heavily in debt, from which it was almost no mental distance to imagine that the fire had been deliberately set by Alasdair himself. His wife and children were supposed to have been away. Perhaps their car had broken down, or their flight had been cancelled, or whoever they were due to stay with—perhaps her mother—had cancelled at the last minute. Alasdair had not gone into the house. He had set the fire from outside, then left, feeling regret, but also hope that this might give his family a chance. And then, the next day, when he turned on the news, he learnt that he had murdered them.

Of course it did not have to be so dramatic. Perhaps Alasdair had stormed out after a fight with his wife. After putting the kids to bed, she had lit a candle, drunk a glass of wine, smoked a cigarette. After she finished the bottle, she drifted to sleep. Whether the fire started from a dropped cigarette or a melted candle—somehow the details didn't matter—the crucial thing was that it was more than an accident. Alasdair had blamed himself, whether rightly or not, causing him to lose his mind and memory, to wander the streets for eight years, to live like a ghost that didn't know why it was haunting. He could easily carry on like this, growing more eccentric, aging fast, until on a winter morning in five or ten years, he would be found under the bridge or in the bushes, his blue lips drawn back from his teeth, his body stiffened and cold.

But that wouldn't happen now. Sam was going to help him. Obviously, he wanted to—in a way, they had been friends—but even if Alasdair had been a complete stranger, Sam liked to think he would have felt the same obligation. In the past, he had been too passive, eager to learn about people's private lives but not get involved. There must have been similar situations in the previous ten years when he had been in possession of information that if used correctly might have saved a friendship, a marriage, perhaps even a life.

He reached the bridge quickly, and not just because he was walking fast. His movements were urgent, his expression purposive; people got out his way. He went down the stone steps, onto the bank, and without any trouble walked the narrow path.

He was surprised when Alasdair stepped out of the dark. He was wearing a small pair of red canvas shorts and a yellow jumper whose sleeves had been cut off. His head jerked forwards in what might have been a nod of recognition. He seemed neither surprised nor pleased to see Sam. It was then that Sam remembered they had parted on bad terms.

"I'm sorry about making you leave," he said. "I was going through a lot of stuff, and I took it out on you. I apologise."

Alasdair coughed. "Yes, you were. You don't look well."

"Oh, I'm fine. I'm leaving tomorrow," he said, and couldn't help smiling. It was slightly annoying that Alasdair didn't respond, unless putting his hand under his armpit could be considered an answer. But Sam wasn't going to be sidetracked.

"I'm glad I found you. There's something I want to ask you."

Alasdair put his other hand under his armpit, but he did at least seem to be listening. Sam got out the leather-bound notebook, then the list of his faults.

"That's mine," said Alasdair, pointing at the list. "Did you read it? You should."

"I did. I also looked at the notebook. I couldn't help noticing how similar the handwriting is."

Alasdair shrugged. "Of course it is. We're both men. I think he's also left-handed."

"What other similarities are there?"

Alasdair looked at the list, then the book, then back at the list.

"The *T*s. And maybe the *F*s. His *P*s are also like mine." He handed back the book and piece of paper. "Is there anything else? I have to find some wood."

"Yes. I want you to look at this picture." Sam gave him the print-out. Alasdair glanced at it, then said, "He looks like me."

"It is you. This is going to be a shock, and I'm sorry, I don't know how else to say it. You were married and had kids and lived in a big house near the park. Then there was a fire. I'm sorry. It's all written here."

While Alasdair read, Sam looked at the river, then up at the windows of a tenement that overlooked the water. On the ground floor he saw an empty blue vase; the first-floor window was blank. A hand-drawn Scottish flag had been stuck to the glass on the second floor. Underneath a black cat stared till it realised it had been seen. Leisurely, it turned its back.

"So, that's my name," said Alasdair. "I wondered about that." He did not seem shocked.

"Alasdair, do you agree that this is you? That it's your handwriting?"

"You could say this. But also not. I think if you look carefully you'll, uh, see that I look different."

"Now you do. But not then. That *was* you."

"No, he was the one with a wife and children. He owned a boat and house and all those things. That was who he was."

"But that was you!"

"But I don't remember it. It didn't happen to me."

This was stupid, utter madness, an amputee pretending he'd been born that way.

"Why does it matter if you don't remember? Does the world only exist in your mind? If I smash you on the back of the head and you black out and later can't remember, does that mean I didn't hit you?"

"Violent," muttered Alasdair, and took a step back.

"Isn't the fact that you can't remember proof that something *did* happen?"

"Have you been to the moon?"

"What? No."

"Maybe you just can't remember."

"Don't be stupid. It's not the same. I know I haven't been to the moon, but you *don't* know what happened to you. I can prove I haven't been. You can't prove this didn't happen."

"You could have used a computer."

"This isn't fake. It's real. Look, I understand, this is a lot, it's too much. It's awful. But isn't it better to know? So you can move on."

Alasdair slowly exhaled, his mouth almost closed. It was like the hiss of a tyre relieved to be punctured.

"So, uh, you think I should remember something so I can forget it? Why would I do that? I don't want this to have happened to me."

"But it did! You were a banker, and there was a fire, and I don't know how it started or how you survived, but it definitely made you into this crazy person who lives under a bridge."

Alasdair turned away. As he walked back to the bridge, Sam shouted, "Did you start that fire? Did you kill them?"

Alasdair did not slow, or pause. He entered the dark.

Sam sat down to wait for Alasdair to come back. The cat in the window offered its face. A cloud blocked the sun.

He wanted Alasdair to thank him. To say he'd be missed. But the reason he sat there for twenty minutes was that he didn't understand. If someone showed him a letter or e-mail written by his parents in which they explained themselves, he'd be overwhelmed. It was helpful to learn about people in general, to know about mothers who felt trapped by having a child, or people who hated consumerism. But these were hypotheses, not answers. They said nothing about his parents as individuals. Why else did he search through books, if not in the hope of finding a letter or postcard from them? His parents had lived on the street for twenty years and must have known hundreds of people. They could easily have written to someone who put the note in a book and then forgot about it. He wasn't crazy to think so. It was possible.

It started to rain. Sam didn't mind. It wouldn't last that long. There was also a chance, admittedly small, that Alasdair would offer him shelter.

Three ducks swam slowly by. The cat feigned disinterest. Above Sam, above the rain, the clouds began to shake. It sounded like a plane was tearing a hole in the sky.

The rain continued. Sam got hungry. He walked towards the bridge. By the time he reached it he could see that Alasdair was gone.

ON THE WAY home he was so distracted that he didn't even notice Abby standing outside her shop. She was holding a small black pipe and talking into her phone.

"The smallest. Miniscule. Hold on, wait," she called.

He stopped and looked at her in a way she didn't like.

"What's your problem?" She stuck the pipe in her mouth and raised her eyebrows.

"Nothing. I mean, sorry. How are you?"

"Average. Bit tired of urine stains. So when are you off?"

"Tomorrow."

"Excellent. You like flying?"

"Not much. The longest I've done is two hours."

"Don't worry, it's easy. Get drunk and watch the stupid films and don't even try to sleep."

"All right."

"Very good. Hey, I got an e-mail from Caitlin. She sent it to me, but it's really for the volunteers. I think it's her idea of a postcard. Anyway, I printed a copy if you want to see."

"Great," he said redundantly, because she was already going inside. She came back with a folded piece of paper she handed to him.

"Enjoy! And send me a *real* postcard. From Bang! Kok!"

"I'm not going there."

"Pity! Bye!"

She waved and went back inside. He put the paper in his pocket. By the time he got home he had forgotten it.

He lay down on the sofa and closed his eyes. He was hungry, and it was almost lunchtime, but he didn't want to go out again. There was really nothing left to do, so he took off his clothes and got into bed. He decided to look through some of his books, starting with his favourites. When he found a passage he liked, he folded either the top or bottom corner of the page it was on, and sometimes, if the passage seemed particularly impressive, he drew a line in the margin next to the sentences. This was supposed to make these passages easy to find when he needed to remind himself of their brilliance. When this would occur he had no way of knowing, but each time he folded a page it was with the certainty of a wine collector placing a bottle in their cellar.

It was thus with great anticipation that he opened a thick book he had not read since 2002. He turned to the first page and read its opening paragraph.

A screaming comes across the sky. It has happened before, but there is nothing to compare it to now.

The old words were comforting. He didn't remember what they meant; it was their familiarity that counted. He flicked forwards to the first folded page.

Wars have a way of overriding the days just before them. In the looking back, there is such noise and gravity. But we are conditioned to forget.

A high-pitched wail cut through the words, a rising, urgent sound. Sam pictured burning houses, people hit by cars. The siren came closer, peaked, then stopped. He pictured its light strobing.

He read the passage again, thought it a well-written sentence but nothing more. He couldn't see what his younger self had found so impressive. It made him feel that part of his past did not belong to him, had not happened to him, the person he was now. Whilst this idea made complete sense to Alasdair, it terrified Sam. If he was not one person with one set of memories, then there was no "he." Whatever "he" thought, however "he" felt, was merely one of a succession of selves that did not form a palimpsest, but instead kept peeling away. From this, it followed that "he" would not really be alive for seventy-six years (the average life expectancy in Scotland at that time). "He" had only five years left, perhaps a decade of life—however long it took for "his" past to seem like someone else's.

That Sam found nothing liberating in this idea should be no surprise. He was protective of his misery.

He was trying to decide whether to pick a different book, one he'd read more recently, when there was a knock on the door. He thought it was probably Alasdair; he hoped, without conviction, that it was Malea. As he reached for the door, he decided to let Alasdair stay in the flat after he'd gone.

Unfortunately, this small act of decency never came about.

"Good evening, Mr. Clark," said the police officer who had told Sam about Sinead. He was with the same, younger police officer I still can't properly recall. It was this man who asked, "Do you mind if we come in?"

"Of course not," said Sam.

They went inside, and their footsteps seemed loud. The police officers stepped around his bags.

"Are you moving?" asked the older one.

"I'm just going away for a while."

"Whereabouts?"

"The Philippines."

The officer nodded but made no reply. Sam looked at his watch. In fourteen hours he would leave for the airport.

The older police officer started to speak, then coughed. He recovered quickly. "Are you a friend of Malea Ocampo?"

The question did not shock Sam. He had imagined bad news too often to be surprised. There was only one thing to ask.

"Is she dead?"

The police officers looked at each other. The younger one spoke. "She's in the hospital."

"What happened?"

"We can't say yet. Can you tell us where you were yesterday?"

"When?"

"Between twelve and three o'clock."

"I was at work."

"And where's that?"

"The bookshop. Look, I need to see her. Which hospital is she in?"

"She's at Western General. But she may be unable to receive visitors." It sounded like a warning.

"Mr. Clark, can you tell me about the nature of your relationship with Miss Ocampo? Have you known her long?"

"About a year. And we don't need to be coy about this. I was a client of hers. I'm sure you already know this."

"Yes."

"And I'm not the one you should be talking to. You should speak to Mr. Asham. I don't know if it was him, but he's hurt her before."

"Why do you say that?"

"Because she told me. And I've seen the bruises."

Sam didn't know if they believed him. My guess is that they took it seriously enough to question Mr. Asham. Why else would he have taken that unexpected trip? If they hadn't done so, he would not have Survived. He wouldn't have had those thirty-five years in Lahore. He would not have died, aged ninety-one, from choking on a frog.

The police officers stood. "We may have some other questions—how can we contact you?"

After they left, the facts unfurled.

She was covered in blood.

She was covered in blood and on the floor.

She was covered in blood and on the floor, and still Asham kicked her.

As the scene expanded, so did the pain. Sam brought his palms to his face, pushed their heels against his chin, his fingertips against his forehead, as if their combined pressure could contain the event. When he closed his eyes, which were already covered, he was attempting a trick that only children can accomplish. They can make things disappear. If they don't like their world, they can just unmake it.

HE WENT OUT and got in a taxi and said, "To Western General." He'd never noticed that the name of the hospital was so martial. He imagined a city in quadrants, each ruled by a warlord, with walls and zones where you'd be shot if you did not belong. Soon he would reach a checkpoint where he would have to give his name, show his papers, provide explanations.

Although the roads were busy, the taxi was not delayed. When Sam arrived, the receptionist asked him what ward Malea was in.

"I don't know. Maybe intensive care?"

She was not there. Nor was she in the high dependency unit. For a few moments Sam was able to hope it had all been some implausibly convoluted mistake involving multiple cases of mistaken identity. Then the receptionist said, with too much triumph, "She's in ward eleven."

Turning corners, trusting signs, Sam moved past people on their best behaviour. Part of this was professional—the good conduct of nurses and doctors—but the patients were playing their part. Whether gliding in wheelchairs, awkward on crutches, or moving in a cautious manner due to hidden wounds, all of them had the composure of people who expect to be rewarded for following the rules.

The corridors kept branching off. It was a tour of the organs. From hearts to kidneys to brains and then the genitals. There were so many scenes that felt private. Alasdair was right: This was where Sam belonged.

He passed slowly down a corridor lined with children and their parents. The chairs were orange, the walls lime green; a poster showed a laughing panda getting an injection.

Ward eleven was at the end of a corridor that had been zealously cleaned. The smell of disinfectant made him feel sick. If he went outside and took slow, deep breaths, there would still be time to visit.

He had turned away when the ward's door slid open. He looked back to see who was coming through, but no one had appeared. It was obviously so sensitive he had triggered it from ten feet away. Now that it was open he could see the rows of beds. At the far end he could just make out a small head with black hair.

At the entrance a nurse asked his name and whom he had come to see. As she wrote it down she said, "And please clean your hands." She gestured to a bottle of hand sanitiser. He squirted some on his hands and rubbed them together; it felt as if sparks were jumping from them. Though not an unpleasant feeling, it made him recall being drugged. All those waves had travelled through him; it had felt so good. Sinead had picked the best drug.

"She's over here," said the nurse. "But I don't know how much she'll be able to talk. We had to sedate her heavily. Are you a relative?"

"A friend."

He waited for a knowing look, a twitch of disapproval. But the nurse only said, "This way."

As Sam passed between the beds, his heart was beating fast. His chest hurt. He was going to be sick. This was far too real. If only Malea would turn, present her face, give him the luxury of a few seconds before he had to speak. That would be enough time to get used to being horrified.

Her head stayed still; she did not move. They were halfway there. He looked to one side, then quickly back, hoping that things would alter in the meantime. To his right a fat man was reading the Bible. Ahead the view was the same. When he looked left he saw a girl stretching a piece of gum between her teeth and fingers. She met his gaze and stretched it more. "I'll see if Malea's awake," said the nurse.

She pulled at a curtain, which resisted then gave with a scraping sound. He was then confronted by a face with aspirations. It was going to be a new face quite unlike the old. In place of the usual brown outside was a red with the highest of hopes. It wanted to contain all other colours while remaining itself. Though blue, black, and green were missing, orange, purple, and yellow were definitely present. Other changes were deeper, structural. The aspect of her nose had changed. One of her eyes was closed, as if whatever was going on behind the lid were supposed to be secret. But there was no mystery about the stitches in her forehead and cheeks.

"Sam," she said. He sat. Perhaps it was the lighting, or the size of the bed, but Malea seemed smaller.

She tried to sit up, and the blanket slipped down; both her arms were bandaged.

"I'm so sorry."

"It's not your fault. You warned me. It was my choice."

"So it was him?"

She closed her eyes for a moment. "He came to my house. As soon as I let him in, he started hitting me."

"Did he say why?"

She swallowed, and it seemed to hurt. She placed her hand on her throat.

"He didn't say anything."

"Nothing?"

He had to tell her. It would mean the end of things but he had no choice.

"I thought he was going to kill me. He just didn't stop."

The only question was when. This wasn't the right moment. She had been through too much.

"I'm sorry," he said, but she couldn't answer. Tears were oozing from her closed eye, falling from the other. He knew nothing about that kind of pain. Sean had been an amateur. Mr. Asham had been angry, but he'd been controlled. Sean's attack had been a beating in the street that could have been stopped at any time. Malea's beating had taken place in her home, in private, without the risk of interruption. Sam imagined Mr. Asham pausing after each strike, considering where to aim next.

"That fucker," Sam said, and it was a relief to have his emotions lurch. Being angry felt better. He thought of punching Mr. Asham, the bastard raising his hands to his face, then being hit in the stomach, the balls. But whatever he did to Mr. Asham would not make amends.

"Here," he said, and passed her a tissue. It was a pathetic gesture, but he was glad she took it, which was more pathetic yet. She wiped her eyes. She was still crying. The normal, compassionate response to tears—what you could do even to a stranger—was to hold their hand, put yours on their shoulder, smooth their hair from their face. But he could not touch Malea. There had already been too many unwanted hands.

She stopped crying. Her breathing slowed. He could hear the low-pitched buzz of other visitors. The loudest voice was a man discussing his operation.

He stood and went to the curtain, hoping to peek through without moving it. Unfortunately, the nurse had been considerate. She had drawn it tight. When he pulled the curtain, it stuck. He pulled again, harder, and then it moved, but with a shearing sound. Behind him, Malea stirred.

"Sam?"

"Yes?"

"You shouldn't wait. Go, I'll see you there."

"Where?"

"At the San Sebastian Church. In two weeks."

I don't know how Malea knew he was also going to Manila. Perhaps the reservation listed the number of passengers on the booking. More likely she heard through one of her clients that he was also leaving. It would not have taken an inspired guess to figure out his destination, or that he planned to go with her.

Joyfully, somewhat emboldened, he said, "No, I'll change our tickets. We can both go then."

"I don't want to. I want to go on my own."

"But why?" he asked, hearing, and hating, the pleading in his voice.

"Because I don't want to see you again. Not here. And if we meet in Manila, we will not talk about any of this. Do you understand?"

"Yes, I do," he said, because being hurt didn't affect his ability to lie.

Her reply was measured, calm and deliberate. "Do you? I do not think so. You did a kind thing for me, and I am very grateful. But I am not in love with you. I am not your girlfriend. I had sex with you because you paid me. If we meet at San Sebastian you should act as if we have never met. If you talk about anything here, I will walk away."

"How am I supposed to do that?"

"I don't know. Maybe you can't."

He wasn't sure she cared. But he was sure she meant it. This wasn't how he wanted them to part. He didn't want to get on a plane without her, let alone spend two weeks in Manila on his own, waiting for someone who either would not show up or would treat him like a stranger if she did.

From close by he heard the tinkling of a little bell. It was a high, sweet sound, almost like birdsong—if not a Daurian redstart, then a lesser coucal.

A woman's voice said firmly, "Visiting time is over."

He looked at Malea. "See you in two weeks?" he said. He was sure of nothing. If he couldn't expect a declaration—there were no feelings to declare—he wanted to be sure they'd meet.

Afterwards he could not decide what the pause that followed meant. It could have been hesitation. A wavering of resolve. But whatever she'd decided, it was easier to say yes. When she said this it sounded like she meant it.

The bell rang more insistently. Sometimes those birds sound angry. If I hadn't been up this morning—I can never sleep the night before the anniversary—they would have woken me. I half expected them to fly through the windows.

Sam didn't want to stand, but he did. There was still time to tell her what he'd said to Mr. Asham. After this, when they met again—not *if*—it would be part of a life she wouldn't discuss. There'd be no chance of absolution; his guilt could only fester.

"OK, see you then," he said, and felt both crushed and relieved. His punishment would be lingering, painful; but it was convenient. Even now, it is not the guilty who decide their sentence.

A last glance at Malea's battered face, its crooked nose, the single eye that stared. Then he was stepping through the curtain, passing down the aisle. The other patients seemed to stare. Had they heard, and if so, did they care? They had their troubles, as did the nurse and the children in that cheerful corridor. They were guilty of some things, innocent of others, like him in most respects except that he Survived.

When Sam left the hospital, the wind was shoving the clouds. It would take an hour to walk back, but he wanted the distraction. That was how he planned to get through the next two weeks. On the flight he'd do as Abby suggested; in Manila he'd walk. He'd go to bars and clubs and lose himself in crowds.

He approached two taxi drivers leaning on their cars. As he came near they fell silent, then tried to make eye contact. When this failed to get his attention, one of them whistled, but softly, not in the piercing, insolent way the taxi drivers do here. When I came back from Vang Vieng last year, there was a woman who made my ears ring. When I stared at her and shook my head, I was more justified than Sam in doing so. Admittedly, he was hungry and somewhat distraught, but there was no need for him to say "cunt" under his breath. I wish that the driver had responded by punching Sam in the face. It would have been well deserved, and maybe more instructive than the beating he had gotten from Sean. I am, of course, not advocating violence as a means of moral education. But it is not *always* a terrible thing to be kicked and punched by strangers, whether they are drunks on a bench, taxi drivers, or flag-wearing men. Despite the pain and damage to the body, in the long run the beating may help. My injuries were very useful during my confinement.

Unfortunately, the taxi driver was too exhausted to care about

Sam's comment. Sam left the hospital grounds and walked by the side of the road. Initially there was the distraction of feeling he'd been wronged. He berated the taxi driver, the man apologised, then Sam repeated the charge. Though it was gratifying to imagine this, it was a thin complaint, no match for what Mr. Asham had done to Malea. If this was not bad enough, what was worse was that Mr. Asham would probably go unpunished. Without Malea's testimony, there was just Sam's accusation. While they were living new lives in Manila—perhaps together, perhaps apart—Mr. Asham would still be selling bread and newspapers behind that shop counter. He'd be there another decade, growing worn, slowly fading, just like his shop coat. Eventually there'd be a morning, perhaps in winter, when he'd realise that the stupid, trivial shop had been his entire life. He'd be seventy, seventy-five; too old to become someone else. Hopefully he'd have a heart attack right there at the counter. His old hands would clutch his chest; he'd make a strangled sound. He'd lie there, alone, in pain; his final sight would be a shelf of fizzy drinks.

Sam was too absorbed in his fantasy to notice himself being surrounded. Their footsteps were heavy, their breathing desperate; he felt like their prey. What was most unnerving was not being able to see their faces. After a flash of profile there was only the retreating back of their heads. And still they kept running past, their bodies lean and sexless. He did not think it was a race. They wore no wristbands or numbers. They were running together for some other reason.

The runners passed. He relaxed. He watched their pale limbs rise and fall until they disappeared. He kept walking, as I am walking, slowly, focussed on muscles and tendons, the press of the ground against his soles. It felt as if his movement were an automatic process in which he had no part. Legs pulled body from the left then right—in his case with little effort, in mine with a degree of care that approaches suspicion.

There isn't much I envy Sam. He was stupid and naïve and hurt so many people. But he was walking twice as quickly as I can. I have walked along this promenade thousands of times, and the vista is always impressive: Only a very limited person can be bored of the sea. But there are still moments when I want it to flow past me more quickly. Instead I must shuffle round the long bend of the coast, the pier a sketch against the sky that mocks me with its distance. The best I can do is remember running as I walk so slowly. It lets me be here, there, back in time, ten minutes in the future. I can be Sam, who had started running. Away from the hospital, away from Malea, but also towards leaving. There were still things to be done. He had to change her ticket. He had to get his bags. He had to go to the airport and get on a plane, but that could not be all. He was going to burn down Mr. Asham's shop.

I don't know why young people enjoy destruction so much. Perhaps they don't feel attached to the world. Or maybe they resent it for existing first.

When Sam got home, he half expected to see police outside. But no one else had died, so he was able to go in, undress, turn on the shower, and stand beneath the stream. If the water was still hot when his knees gave way, it was not because he couldn't stand—he could—but because standing was pointless. There was no need to keep muscles tense and ligaments stretched while maintaining his balance. He got just as wet when sitting, and in many ways it was better. The water struck his skin with greater force.

As the pier comes close I see the queue for the tunnel and shiver.

Was the water getting cold? Not yet. As soon as he felt it doing so he would get out. He would put on his clothes and shoes, and then he would be out the door.

It is not a big queue, maybe thirty people. Usually there are hundreds. That it is here every day, sometimes shorter, usually longer, reminds me of a book I read so long ago I can remember nothing of it except a single scene. It took place in what was then Portugal, or maybe what was Spain. It was during a time of crisis so great that people were choosing to die. The bells of the churches rang at all hours. Outside people queued in the thousands, calmly waiting, sometimes for days, to be mercifully killed by the priests.

When Sam felt it—the cooling, his skin's brief frown—he wondered if he was mistaken, but only for an instant. Then he put his hands on the side of the bath and stood, an older man's precaution that gave him momentum, too much, because he slipped and hit his elbow on the side of the bath. It was an excellent collision. A different angle and lesser force would not have damaged the nerve. Pain streaked the length of his arm, and he almost passed out. Even under the tepid water he broke into a sweat. Not until the shower was cold did he dare sit up and consider whether his arm was broken. He moved it slightly. He did not think so. But there was a worrying tingle between his elbow and wrist. It felt as if some change had taken place.

Just because the queue is small doesn't mean I have to go in. There will be other days.

It took longer to dress himself using only one hand. There was time to think. Would Sinead have a funeral? If so, who would attend? Her mother? Toby? Yes to the latter, because Evelyn would want to go. She'd probably find it satisfying.

And who says I need to go in? It won't tell me anything I don't already know. It's not as if I've *forgotten*.

He forced sockless feet into shoes and then was out the door. His hand felt brittle, electrically charged, but at least he was moving. He didn't stop when he reached the bridge.

Mr. Asham's was the only shop open. Sam had expected this, and in fact preferred it. The oil that destroyed the place would come from its own shelves. Afterwards, as Mr. Asham looked at the black and twisted metal, the ruin of three decades of work, he might remember Sam smiling broadly when he came to the counter. Whatever his suspicions, they were sure to be eclipsed by the slow, depressing work of rebuilding, those many unhappy weeks when Mr. Asham would struggle to believe the damage could be undone. Only after the shop had reopened and there was hope of better days, a new beginning, would he receive a postcard with a drawing of the queen that depicted Her Majesty throwing a Molotov cocktail.

My legs hurt. I want to rest. Something is wrong with my ears. They keep popping as if the pressure is changing too fast.

But as usual, Sam's mind was split. Although he wanted to see Mr. Asham, the prospect was terrifying. If you have never been badly beaten, you may think it is like being hit or kicked several times, something most people can imagine, even if they have never been attacked: We have all slipped and fallen or been hit in the face with a ball. A proper beating is like this to the degree that a normal bowel movement can be said to resemble dysentery. Whilst the same parts are involved, the fear and pain are so intense as to be unrelated. It cannot be imagined. It is a death you survive.

My ears are no cause for worry. They are my body's version of an excuse. To call its bluff I stop and take deep breaths. I swallow. I yawn. If my Eustachian tube was blocked, it is clear now.

But instead of Mr. Asham there was a short grey-haired woman wearing a green sari behind the counter. Her presence made Sam relieved and suspicious. Just as people forgot that Mr. Asham was a man who wore tweed suits, so they forgot he had a wife called Rabia. Although his son often worked in the shop, she was rarely seen. I don't know whether this had to do with Mr. Asham's beliefs about the role of women in the workplace, or a wish to keep his home and work life separate, but the result was that every time Rabia appeared there was an instant of disbelief. She was incontrovertible proof that he was more than a Pakistani man who stood behind a shop counter wearing a blue coat. He was a father, a husband, someone who was loved.

Although I haven't made my decision, I still join the queue.

Sam went to the shelves of cleaning products. He looked at soap, detergent, furniture polish, then washing powder and bleach. He could not see anything that would catch fire. When he asked Rabia if they had any oil for lamps or heating, she said, "Not until winter." The only flammable item Mr. Asham sold was the liquid people used in their cigarette lighters. Although there were three cans of it, they wouldn't be enough. There would be no fire.

We step forward. Wait. Step forward again. I watch as a young woman, less than thirty, steps out of the queue. There are many reasons why she might be leaving after waiting half an hour. That she has had second thoughts is only one possibility. As for the two young men in front, they don't seem worried at all. They have their arms round each other's shoulders and are singing together. I don't know all the words—my Urdu is pretty thin—only that it is a song about heaven. I think it's meant in a general, non-religious sense, because it's also about love. I'm guessing they are here for the same reasons most young people come. They think it will be funny to see themselves looking that way, just as people at funfairs used to enjoy seeing their images distorted by mirrors that made them look taller or fatter.

"Is something wrong, dear?" Rabia's tone was warm, solicitous, wholly genuine. He managed to say, "No, it's fine," but then his voice cracked and he was crying in a desperate way that made Rabia step back.

I want to tell these young men they should reconsider. I don't know them; I can't guess how they'll react. They'll probably find it amusing. There's even a chance it will help them in some subtle way. Add a little caution to their confidence.

"What is it? What's the matter?"

But I fear the old cliché about knowing the future is true. If we are to be hanged one day, let the knowledge come gradually—in the beam of a telephone pole seen on the way to work, in the overhead lines of a railway crossing—so that over years, decades, we build a sketch of the scaffold, become familiar with that image.

Sam swallowed. "No, I'm fine. But thanks." Rabia was a kind, maternal figure who hopefully had no idea about the person she was married to. Not that this was impossible. There are always excuses.

These young men definitely shouldn't go in together. Whether we are in love, or lust, it is only with the person who exists in the present.

"O-kay, dear," Rabia said. For a moment Sam felt a flash of anger; she was being patronising. As if he needed her permission to feel fine.

When they next kiss their lips may not feel as soft. Their hands may feel rougher, far less nimble. As if they belonged to someone else.

Sam saw fire on the shelves, the floor; the windows cracked, then broke.

They step forward, as do I. There are only five people ahead of them.

But there was going to be no fire. And fire was not enough. Fires happened all the time. They were accidents. They were not a judgement. People would look at his burnt-out shop and say, "Poor Mr. Asham. What a shame. Such a nice man."

There are four people ahead of the couple. Two old women, a teenage girl, and a middle-aged man. I wonder what he will choose, if he will choose at all. Apparently the machine can decide.

Outside the shop Sam looked in both directions, wondering which way to go. It didn't really matter. He'd have to wait till three or four in the morning, when the street would be deserted, before he could do anything. As he entered the park the air smelt of smoke and cooking meat. He heard a guitar, a drum, several shouts, some laughter. He walked toward the nearest light till he could see their faces, orange and partial. Sitting with them would be a nice way to spend his final hours in Comely Bank. They might be interested in where he was going; if they asked him why, he'd tell most of the truth. Everything except Malea. Everything except Sinead, Mr. Asham, his parents, what he was going to do when they were in their beds. He stood a moment and listened, heard talk of a protest, a party at Josie's. They were laughing at her new haircut when he walked away.

Now there are just two old women in front of these young men. They do not seem to be together. The woman in the very front hasn't turned; if the one behind her has spoken, she has done so in a whisper. To me, this isn't surprising. Though some might think these two women—both old enough to be Survivors—must have a lot to talk about, in my experience such similarities often have the opposite effect. We have little to say to ourselves.

There was no one by the pond. On the water he could see a ghostly blur of swans, moving without sound or effort, pulled by invisible strings. He sat on the grass and watched them drift, apparently without purpose, sometimes drawing near but never colliding.

The first old woman enters the tunnel. The other, now first in line, turns to the young men. "I don't know why I'm bothering. All I need to do is look in the mirror."

Sam's head was heavy. He lay on his side. The swans were liminal.

She says this while stroking her cheek. The gesture is so self-adoringly coquettish that the young men don't know how to react.

He saw lighter patches of dark.

They are wondering if it is possible for her to be so sweetly deluded about her true age. If so, what should they say? Surely it can do no harm if they agree.

They were not separate.

She lets them doubt a little longer. When she laughs, they quickly join in, no doubt relieved. It would have been a small lie, a white one; but many people of their generation seem unskilled at this.

Not—

"I guess this is time travel," she says, and we laugh immediately.

When Sam woke it was because of the pain in his ear. The lobe felt as if it had just been pinched, but by something stronger than fingers. He sat up and there was a hiss, and then part of the darkness was hurting his legs, and though he moved quickly it got him twice before he was out of range. Then the hiss returned, but it was now accompanied by the snapping sound of a sail being bullied by wind. The swan was furious.

The green light comes on over the door. "See you in the past," she says, and disappears inside. The couple dutifully steps forward, one of them whistling the tune they had been singing. "Skip to the next track," says his friend.

Sam ran and did not look behind because there was no point. He couldn't run any faster. His ear was bleeding and maybe his legs, and if he had the chance he'd kick that bird to death.

"Which one? 'Best Boy in Kuqa'? Or '3099'?"

He ran until he reached the gate.

"What about something older?"

He stopped and put his hand to his ear. He wiped the blood on his sleeve.

The young man thinks then starts to whistle a tune I know so well I join in. Though this makes him falter, he does not stop. He whistles four or five bars more, after which he turns to me slowly, eyebrows raised.

Sam didn't know how long he'd slept. Although it was still dark, he thought dawn was near. He looked down the road and saw the face of the clock on the church. It was just after four; little time was left.

"Are you a fan?" he asks.

Sam walked quickly to the bookshop. He took two cans of paint from the back office, searched through drawers until he found a brush.

"I have to be," I say. "She's my friend."

A last look at the office, the shelves; then he was on the street and walking towards Asham's shop.

"Really?" they say, and sound as thrilled as if I, not Shun Li, had written the song.

The street was deserted. No cars passed. Every window was dark.

"That's amazing. What's she like?"

He opened the can of paint, and it was so white it glowed. He dipped the brush in, wiped off excess, drew a vertical line.

"Don't ask him that! That's private."

Next to it he drew another line, then joined the two to make an *A*.

"Oh no, it's fine," I say.

He made a mess of the *S*. The *H* was slightly better.

A proper answer would take much longer than the time that remains.

As was the second *A*.

"She's wonderful," I say, then add, "but she's so competitive! She even hates losing at cards."

The *M* was just so-so. He wasn't sure about the next word. *HITS* or *HURTS*?

In truth, I've never seen her play. I just like the idea of this becoming a rumour.

It had to be the latter. Someone might add an *S* to the start of *HITS*.

"No!" they say in unison.

ASHAM SHITS WOMEN was not much of an accusation.

"Oh, yes. She's awful when that happens." They shake their heads in scandalised delight.

He painted the *H,* the curve of the *U,* and then he saw the lights.

Behind them, above the door, the bulbs are blinking green.

The car was far in the distance. It was travelling slowly, and there were three junctions where it could turn.

"If I win, I have to leave the room because she just loses control. She's not herself."

The car passed through the first junction, stopped at the second.

"One time she broke a vase. Just threw it at the wall."

They grin and say, "Incredible!" They do not believe me. They like this because it's gossip, not because they think it's true. Anyone who has seen an interview with Shun Li will know better.

The car passed through the junction. If they hadn't seen him, the reflection from the letters, they would do so in seconds.

Only in Shun Li's earliest work is there anything resembling a solo. Everything she's done since then is scrupulously cooperative, not just in how it's presented—as the work of the Nanjing Ensemble— but also in her interviews (always with at least one other ensemble member). As for the music, though the *guqin* is always present, its voice is often the quietest.

The car lights caught the paint.

Such a person does not break vases after losing at *bashi fen.*

It was a white car with blue and green squares down each side.

Even if they believe me, they're thinking of someone else.

On the front of the car, above the lights, was the word *POLICE.*

And though the point is made, the joke is done, I say, "And you should see her when she's getting a taxi!"

Sam stood, paintbrush in hand, above the defaced pavement. And saw the car glide by.

They smile, but do not laugh. Their eyes start flicking away.

He watched its lights recede.

Before I can make up something else, the man behind me speaks.

When they vanished he bent and put the lid on the can of paint.

"Excuse me," he says. "You can go in now."

He picked the can up by its handle, drew his arm back, then swung the can at the window. In the quiet the sound of breaking glass was greatly amplified.

They turn and see the green light. They rush to the door, enter.

He wanted to hear it again. To repeat the sound ten or twenty times.

"Are you all right?" the man behind me asks; why, I do not know. I'm sure he's many things, but not a mind reader.

He ran to the place where he had lived. He scrubbed the paint from his hands. Then he got his bags and left without shutting the front door.

It takes a few seconds to realise what the man means. It's only a small thing. I just need to step forward.

Sam walked until he saw an orange light approaching. He held up his hand and the taxi stopped and he got in. "To the airport," he said, and then the taxi was going fast through the unpeopled streets. The buildings were dark, their windows blank. There were no bright rectangles where people stood holding signs with his name.

My foot must have gone to sleep. Despite me telling it to move, it is like a stone.

He rested his head on the door and listened to the taxi's engine. Though the hum of it rose and fell, it had a regular throb.

"Sorry," I say, and the man behind me says, "Take your time. No rush." And I think he means it.

The throb of the engine grew louder. Was he already on the plane? Moving eastward, crossing time zones, headed for the day.

I press my foot into the floor and will the blood to move.

Where would he be at sunrise, over which city? Certainly in Europe. Probably Germany or France. Places he had never wanted to visit, but now that he was leaving, about to *travel,* they seemed possible. He and Malea would go together on their honeymoon.

The light is green. My foot is dead. The man behind me coughs.

Sam opened his eyes—but briefly, so there was a flash of shops, a petrol station, a leap of flames. His eyes closed; when they reopened there was only dark.

"You better go first," I say. The man hesitates, then does.

"Kids," said the driver. "Like bloody animals. Running around in packs."

Either blood or something equally vital returns to my foot.

"Doing God knows what in the park."

I raise my foot and move it forward. When I place it down it feels like hundreds of spines are pushing into the flesh. It is that special variety of pain that makes you laugh in embarrassment. As if your foot had committed some ludicrous act you wanted to distance yourself from.

"Off somewhere nice?"

But the only way to make this go away is for me to lift my foot, put it back down, feel the hurt again.

"Manila."

Three, four steps.

"Beautiful. But watch out for the lady boys!"

Then I am at the door.

"Me, I won't get a holiday. Not this year."

Turning to look at the queue, I see thirty people waiting. About two-thirds are elderly, the rest quite young.

Next thing Sam knew they were in a place of light and glass that seemed to be from another time.

The one person who meets my gaze is the jovial woman who has just emerged from the tunnel. Her eyes are red; she holds her throat. I cannot read her expression.

"Where are we?" Sam asked.

It may be a look of warning, even reproach. As if I should have talked her out of something that I mean to do.

"The end of the road," said the driver, and laughed at his non-joke.

Except this is what I want to see. And I've never been good at reading faces. Upset, anxious, guilty: To me they look the same.

Sam rubbed his eyes. People were hurrying, pulling suitcases. A sign read: *DEPARTURES*.

Then the woman is gone and I am back to looking down the line. Though most people will have come on their own, or in couples, from the way people are talking to each other you would think they were well acquainted.

Sam walked through doors that opened into too much light. People stood in lines that seemed ready to dissolve. They glared at their too-heavy luggage in mistrustful silence.

For me this kind of friendliness typifies the difference between the old world and now. But there are plenty who disagree. Every year I have at least one student who insists it is not a matter of Before versus After, more of East versus West. He or she will come to the lectern after class and say, *But the whole world was not destroyed. We did not rebuild from nothing. There were Chinese and Indian traditions. There were Asian values.*

Sam's gaze travelled across the airline desks.

It's the kind of thing you want to hear from your students: a big, original-seeming idea that challenges orthodox positions. But the rebuttal is quite simple: The societies that exist today bear virtually no resemblance to what came before. To say they kept their streets and buildings, and most of their people, is to miss the point.

He could not see his airline.

Because their change was not spectacular. It took place unseen, within cells, in the dark of brains. Everyone, in every city, was of the same two minds. There was terror and there was relief. They rushed through each person in surging tides till all things were submerged.

It was difficult to concentrate with so many passengers sweeping through.

Obviously this wasn't always for the better. The suicides went on for weeks, months, like echoes slow to fade. Even now they remain. An old man is found on the shore; an old woman steps from a cliff. I suppose they'll still be heard for thirty, forty years. Fainter, less often, till there is silence; no Survivors left.

He saw the desk and joined its line. The whole thing was insane.

I turn and raise my hand to no one in particular. Which is to say I raise it to them all. Straight ahead, at eye level, my palm facing down. It is a gesture with a terrible history, but this no longer matters. Without a frame of reference, it is a salute.

The man in the front of the queue had very large ears.

I know this is foolish, not really a joke. But when a few people raise their hands in answer it pleases me far more than it should. Thus distracted, I finally step through.

He watched the ears as the queue moved forward.

I enter a corridor whose walls are covered in something grey and uneven. I think it is a kind of lichen. When I brush against it there is an intense smell of rosemary that is almost cloying. I cough, and the irritation passes. A second door slides open, and I step into a small room. "Good afternoon," says a voice that has been made to sound like both a man's and woman's. It thanks me for choosing to take part in the project, then informs me that if I do not wish my image to be saved I should press the yellow button.

What would happen if he touched them?

The button winks invitingly. Although my hand twitches forwards, it won't get any closer. My image can't do harm.

He'd be hit. Badly beaten. The thought was appealing.

"When you're ready to proceed, please step into the circle."

The man in front was almost at the desk. His ears were quivering. His head turned from side to side, looking for the smile, the signal, that he could cross the line on the floor.

As I look down a white circle brightens, then dims, at exactly the same rate as the button. I wonder how much time a person is given to decide.

The woman behind the desk beckoned.

I step into the circle. The light no longer dims. It is now a bright ring that holds me in place. "Please remain still," says the voice. "This will not take long."

Sam's feet touched the line. He looked at the desks, the heads locked to screens, the faces that paid attention whilst they ignored.

Invisibly, and in silence, my face is being captured. It will be transformed.

Sam opened his passport in readiness. He turned to the back page. The photo was eight or nine years old, his face a little fatter. He was not wearing glasses. His hair was shorter. It was him, and not.

Even as I wait, the years are being taken. With every second, another is gone, no doubt two or three. I must already be middle aged, my hair plentiful.

He had just started at the bookshop. He had been seeing Emma, who went to Madagascar to observe lemurs.

I am no longer a professor. I am just a lecturer. Then a librarian. Then I am in my cell. In court. In that square where flags were waved.

He understood why Emma had left, but he still blocked her e-mails.

I am back in that crowded bar watching the end of the world. I am drunk. Crying. As confused and helpless as a newborn.

The man at the desk called him forward. Sam handed over his

passport, then put his bag on the scale. He was told to have a pleasant trip.

After that, or before, there are just flashes of someone else. A person I recognise, although we met for only a moment, as if we stood in different sections of a revolving door. Him exiting as I entered.

Sam stepped away from the desk, then stopped. He had no idea where to go next. Then he heard a scrambled voice telling him to go to gate twelve.

The announcement does not need words. Instead there is a single note that lasts three or four seconds, a clear chime that makes me think of a metal strip with a mirror's shine being struck with great skill. It tells me the capture is complete. It asks me to prepare.

This was all he needed to hear. The airport was just like the hospital: All he had to do was trust the signs. Although the corridors were busier then the hospital, prickling with hurry, as he stood on stairs that lifted he felt the same feeling of surrender.

Without warning, the circle starts to turn. Very slowly, anticlockwise, which seems appropriate. After a quarter of a revolution it stops and the wall slides away.

There was little time to worry, certainly not enough to panic.

I step through. The tunnel is a long grey tube. Its gentle slope is an optical trick, or at least so I've heard. Something to do with reflection.

At the gate he was thankful that the flight was boarding. He did not want to sit and wait; he wanted to keep moving. Soon he would be rising. Everything would quickly shrink until it wasn't there.

The light of the tunnel is the diffuse kind that has struggled through clouds. The silence is similarly effortful. There should be sounds of waves, cries of gulls, voices from those passing. The walls aren't thick enough to block these out. This quiet is manufactured. Even though I understand why—to reduce distraction—it's still irritating. Even the best-intentioned trick contains some kind of insult. One person saying to another, "I am smarter than you."

"You are an idiot. A fool," said a woman behind Sam. He turned and saw a woman with a magenta headscarf speaking into her phone. "Beverly, this is it. No more. You have given me no choice. I am not going to wait."

I hesitate on the threshold. Nothing is happening. The walls are dark, and there is a silence made of sounds beyond my perception. But nothing is wrong; I'm just nervous. As soon as I step from the entrance, the walls come to life. Either there's a hidden sensor, or someone is watching. With all us old people shuffling through, I suppose there must be.

When he reached the end of the line, he dropped his boarding pass. He bent quickly, retrieved it, then straightened, and for an instant he was falling.

There may have been fainting spells or a heart attack. If so, I doubt they happened here. When people saw their faces, as I see mine, there would have been no alarm. No matter that their eyes, like mine, were multiplied hundreds of times. At this age, there should be nothing upsetting about the sight of one's own face. No surprises, only recognition.

"Sam?" said a voice he knew. He blinked, and the world became steady. "What are you doing here?" she asked. His delay in replying to Boring Lesley was not because he had forgotten she had found this job at the airport; it was because he had forgotten she existed. By the time he recognised her, it was too late. She stared as if betrayed. Boring Lesley, in that instant, became interesting. Either he was important to her in some fashion, or she was oversensitive. When he handed her his boarding pass, she tore it angrily.

I walk beneath my gaze. In the far distance, at the end of the tunnel, a figure appears. A man about my height, with grey hair, slowly walking towards me. When I pause, he also stops. I stare, and he stares back.

She thrust the jagged stub at Sam and pointed down the tunnel.

And what will happen now? Do I turn and run? Even if I were able to, it really wouldn't help. The only thing to do is go on. That's why I'm here, what I want, what I am afraid of. Thankfully, little is required. I do not need to be brave; I do not need to make eye contact; I do not need to speak. All that's required of me is to shuffle on.

He followed the slope of the tunnel down into the plane. His seat was at the back and by a window. It was occupied by a middle-aged Filipino man whose eyes were closed. He was breathing loudly through his mouth. His neck was heavily bandaged. "Excuse me," said Sam. "I think that's my seat." The man did not respond.

He's younger than he looked at first. His hair isn't as grey. He's clean shaven, taller. As for his walk, it isn't a copy of mine. It has been given more thought. His back is straighter; his arms swing more. The length of his stride, though somewhat shortened, is still greater than mine. The overall effect is more that of an interpretation rather than an impersonation. It is very impressive, though not, alas, correct: Until ten years ago, I still walked with a limp. Of course there's no way for them to know that just from an image. They only contain so much.

Sam repeated himself more loudly. The result was the same, except that the corners of the man's mouth lifted, not a proper smile, but suggestive of mirth.

Now I can see his features clearly. His hair is almost dark. He has stopped moving, seems to be waiting. But of course he is not. He cannot wait any more than he can laugh, cry, do a conjuring trick. Which is all he is. The most that he can do is *seem* to be looking at me.

The man's eyes opened. He blinked. "Yes?" he said, and looked at Sam with so much hostility that his gaze was like a blade pushing through his body.

But there is no reason to avoid his gaze. I can look in a mirror. He is the one who should find it hard to make eye contact. The fact that he can look me in the eye so coolly, almost with amusement, only underlines the falseness of the trick. And of course this should not be disappointing. And yet it somehow is.

The bandages around the man's neck made his head look disembodied. They were so thick their primary aim seemed to be concealment. Sam thought of a terrible wound, a hole in the throat, the vocal cords exposed. The man pointed at himself and spoke. "Is this you?" he asked while jabbing his fingers into his chest in an emphatic manner.

Now there isn't much resemblance. He is in his mid-thirties; his head of hair is dark. For some reason he has a beard, why I've no idea; I've never even had a moustache. I suppose the program has to guess some of these things based on the fashions of the period. Though I'd also like to think that someone has made the program stick facial hair where it doesn't belong, either as a joke, or to remind people that this "person" wasn't, won't be "them."

"Are you here?" asked the man, and raised himself, a slight motion that still seemed to cause him discomfort. "Yeah," said Sam, and then the man became contrite. "I'm sorry," he said. "I didn't mean to. She told me to sit there, and I didn't check, I probably should have. I'm really not myself." He brought his hand to his neck, swallowed, and looked in pain once more. "It's just easier if I can lean against something, then maybe I can sleep." He closed his eyes, then opened them; only then did he start to gather his belongings. He had several magazines, a bottle of water, some thick wooden beads. One of the man's hands was also injured; its bandage was coming loose. As he stood, he dropped the bottle of water, and then, when he bent to retrieve it, one of the magazines as well. There was so little space between the edge of his (or rather, Sam's) seat and the one in front that he had to twist his body to the side as he bent down, and though he did so carefully, it was still so painful he gasped. When the man straightened, he was pale and sweating. He looked both close to tears and ready to collapse.

With heavy legs, and almost staggering, I reduce the distance. At ten feet the beard is gone. He is thirty-three, thirty-two, thirty years of age. He is in the streets of Manila. He is on the plane.

Sam looks at the man, and I look at him, and then he steps aside. From the man on the plane, from me in the tunnel, so that we can pass. In the present this is a thoughtful gesture: I imagine most people would prefer not to step through themselves. Sixty years ago, Sam stepping aside meant quite the opposite. It was a last aversion of the eyes, a final turn of his back.

The man stepped into the aisle as I step next to Sam. There are only six inches between us, six inches that are sixty years, a gap between worlds. We stand next to each other, face to face, I with too much to say, him with not enough. I thought this would be upsetting, traumatic. But now that I see him, this less than a ghost, I realise there's nothing to fear. There's no need to destroy a relic. So long as it knows what it was, it is being punished enough.

Sam took his rightful seat. He leaned against the window. Nothing more was required of him, nothing except patience. With this in mind, he took off his shoes, fastened his seat belt, then spread out the blanket. He wasn't sure if he'd turned off his phone; when he put his hand in his jacket pocket it met the smoothness of paper. He took it out and stuffed it into the seat pocket—he wouldn't need his ticket anymore—then put his hand back in. The mobile wasn't in there, so he tried the other, and again found paper. He brought it out with the phone and saw it was his ticket. He leant forward and retrieved the first piece of paper. It was Caitlin's e-mail.

Hello from sweaty Cairo! The traffic's crazy, and there's too many people, but this place is amazing. Walking the streets is like being in two or three different eras at once, there are streets with old mosques that are centuries old and then there's ones that just sell iPhones. There are massive hotels with white limousines outside and then there are these huge graveyards where thousands of people live in tombs and sleep on the graves. So far everyone's nice except for some of the creepy men—a woman in my hostel was groped on a train and bus on the same day. She said it wasn't just because she was foreign—it happens to women with headscarfs too, which is a shame because I've started wearing these. After an hour in the afternoon sun my brain was really throbbing—I almost fainted in the spice market on my first day. I like moving through the crowd as if I'm in disguise, it makes me feel like one of those nineteenth-century travellers who pretended to be Muslim. Best moment so far: sitting by the Nile at sunset and hearing the call to prayer. It's such an amazing sound that I expect everyone to just stop and listen, but of course it's as normal to them as church bells are to us, although I still think there's something special about hearing a voice. Must go— am off to Yemen tomorrow with two Dutch girls I met in an *ahwa*. I had no plans to go there, at least not for ages, but they told me about this little island called Socotra that has prehistoric trees and pirates and at first I wasn't sure but then I googled it and found this picture and knew I had to go there.

Maybe it will be disappointing, but I want to take the chance. I don't believe in fate, but if I'd come here earlier, when I planned to, I definitely wouldn't have met them, and so wouldn't have this chance. That's what this trip is all about: meeting new people, taking opportunities, trusting to luck. Say hi to everyone, will write more soon xx

Sam folded the paper. He was glad Caitlin was doing well. She was in a new place, with new people, becoming someone else. Obviously, he couldn't take all the credit. But he had played his part.

The plane began to move. Next to him the man crossed his legs, then uncrossed them. "I don't like flying," he said. "I know it's safe, but that doesn't help, I still have stupid thoughts." Sam nodded, then looked away. Outside the lights were picking up speed, as if they were racing the plane. Though they went faster, they could not keep up, unlike the airport fence, the trees, the hills that hulked in the gloom. These kept pace with him and the plane like loyal, cheering crowds. With a vertiginous lurch, and a moan to his left, Samuel Clark departed. As the plane climbed the sky lightened further, till there was a scarlet line to the east. At first it was as thin as a paper cut, but this soon widened, acquired thickness, bled beyond the edge of land that still made the horizon. The plane had barely begun to level when the sun emerged. It welled up like an orange tear. The wings of the plane glowed. Sam watched fields and rivers burn, trees, cottages, cows. No place could escape those flames. Not Glasgow, not Edinburgh. Comely Bank was ablaze. What had been solid during the night was melting, being transformed, just as the fire was changing as it found new fuel. Light that had been red, then orange, now shifted to gold as it swept over the bridge, down the street, pushed through windows, slipped through curtains, seeking, finding faces. Mrs. Maclean would already be awake, as would Mr. Asham, who had probably not slept. The light could even reach under the bridge, but Sam hoped it wouldn't, not yet. He wanted Alasdair, Toby, Abby, and Spooky to sleep as long as they could, to wake only after the light had run out of surfaces to touch. He wished for it to first visit Sean and Rita's bench, then brighten the paint outside Mr. Asham's, flicker on the bookshop window, glance off the French delicatessen, burst into his former home, gild the surface of the pond, heat the church's steeple. Only when almost all was lit, aflame, should those relics wake and understand that the day had come with neither warning nor remorse. It seemed fitting that these pieces of the past should linger for an extra instant: *Time past as time present,* as old fools might say.

But the relics wouldn't be the last to wake. There was still one place he hoped the light hadn't touched. If it strained credibility to ask that the entire hospital remain unwoken, unawares—as if everyone inside had fallen victim to a resurgence of *encephalitis lethargica,* the sleeping sickness of the 1920s they dubbed a "global catastrophe"—then he would settle for the daylight sparing that small room which was not a room, just a curtained-off space. Though the light might reflect off the white surfaces of the ward, bouncing between wall, ceiling, and doctor's coat until it was so powerful it bleached the retina and killed the eye, still he hoped it could let Malea sleep an hour more, even a minute—duration didn't matter. A single second was as much a reprieve, a suggestion of grace, as the sudden tilt of his world as the plane banked steeply right. This long, slow turn culminated in a heading committed to journeying east; it swapped a view of burning land for that of water with the sheen of scales. With each second, more land slipped from view, not just in the present, but also the future, because Sam wasn't coming back, not ever, not even if they had kids. He saw green fields, a rocky beach, then waves, but this wasn't the end of the land. There were fifteen seconds before they passed the island that was its full stop. After that there was just water; ash coloured and so infinite seeming it was hard to believe there would be anything solid again. Looking out from the end of the pier, the feeling is the same. No boats interrupt the waves. The space is so open, so empty, it demands to be filled; part of me has to oblige. As much as I am here, standing on wood, pressed against metal, I am also at the edge of vision, paused at the horizon. It is a necessary, futile expansion that makes me feel foolish. There's so much more that I could do. And yet we remain. Dead, dying; alive.

Acknowledgments

THANKS TO THOSE WHO READ this book in all its incarnations: Ronan Ryan, Jason Morton, Lynsey May Sutherland, Krystelle Bamford, Jon Sternfeld, Magda Boreysza. I'm also grateful to Gail Durbin for help with some of the "found" photos in the book. Thanks to Duncan Macgregor for help with graphs and other moral guidance.

Thanks to three people without whom: Beth Weinstein, Nicole Sohl, Ryan van Winkle.